reviews of lemongrass hope

"*Lemongrass Hope* is that fine and fresh thing—a truly new story. Kate is struggling with family life and love under stress in the here-and-now when her fate is struck by lightning, holding out the chance to love again through a meeting of souls in a time not her own. What she must consider is that dreams come true demand an excruciating choice. Amy Impellizzeri is a bold and tender writer, who makes the impossible feel not only real, but strangely familiar."

> — JACQUELYN MITCHARD, *New York Times* best-selling author, *The Deep End of the Ocean*

"The nonlinear structure makes her story unique... The complex decisions at each turn build reader interest and investment in the characters... A layered, bittersweet romance that questions consequences and explores second chances."

> — *Kirkus Reviews*

"Amy Impellizzeri's literary experiment, *Lemongrass Hope*, show-cases everything that is right and wrong about married existence, while turning on an alternative lighthouse as a beacon of optimism. This bizarre time-traveling experience delves into the psychological unrest that often occurs in a long-term relationship . . . The mind-bending journey is fascinating."

> — *ForeWord Reviews*, *Fall 2014 Issue*

"Amy Impellizzeri has crafted a heartbreaking story of choices. Compelling, thought-provoking, and filled with enchantment, *Lemongrass Hope* takes you through magical waters, and leaves you wondering about your own second chances."

— **KAREN BROWN**, author of *The Longings of Wayward Girls*

"What a *great* story . . . I love a book that can surprise me and give me a shiver. The epilogue gripped me. I thought that part was brilliant. Then when I went back and re-read the prologue, it gripped me even more . . . Really honed in on a primal longing in this modern-day world that I think is deep within many of us."

— **AMANDA MININGER**, author of *Touch*

"*Lemongrass Hope* is one of the most exceptional books I have ever read. My love for it grew from, 'This is a great book' to 'This may be one of the best books I've been asked to review' to 'Okay, this is one of the best books I've ever read.' It is extraordinary. Mind-boggling, captivating, emotional, addicting, and positively heartrending."

— **THE LITERARY CONNOISSEUR**

"This story is so heart warming, the characters so genuine, the story so fresh and captivating . . . I just finished this book a few days ago and the story is still with me. It truly is a book of hope, belief and choices."

— **ALL ABOUT A BOOK**

"Wow. You have to read this book."

— **THE BOOK CLUB BLOG**

lemongrass
hope

a novel

lemongrass hope

a novel

amy impellizzeri

Wyatt-MacKenzie Publishing
DEADWOOD, OREGON

LEMONGRASS HOPE

Amy Impellizzeri

ISBN: 978-1-939288-53-0

Library of Congress Control Number: 2014933433

Cover Photo: Lindsey Raughton is an accountant and photographer living in
Montgomery, Alabama. The photograph of a Marula tree used for the book cover
was taken in Kruger National Park while on a family vacation in South Africa.

Wyatt-MacKenzie Publishing
DEADWOOD, OREGON

Wyatt-MacKenzie Publishing, Inc.
www.WyattMacKenzie.com
Contact us: info@wyattmackenzie.com

dedication

To Hope,
as much a colorful character in my own life,
as it is herein . . .

prologue

Destiny.

That's what I'm thinking about tonight as I look at this gorgeous—more than yellow, not quite golden—sunset.

No, that's a lie.

I'm thinking about loss.

Choices. Destiny.

But mostly loss.

It's ironic of course that I cannot stop thinking about loss since we finally—*finally*—found our way back to each other.

And I'm not surprised at all that this is where we find ourselves.

Right here. All over again.

Because again and again, we find our way back.

I have always been convinced that starting over was all we truly needed.

But like I said.

Tonight I'm thinking about loss.

Choices. Destiny. And loss.

Oh, and one more thing.

That dress.

I can't stop thinking about that damn dress.

part one

June, 1997

SHE HAD BEEN STUDYING HIM. Arguably for too long. But certainly long enough to see that the cycle was repeating itself. In a loop.

Slouch, frown, straighten, smile.

Repeat.

Repeat again.

He was tall, which made the slouching over his drink at the Botswanan bar even more pronounced. For long periods of time, he would sit like that, quietly frowning, and then, as if on cue, he would straighten up, smile and look expectantly at the doorway.

Despite his obvious sadness, there was that hopefulness trying to fight its way out of him. And that—instead of the fact that she had been studying him for far too long—was what Dee would remember afterward. Indeed, it was why she even wanted to talk to him. With her Bahamian English. She was far from home and he seemed to be as well. He shuffled through a money clip filled mostly with American looking dollars, as he looked for Botswanan pulas to pay for his drink.

"You are from America." She said it rather than asked it, as she arrived finally to sit down next to him on an uncomfortable wooden stool. A stool that tilted left and right like a wave-crashed boat when she landed on it, as it had no firm anchor in the dirt floor below.

"I am. And you?" He looked at the nearly empty glass she had brought to the teetering stool with her, asking where she was from and what she was drinking in one efficient question.

"No, thank you." She flattened her hand over her glass to show she was finished.

Drinking, not talking.

She continued on in careful English. "I live in the Bahamas, now. But I am from here. I've come to bury my mother."

"I'm sorry," he said obviously.

"It is my last trip here I am sure. Such a long, difficult trip. I don't like long and difficult. That is why my home is in the Bahamas now."

She smiled and introduced herself belatedly, holding out her hand to him. "I am Dee."

He took her hand and looked her in the eye for the first time. "Ian. Nice to see you, Dee."

As he shifted his glance back down at the bar, Dee searched for words to continue the conversation. She was anxious for a diversion from her own grief. Her need for distraction was what had brought her here in the first place, immediately upon arriving in Botswana. Even before she went home to join in the funeral arrangements, she had been drawn here somehow.

She pressed on. "What about you, Ian? Have you come for a happy visit or a sad visit? I see a little of both in your face."

Because he didn't answer right away, Dee was left to worry that her frankness had put him off.

Doesn't he feel it, too?

The familiarity? The warmth?

She started to stand up, reluctantly abandoning the seasick stool and the tall man.

I'll just leave him alone.

Alone with his slouching and imprisoned hopefulness.

But no. He answered then, finally.

"It *is* a little of both. This is a trip I've been looking forward to for quite a while. But now that I'm here, I'm—I'm having trouble forgetting someone."

"Tell me about her," Dee commanded as she sat back down.

Ian ordered more drinks for the two of them. And as he got drunker, he told Dee. About how it had happened. About how it had ended. He explained that on some days, he was saddened by the suddenness of its ending, and he confessed that most days, he had to acknowledge that it had seemed doomed from the start.

He had loved this American woman with his soul. He didn't say this lightly, he explained, since he had never understood really what that meant; never really believed it meant anything at all, until he had met *her*.

"I want to go back one day, and fix things. Eventually."

Dee nodded when he said this, grateful that she could finally offer some comfort and encouragement.

"Marula fruit," she smiled. "You need marula drink instead of that." She pointed to his glass of bourbon and he smiled again, straightened up and glanced over Dee's head at the door again for the first time since Dee had sat down.

"Yes," he said. "That's exactly why I've come here."

2011

KATE FELT HIM BEFORE SHE SAW HIM.

The rush of October air from the hastily opened door in the coffee shop blew a crumpled napkin containing her son Michael's baby tooth out of his hand and made Kate shiver at the same time. With her back still to the door, Kate bent down to scoop up the shrouded tooth, eager to quiet Michael's renewed tears and replace the napkin in his clumsy hands. But in doing so, she dropped her oversized handbag onto the floor where it flayed open, all of its contents exposed grotesquely.

"Michael. It's ok." Kate stroked his hair and pulled Michael to her chest, his tears and bloody slobber streaking her sweater like some horror movie version of a water color design. Michael's tooth remained balled up in her hand.

His first lost tooth.

The tears, the moment, the crouching hug. It all felt familiar somehow, and Kate's shoulders shook again with a sense of déjà vu.

Next to her, Kate's younger son, David, started playing with an elaborate display stand of coffee mugs for sale. When she turned to stop David, she found herself facing the man whose entrance had blown the napkin out of Michael's hand and had set this confusion in motion.

Kate stared at him, waiting for him to notice her. See that it was *her*. And then—

"Kate." He looked sad—*defeated,* she thought—as he said her name.

Or is that my imagination projecting onto him?

After all, she felt disappointment that this messiness was how they happened upon each other now, after all this time.

"I wish—" He surveyed the scene in front of him.

Wish what, Ian? Because I wish, too. I wish so many things.

Kate pulled both of her sons to her and glanced over Ian's shoulder at the door, wondering if she should leave or try to start the overdue moment again. She stared at him, willing him to finish his sentence, so that she would not have to speak. So that she would not have to think of something to say. It didn't work.

"Wish what?" This time Kate said it out loud.

"That we could turn back the clock again. Start over."

A phone buzzed then atop Kate's abandoned bag and she instinctively glanced at it in time to see it lighting up with a familiar but infrequent number.

Benton.

It's like she knows I'm here with Ian. She has the most uncanny sense of timing.

Kate let the phone go to voicemail just as she dropped Michael's tooth on the floor again and the tears renewed and the déjà vu shiver made its way from her shoulders all the way down her spine.

Two Years Earlier - 2009

I COULD ALMOST BELIEVE AGAIN.

On a cloudless afternoon, where everyone's mood was finally in sync with the weather, Kate felt transported.

She dug her toes into the beach sand inches away from Michael, while reading her Book Club's latest selection, Elizabeth Gilbert's *Eat Pray Love*. Kate smiled a little remembering how she had impulsively kissed her husband, Rob, goodbye back at the hotel when he gallantly offered to stay behind with their napping toddler, David, so that she and Michael could enjoy some quiet time together on the beach.

They had reached a place where small gestures were big again.

Gallant offers. Beach sand. Impulsive kisses.

Small. Yet big.

Kate and Michael had spent nearly an hour constructing a rather elaborate structure. It was hardly a sand castle, but more of a sprawling sand *ranch*, which Michael was now delightedly running his trucks and beach toys around in a few moments of vacation bliss. Kate was about to interrupt to re-lather Michael with 50-plus sunblock before she settled into her chair to read, but with the realization that there was absolutely no reason to ruin Michael's contentment, or her own, Kate instead sunk into her chair and her book and tried to imagine a world where pizza from Naples, Italy could solve heartbreak.

She knew some of the women in Book Club—Lex, for

example, would find this part ridiculous—she heard some cynicism in the back of her own mind as well.

Your marriage has completely failed and you are in Italy eating your way to recovery? Sounds like the beginning of a bad made-for-TV movie on eating disorders.

Kate could already hear Lex taunting as she re-read the page, and for a moment Kate nodded along to the voice in her mind's eye before catching herself.

Don't be hypocritical, Kate told herself sternly. *You are here seeking magic cures of your own.*

Magic cures. The very phrase led her mind to wander off Gilbert's narrative again, as Kate wondered if there wasn't some place more mystical that she could have escaped to. When she booked this trip, California had seemed as good a solution as any. But now, she wondered where else she could have gone.

Stop daydreaming about mystical places, Kate chided herself. *What am I doing here? What am I really doing here?*

While Michael played, Kate kept reading and re-reading pages of her book, distracted by her brain's involuntary responses to the words on the pages. Gilbert's pained descriptions of her divorce kept reaching out to grab Kate and sicken her.

She and Rob had traveled all the way across the country to a resort that she was somewhat embarrassed to admit to her friends as she was leaving town, was actually called "Paradise Resort." And while she reluctantly admitted the name of the resort, what she did not admit to her friends upon her exit from the East Coast, was that the trip was designed and planned with the hope that time together and distance from their daily lives could heal Kate and Rob. Could repair a marriage they had not conceded to anyone was strained far past its logical breaking point.

How did we get here?

This was the question they both asked each other with increasing frequency these days.

But there was another unspoken question that swirled around Kate like a pesky fly. She swatted it away, trying not to acknowledge it and trying not to let it land on her brain, for even a moment. But it made its way in there anyway. Despite her swatting and ignoring.

Did this marriage ever really have a chance?

Every day started and ended the same way—an eruption, an argument.

"I'm juggling a lot here, too, Rob. But at least I'm trying," Kate had seethed a few weeks ago through clenched teeth after Rob made the usual excuses about deadlines at the law firm where he was trying to make partner, and Kate's "noble but completely unrealistic" expectations about "having family dinner every night."

"Kate, I would hardly characterize your constantly picking fights with me as 'trying.' I mean, really, Kate. Let's be honest here. It's as if you have given up any hope on this marriage. Do you know how completely disheartening it is to live with a woman who is convinced at every moment that this marriage is about to end?"

Kate had been struck by those words. Well, not the words so much as the pain and anger unleashed at her over a pounding fist on the kitchen island. So Kate had looked ahead at her college teaching schedule, and had asked Rob after work the next day if, after he made it through the next deadline at his firm, they could book a trip. This trip.

To get away.

This vacation was an energetic attempt to get away from the rooms in their own home, each one tainted by a fight more vicious than the last one, and to breathe salt air and eat out every night. They had, no doubt about it, come here to "Paradise

Resort" expecting something magical to happen to their family.

After glossing over the same page of Gilbert philosophy for a fourth and fifth time, Kate closed her eyes, listening only to the ocean waves rhythmically collaborating with the seagulls overhead.

Wasn't it happening?

Whatever she had allowed herself to hope for when booking this trip—wasn't it happening?

After all, Rob had agreed—no, offered without Kate even asking—to stay behind with David for his nap today. He had been patient with Michael who dressed and re-dressed for the beach, changing his mind about which bathing suit was his "favorite" one on this day, a task that would have aggravated Rob at home.

Kate was enjoying dressing up at night for dinner and being attentive to Rob, in addition to the kids. Rob seemed happy that Kate was, well, happy. The kids were not the least bit affected negatively by jet lag, falling asleep dutifully by 9 pm, exhausted by the full days of sand and ocean. They even slept in until 8 am, a welcome respite for Kate and Rob, who needed sleep as much as they needed alone time.

Kate was, in fact, eating, praying, and loving.

And she felt optimistic, renewed. For the first time in a long while, Kate felt . . . hope.

❧

After about an hour of vacillating between Gilbert's memoir and her own thoughts, Michael announced that Kate's interlude of peace was over by throwing his plastic truck at her leg.

"Michael!" Kate yelped, massaging her shin where the truck had landed with a thud.

"Mommy, I'm *hungry*, I want to go back and get *Daddy.*" Michael's sweet voice had turned whiny and grating but Kate's reserve of patience had been refilled by the hours on the beach.

She reached over, and scooped Michael up in her arms. She hugged him but her voice was stern. "Michael, we don't throw things. Yes, we'll go back to Daddy and David and yes, we'll eat, but first you help me put all these toys back in their —"

"*Michael! Get up!*"

Michael had wriggled out of Kate's grasp and was face down in the sand, rolling in it until even his eyelashes and lips were coated in grit. He spit out the sand and yelled loudly, "I want to go *now!*"

Aware that a few people were shuffling uncomfortably in the beach chairs next to her, Kate's reserve of patience ebbed out to sea. *Damn*, Kate thought. *And there it goes. Just like that.*

A tightness grew in Kate's chest. She was torn between wanting to yank Michael upright in anger and wanting to turn to the gawkers on the beach and yell at them, *"Really? None of you has ever had a 4-year-old?"*

She chose neither.

She leaned into Michael and whispered through gritted teeth, *"Michael, everyone on the beach is listening to us. That. is. enough."*

She started to pick up the toys, and announced in an appropriately parental yet patient voice—loud enough for all the beach voyeurs to hear, "I understand that you are frustrated and hungry, honey. And four. But, nevertheless, we need to pick up these toys and head back to the room. *Nicely.*"

"Nevertheless" was probably overkill. Now everyone knows this is for their benefit, not his.

Michael watched Kate picking up the toys. He stopped rolling in the sand, but he sat defiantly, determined not to pick up a single toy. Kate could feel everyone on the beach staring at her. They had stopped everything they were doing in order to watch her gathering up the plastic toys, catering to her obstinate son.

A gray-haired older couple, who could have been someone's grandparents, were looking at her, shaking their heads. The tan, lithe, and clearly childless couples on the beach were looking at her like she was walking birth control, and the nearby parents were looking at her with smugness and unabashed "so-glad-that's-not-me-today" smiles.

Kate caught all of their looks from the corner of her eye and then she caught a glimpse of *him.* Turning her head quickly, Kate thought she saw Rob watching her from a few yards away on the beach. She was startled for a moment, before realizing it was not Rob, just a dark-haired, handsome stranger on the beach.

Kate welled up a bit as she continued to throw trucks and plastic sand toys into a bag, weakened emotionally by the embarrassment of Michael's very public tantrum and the realization that dark-haired handsome strangers were about as familiar to her these days as her own husband.

And suddenly, the ocean and the seagulls and the background beach noises swirled in her brain causing a frenzy of static that drowned out hope and anything else she had been starting to feel just moments ago. *I have no control over anything anymore,* she thought. *It's just . . . happening.*

Desperate not to begin crying on the beach in front of all of the watchful glares, Kate could think of only one thing to do.

She leaned down to Michael and tried to keep her voice inaudible to the beach do-gooders and voyeurs. *"Michael, if you help me pick up these trucks—we will go get ice cream for lunch. Now."*

Michael smiled—deviously, she could swear—much too deviously for a 4-year-old—and leaned over to plop a few trucks back into the bag she was holding open.

Kate tucked her book and sunblock into her beach bag, and as she and Michael headed back up to Paradise Resort hand in hand, she glanced around at the admiring looks she was getting from the grandparent set on the beach. They were nodding approvingly at the stern way she had parented her child, at her persistence, and its results.

You. Are. A. Fraud. Kate heard in her ears.

And this voice was louder than any messages she had tucked away from the time she had just spent with Elizabeth Gilbert, and stopped in its tracks any chance that she might start believing in magic cures again.

"MOMMY, DO YOU LIKE ELEPHANTS OR LIONS?"

"Elephants."

"Do you like chocolate or vanilla?"

"Chocolate."

"Do you like the number four or eight?"

It was the day after the beach showdown and Michael was firing questions at Kate, while she stared out the passenger window taking in the California sights. They had woken to overcast skies and decided that today would be a better zoo day than a beach day. But now the weather was starting to clear, revealing a gorgeous and sunny day.

"Oh boy. You guys playing this game again? I thought he'd given it up," Rob muttered and Kate gave a little nod as she continued playing along.

Michael *had* given up this activity—dubbed "The Question Game"—not too long ago.

And truth be told, Kate would have expected to be glad when and if Michael ever gave up The Question Game. She was so wary of it when Michael first made it up.

At least she thought he made it up. She actually wasn't too sure where it had come from, this variation of "I spy" seemingly gone awry.

I spy with my little eye a yellow flower.

Mommy, do you like yellow flowers or red flowers?

I spy with my little eye a blue car.

Mommy, do you like cars or buses?

And so it went.

Kate didn't like encouraging Michael's developing "either or" attitude and in the beginning used to answer with responses like "well, it depends, honey." Or "certainly, all flowers have their own unique beauty so color doesn't matter."

But it was rambling responses like these that would lead Rob to roll his eyes and disengage completely from the game. Not that Michael directed his questions to Rob—they were all for Kate—but still, Rob almost completely ignored them as they bantered back and forth for most car rides.

And then one day, Rob chided Kate out loud and impatiently. "Oh for heaven's sake, Kate, there's no moral lesson here. There are just red or yellow flowers. Maybe he's planning your Mother's Day corsage. Maybe he's checking to make sure you're even listening. Why can't you just answer the questions without turning every single minute into a teachable moment?"

On the day Rob finished his "teachable moment" lecture, Kate had responded the way she did best these days.

She ignored him.

Kate stuck to her guns and continued to answer Michael's questions with long-winded non-answers.

Until the day she noticed he was no longer playing the game.

How long since Michael had asked a single question in the car?

She couldn't say for sure. But one Saturday morning while running errands with Rob and the kids in the car, Kate realized that Michael had not asked her a question all morning, and as far as she could remember, all week. Perhaps longer.

She had waited to ask until driving to preschool Monday morning when Rob wasn't in the car with them. "Michael, why don't you play The Question Game with me anymore in the car?"

"Oh, Mommy, you never answer the questions anyway. I don't like that game anymore."

Hurt and a bit defeated, Kate suggested, "Well, why don't we try again?"

Michael jumped back in enthusiastically, "What do you like better—tables or chairs?"

"Chairs, definitely chairs," Kate answered with confidence, though a bit chagrined at the thought that Rob had been right all along.

Michael smiled broadly, and as Kate caught a glimpse of his smile in the rearview mirror, she swelled with happiness.

Happy that The Question Game would now resume, and that she now knew how to play, and that in this instant, Michael thought she was the best mother ever.

Even though being the best mother ever was increasingly beginning to mean providing clear-cut, black and white answers, and hoping always that they were the right ones. Something she wasn't entirely comfortable with, even though Rob seemed just fine with it.

Ian. She thought with an ache in her heart on the day The Question Game resumed, and nearly every time they played it after that.

Ian would hate this game, too.

IAN AND BENTON HAD ALWAYS BEEN LINKED in Kate's mind. It had much to do with how they had both come into her life.

And how they had both left.

Kate first met the beautiful Benton in 1996 while working as a waitress in an Italian restaurant in Manhattan to put herself through grad school.

The day they met, Kate was sitting in Bryant Park in midtown Manhattan at lunchtime, editing a history paper over a cup of coffee. She was getting ready to start a shift at the restaurant, and was hoping to finish her paper before then.

Benton came and sat down next to Kate. Right next to her. Almost on top of her. Benton was tall and thin, and had long hair the color of autumn: the right mix of red and brown with flecks of gold. She had friendly eyes and a bright white smile and was dressed all in navy like a banker, even though she looked like no banker Kate had ever met.

"See, I knew it," Benton had said confidently, waving her long, manicured fingers over the textbooks and handwritten notes scattered across the park table, nearly knocking over Kate's cup of coffee without apology.

"I *told* my friend last night that you were *not* a starving actress. That you were an academic. An intellectual. He said that you were too pretty to be an intellectual—that you were for sure, a 'wannabe actress.' His words, not mine—so gauche, no?"

Kate laughed in spite of herself. In spite also of having no clue what this gorgeous but obviously deranged creature was talking about.

"Benton. Benton Daly." She held out her hand, but as she had plopped herself almost on top of Kate at the small Bryant Park table, Kate actually had to push her chair back to shake Benton's hand comfortably.

No matter. Benton didn't bother adjusting her close seat as she continued on. "You waited on my friend and me last night at Rocco's. We were absolutely mesmerized by you. Couldn't figure out your story—and I'm usually so *good* at people—but you had us stumped. I heard you talking with the gentleman across the dining room and you actually sounded like a professor who was moonlighting as a waitress in the theatre district!"

Rocco's.

The steady streams of people who poured in and out of Rocco's were as unfamiliar to Kate as the faces that lined the streets of Manhattan as she walked back and forth from her apartment to the restaurant to class. The night before, a favorite professor had come in with his wife and another couple and Kate had chatted a bit with them between courses. In truth, she was distracted by impressing her professor, knowing he would soon be reading the very paper she was now editing at the park table, which explained why Benton did not stick out in her mind—gorgeous as she was. Sitting there with Benton, Kate couldn't actually remember her dinner companion. A handsome man, no doubt, but Kate just couldn't remember him.

Later, she would enjoy telling the story of how she met Benton in Bryant Park over and over again to Ian. He would say, "Wait, show me exactly how she sat down. And you had to actually push your chair back to shake her hand? And you couldn't remember me? Not at all?"

Fake pout and then tender, long kiss.

Kate would always shake her head, of course, equally as incredulous as Ian was that she did not remember him as

Benton's dinner companion at Rocco's that first night.

Especially since that was the night he had always told her was the night he first fell in love with her.

❧

After that comical meeting in Bryant Park, Benton and Kate became fast friends. Reassured by Kate's grad school career that she was indeed an intellectual and not a "wannabe actress," Benton had invited her into her warm circle of friendship and Kate found her as hard-working and smart as she was charming and kooky. Benton had recently graduated from law school and was busy suppressing her impeccable sense (and love) of fashion by working as a smart-ass corporate lawyer at her father's best friend's white shoe law firm. The daughter of a wealthy banker, she was happy to pay her dues at a high profile midtown firm, but had aspirations of grandeur and entrepreneurship and starting her own organic clothing line. Kate loved to talk to her and listen to her and dream with her.

And at that time, it never occurred to Kate that Benton was someone she would ever lose touch with. Young Manhattanites just embarking on new lives, they talked every day about sample sales, the Hampton shares they couldn't swing with their grueling work/school schedules, the bosses they hated, and the big—make that *huge*—dreams they had of doing big—make that *huge*—things with their futures.

The brown-haired, blue-eyed Benton boasted some one percent Mexican blood in her veins thanks to some (possibly) tall tales by her lovely blue-eyed grandmother. So every year she threw *the* Cinco De Mayo party in Tribeca. In May 1997, Ian was Benton's neighbor in the posh midtown apartment building she lived in just blocks from her firm. He had also been her purely platonic dinner companion that fateful night at Rocco's many months earlier.

But on Cinco de Mayo, 1997, Kate was not summoned away from a stack of papers she was meant to grade for Professor Tipton as his highly esteemed, and equally underpaid Teaching Assistant, to meet Ian. *That* night, Benton had invited Kate to meet a newly single attorney colleague of hers.

"Come on, Kate. Forget about this ugly stack of papers and come to my party tonight. I want to introduce you to this guy from my office named Rob Sutton."

~

"I'll have a Manhattan and would you please get this lady a . . ." The tall, good-looking stranger turned to Kate who was waiting at the bar for Benton at the Cinco de Mayo party.

"A glass of white. Do you have any sauvignon blanc by the glass? New Zealand preferably."

"There you go. New Zealand sauvignon blanc." He finished their order and looked at Kate with amusement.

Perhaps trying to impress him or perhaps just trying to make conversation while she waited for her blind date, Kate continued on, "Did you know that according to Oz Clarke, New Zealand makes the world's superior sauvignon blanc? Even more impressive given the history of wine-making in the country. The government actually paid the grape growers to pull up their vines in the 80s."

"I did not know that. I will give more attention to New Zealand wines in the future." The stranger turned back to the bartender who was uncorking a wine bottle. "Would you mind making that two glasses of wine? I've just been persuaded to try something new."

When the wine was served, he clinked glasses with Kate: "To New Zealand wine growers."

"So. How do you know Benton?" Kate asked as she finished her first sip.

The handsome stranger looked at her with genuine frustration.

"You really don't remember me do you? She said you didn't, but I was hoping she was just kidding."

"Who? Who said what?" Kate looked at him carefully over her wine glass, trying hard to decipher what he was saying, believing for a moment that he had her mixed up with someone else, until he reached out his hand.

"Ian. Ian Campton."

"Ian!" Now it was Kate's turn to look amused. Ian had been somewhat of an urban legend for her. She was convinced that he didn't exist since she could not for the life of her remember Benton's alleged dinner companion from that first night at Rocco's.

"Of course. Benton's neighbor. So nice to *finally* meet you." Kate winked when she said it, hoping to soothe Ian's apparently wounded ego, momentarily at least.

"Well, actually, to be honest, I'm only her neighbor for six more weeks. I'm just subletting from a friend who lives in Benton's building right now. I'm back to Africa next month for a six-month stint. Longer if all goes well."

Thud.

Kate had to keep from looking around to see if anyone else had heard the sound she could have sworn her heart had made. She had just met this man (officially at least) and she couldn't stop looking over his shoulder for her planned blind date, and yet, she was genuinely sorry in that moment to hear that Ian was leaving the city in a little over a month. In truth, she had, ever since meeting Benton in Bryant Park and hearing her story about eavesdropping on Kate and Professor Tipton at Rocco's, enjoyed imagining Ian as a handsome dark-haired stranger walking around New York City, confused about the waitress who was too smart to be an aspiring actress in mid-town

Manhattan. And now that she had finally *met* the handsome stranger, she could tell just how palpably his absence might be felt, if only in her own imagination.

Kate sipped her wine casually and asked as nonchalantly as she could, "Why Africa?"

Ian laughed and shook his head.

"What's so funny?"

"I'm used to people being easily impressed when I tell them I've been to Africa and I'm headed, you know, back there. I like to believe that everyone I tell thinks it's thrilling and sexy and gushes over this very exciting news of mine. But not you. You're just: 'Why Africa?' Very humbling."

Kate wanted to put her hand on his, and reassure him. This sort-of stranger in the bar who was going to Africa. She wanted to tell him that he was thrilling and sexy, and that she had been able to figure that out in about an instant, now that she had *met* him, but instead she apologized the best way she knew how.

"Oh, I'm sure you will get a much better reaction to your travel plans from other people. I don't tend to react to things the way everyone else does. I get it from my mother, actually. I'm very analytical. Very practical, I like to think—but the way some people view practical, you would think it's a crime."

She clammed up then, afraid of already having said too much.

By "some people," she had meant Ted, of course. Very un-practical Ted. When Kate first met Benton, she had been dating Ted for a few months. They broke up soon after, but she was still stinging a bit when she "met" Ian that night in Tribeca. Not by the fact of the breakup, but by the way Ted did it.

Ted was a musician.

"An artist, really."

His words.

Kate had often asked, "But how are you going to make a

living with your music?" And Ted had often called Kate "too analytical," spitting the words out as bitter-tasting vulgarities. One night after deciding not to introduce him to her parents, even though they were coming into the city from the suburbs for dinner, Kate realized that her future with Ted was probably going to be measured in a matter of mere weeks, rather than years or even months.

And so on the night Ted broke up with Kate, she had long been ready for him to go, and had been scheduling her own breakup conversation as a matter of fact (*no really!*). But unlike Ted, Kate was hoping to have a friendly break-up where they agreed to lie to each other and say, "We will still be friends"; where they both agreed that they were special and wonderful people who were just "growing apart" and needed "some space."

But not Ted.

He left amidst some disappointing and vitriolic diatribe about passion and art for art's sake, and how Kate was lacking passion and an artist's soul and was therefore completely unworthy of him. While Kate agreed with him to some extent, it just seemed so, well *mean*, to say it out loud. Kate couldn't help thinking of Ted's tantrum while she apologized to Ian for her reaction to "Africa."

"Seriously, why Africa?" This time, she reached out and touched his hand.

Ian looked at her very carefully as if he were studying her— no, as if he were looking for something. She felt electric and peaceful all at once and wanted to hear more about him, and about Africa, and in that moment, Kate didn't feel analytical at all.

But they were interrupted just then. Benton walked over, escorting a self-conscious-looking but handsome dark-haired man in a navy lawyer suit. Ian turned away and broke his gaze, and the moment passed. Kate told herself that it would be silly to stand here and talk to this stranger about his African adventures based solely on some "peaceful electricity" that seemed to have passed between them. She excused herself as politely as she could to Ian and turned to Benton and Rob who had just arrived at the bar.

"Kate, this is Rob!" Benton yelled over the music and the margaritas she had already consumed. Kate shook Rob's hand and motioned him away to a quieter area of the bar—away from Ian, but as she glanced over her shoulder at Ian, she saw that Benton had stayed to talk with him and mitigate her arguably rude departure, and that Ian was still looking in Kate's direction in a curious and interested kind of way.

2011

"MOMMY, CAN YOU FIX THIS?" David brought a small, plastic broken action figure into the kitchen and looked up at Kate so confidently that Kate almost burst into tears.

The toy's arm was cracked in half leaving only some sharp edges, most likely the result of a territorial dispute between the boys, and David was holding both the broken figure and its ragged arm up for Kate to see.

"Well, I think I can, honey. Why don't you leave it in here and let me glue it—we'll see how it looks tomorrow. You have to promise me to leave it alone until tomorrow, ok? Or it'll never work."

Kate took the action figure pieces and stashed them on top of the refrigerator out of view and reach of both boys. The jubilance and reassured look on David's face buoyed her for a moment until he headed back to the basement to break some more toys. As soon as David was out of sight, a feeling of desolation blanketed Kate again.

She reached up for the toy and the arm remnant and threw them both into the garbage. She started to walk away from the trashcan, and then turned quickly back to bury the items below some newspaper and paper towels so the boys wouldn't catch a glimpse of their toy—the one they had likely been fighting about just a few minutes ago. Kate made a mental note to pick up a new "fixed" action figure the next day, and then she went back to what she had been doing before David walked in and allowed her to be a superhero for just a moment.

What she was doing was arranging food in the refrigerator: moving milk, and discarding leftovers. She was trying to make room for the acrylic bakery bowl of rice pudding she had just brought home for that night's Superbowl party. As she shuffled cold food containers, Kate allowed herself a smug smile of satisfaction that she had moved beyond caring that she had run out of time to actually *make* rice pudding, her favorite dessert, and that she wouldn't be trying to pass this off as her own. That would take energy she simply did not have anymore.

Out of the corner of her eye, Kate caught a glimpse of their family photo from two years earlier at Paradise Resort, sitting on the kitchen counter. She stopped rearranging the refrigerator to stomp across the kitchen and heave the picture into the trashcan on top of the newspapers, the discarded toy and its broken arm. She made no second trip to hide the framed photo in the garbage can.

Over the last two years especially, ever since they arrived home from Paradise Resort, she had found herself faking it more and more.

It being perfection.

It being hope.

She desperately wanted to be one of those for whom it was easy. One of those women who moved through motherhood, and wifedom—hell, life—more effortlessly than Kate. For Kate, it just seemed like so much work. So, instead, she committed to making it *look* easy, which was even *harder* these days.

Hiding the cleaning lady, pretending instead her immaculate home was the result of her hard labor. Making sure to throw out the card of the interior decorator who had worked a little magic hanging curtains in every downstairs room of Kate's home. Leaving out ironing boards decorated with Rob's shirts on paper-wrapped wire hangers, which actually and humorously seemed to impress Rob when he got home from work, when in reality she regularly paid Mr. Horsham of Horsham Drycleaners $2.50 per shirt for same day service.

More than once, Kate had even passed off take-out as her own creation for dinner parties or potluck get-togethers. But tonight, she had decided she would proudly display the rice pudding in the same disposable bowl in which the bakery had sold it. She did not feel like faking anything tonight.

So it's happened, she thought. *We've finally gotten here—to the place where I can serve bakery pudding in an acrylic bowl without apology.*

The irony was painful. She had worked so hard while hoping things would turn out differently, trying to create a façade that she was comfortable in this skin, in this life, and now—

Well, no one would care. That was the funny thing. They'd compliment the pudding and the bakery choice and they'd mention that they loved that bakery and bought cannolis there for Christmas Eve. They would not think any less of her. That was not why she faked it. She wasn't worried about what her friends would say. She wasn't even worried about what Rob would say. She faked it because *she* wanted it to be different. But it wasn't. Time to admit that to everyone.

Her friends might see the bakery pudding and ask about her week. They might ask how it was all going. "Oh, did you have a busy week? Were the kids sick?"

And would she have it in her to lie? Would she recover quickly? Or would she simply blurt out the news that Rob was cheating on her, and had been for some time now, and that it had all been a bit of a distraction this month.

This particular month in 2011 when she was trying on her new life as a stay-at-home mom for the very first time. Like a winter coat that she had spent too much money on and was now deciding whether it truly fit or was warm enough. Or whether she should take it back and buy extra coats for the kids instead.

It had been ten years of waiting for this month, and here she was, not feeling very warm at all.

1997

THE MORNING AFTER KATE MET ROB at the Tribeca Bar, she woke up a bit hung over and tired from the Cinco de Mayo party. Her phone lit up with a call from Benton, asking somewhat mysteriously, "So guess who asked me for your number last night?"

Kate's brain, foggy from the party and the wine, tried to imagine why Rob was asking Benton for her number since Kate had, in fact, *given* it to him the night before.

They had talked and laughed at the quietest table they could find in the middle of the party, and the date ended in Kate's apartment with them making out just long enough before she insisted on walking him out to the street to hail a taxi a few minutes before midnight. They exchanged cell numbers and Rob had kissed Kate while they stood on the corner as his taxi waited, and he told her he'd call her "tomorrow." He had called just after midnight, still in his taxi on the way home. "You are something special, Kate," he had slurred. And then, "I told you I'd call you tomorrow."

Kate was still thinking about that somewhat dreamy and drunken exchange, when Benton woke her out of it. "Ian wants to call you, Kate. I figured what's the harm? He's leaving in a few weeks anyway. So I gave him your number. That's ok, right?"

And suddenly all Kate could remember about the night before was the intriguing man at the bar who had changed his order to New Zealand sauvignon blanc for her and who had looked at her in that searching way, after he had announced that he would be leaving for Africa in just six weeks.

∾

When Ian called later that same day, and asked her out, Kate agreed without hesitating. She was flattered (especially since he had obviously seen her with Rob at the party and seemed not the least bit daunted). She was also anxious not to have any moments of kicking herself by the time Ian left for Africa. When Kate began dating Rob, as she had already decided to do, she didn't want to have any dark, mysterious Ian clouds lingering around her head.

No doubts.

That's what Kate told herself as she scheduled her first date with Ian fewer than 24 hours after meeting him—*finally*—at the Tribeca Bar. For that same night.

Ian picked the place which turned out to be a quiet Indian restaurant downtown. They ordered a samosa platter and talked about their favorite spots in the city. Kate tried not to bore Ian with tales about her grad school schedule, but he continued prodding her about classes and her upcoming teaching gig. He was attentive and interested, reminding her that his first memory of her would always involve eavesdropping on her apparently successful attempt at impressing her history professor.

"Why history? Why teaching?"

The waitress poured generous glasses of wine and they decided to order dishes to share.

Hmm. A pretty intimate first date decision, Kate thought, but did not say aloud.

When the curry dishes arrived, Kate reached across to Ian's plate, scooped up some rice and chicken in naan bread and picked up again where they had left off the night before. "So, tell me. Really. What's the deal with Africa?"

Ian stopped in mid-scoop of his own food, then put it back down on his plate to explain.

"Well. I write for this little travel mag, and a year ago, I went to Botswana on assignment to do a piece on an amazing new camp resort in the Okavango Delta."

"Un hunh, the Avocado Delta, of course." Kate continued scooping and eating.

"Good try. Okavango Delta. This beautiful couple, Sandy and Doug, lives among a trio of elephants that they rescued. They are trying to create a foundation of sorts to preserve the African elephant and other wildlife. In the meantime, they live with the trio like parental figures. It's astonishing, really."

Ian paused as if he were waiting for Kate to respond. Or close her mouth.

She sat across from him rapt.

"Yes, what about the trio of elephants?"

"It seems you did not actually read my amazing piece on all of this in Time Travel, Inc."

Kate laughed. "Is that for real? The real name of your magazine?"

"Well, yes. Seems it caused a bit of confusion with my Botswanan guide, as well. He saw me faxing some notes back to my editor and asked if I was really writing about time travel."

"So you told him yes, naturally."

"I actually did." Ian looked only mildly sheepish when he said this.

"Anyway, that Botswanan guide invited me to drinks the next day. They make a drink down there from the fruit of the marula tree. It's known to cure disease and do all sorts of things. So, over this decadent marula tree booze, my guide told me a story of a mystic in the delta who swears that through some combination of the fermented marula tree fruit and Botswanan agate, he can make things happen."

"What things?"

"Well, time travel, of course."

For a moment, Kate thought Ian was mocking her, or perhaps was a complete lunatic, but then he burst out laughing. "I know, crazy right? That's what marula drink will do to you. At any rate, I have spent the last six months trying to convince my editor that there is another story down there in the delta— something about the mystic and the agate and the marula. And I've finally succeeded. If nothing else, I'm going to treat myself to one helluva marula drunk."

Kate stopped eating and blinked hard at her plate of curry. She could not help but wonder what it would be like to drink marula booze in the Botswanan delta with this handsome man who seemed like he just might believe in time travel.

And who was making her want to believe as well.

As Ian reached over and scooped food up from Kate's plate comfortably, she said, "It doesn't sound that crazy, actually." Ian looked up quickly at her and his shoulders relaxed visibly.

"No, I guess it doesn't."

Later that night, fuzzy and happy from the evening, Kate leaned her head against Ian's shoulder in the cab on the way home, and said "Well, I have to say, Ian, I will miss you when you leave for Africa. It's been a really lovely night."

Ian lifted her head from his shoulder and kissed the top, just after he said, "Well, Kate, you could always come with me to Botswana."

When the cab reached Kate's building, Kate fumbled with a goodbye and then Ian interrupted her. "I just really want to kiss you, Kate. Would that be ok?" She nodded with awareness, lucid suddenly, realizing that no one had ever *asked* to kiss her and that asking for a kiss was quite possibly the sexiest thing any man could ever do. And while she couldn't be sure what

Ian was thinking, what Kate was thinking was: *It might be very nice to believe in time travel if that meant I could hold onto this one singularly perfect moment for the rest of my life.*

1998

"SO. WHERE DO YOU SEE YOURSELF IN FIVE YEARS?"

Kate was sitting across from Rob in an urban coffee shop warming her hands on her coffee mug, trying to get rid of the winter chill from the air that kept blowing in every time someone walked in.

"Well, I'll be married to the girl of my dreams, planning an impromptu trip around the world to prove to both of us that we can still be spontaneous, and I'll be a successful partner at *this* law firm."

Kate laughed. "That's a terrible answer. They'll hate you if you say that."

"I know." Rob ran his fingers through his hair and looked down at his coffee mug. Kate saw that he was more nervous than he had been letting on about his interview with a new firm the following day.

They had been dating for six months and Rob was thinking about leaving the law firm where he had started his career after law school. Where he had worked with Benton. Kate was helping him prepare for his interview.

She reached across the café table to take his hand. It felt warm against her cool skin. "Hey. What's the worst that happens tomorrow? Is your current firm that bad? I mean as far as Manhattan law firms go?"

"There's no future there. I could work to my grave and prob-ably be on the same rung of the ladder in five years. That's nothing to look forward to. It's time to move on and start looking ahead."

"You're always looking ahead. You're like a speeding train. You need to slow down once in a while. Smell the proverbial roses."

Rob shook his head. "I'll slow down, when I get where I want to be. I want security. For me *and* that dream girl of mine. What about you, Kate? Do you ever think about the future. Our future?"

The coffee shop door opened, and Kate shuddered with a chill again. Without looking up at the door, she warmed both of her cold hands in Rob's hands, abandoning her coffee mug for the moment, and nodded.

Of course I do. I think about the future. When I'm not thinking about the past.

IAN CALLED KATE THE MORNING AFTER THEIR downtown Indian restaurant date, and the next and the next.

Kate thought fleetingly, briefly, that it was odd that she did not hear from Rob during that time. She would have ignored Rob's calls, of course, so wrapped up as she was in Ian. But still, Rob didn't call.

Only Ian.

It was all she could do to get through the last few final papers she had to finish before her grad school career officially ended. Most days, Kate typed them in the school computer lab while Ian sat next to her making notes and doing research for his upcoming trip.

One late-May evening, Kate was proofreading her final paper in her apartment, and Ian was staying up with her through the night in a show of solidarity and support. He was nodding off on the sofa while she was going through the citations for the last time, when her house phone rang shrilly at two in the morning, and they both jumped.

Ian looked quizzical and Kate returned a questioning shrug as she walked across the room to the phone. For a moment, she actually wondered if it could be Rob, and she was horrified thinking that Rob might be calling her finally, after all this time, at 2 am and what horribly untrue things Ian might think if that was the case.

She reached for the phone and then—

"Benton? Are you all right?"

Benton was teary through her "Hey."

"Benton. What do you need? You need me to come meet you?"

"No, no. I just need an ear. You busy?" Kate glanced at Ian and her citations and the clock and sighed without noise.

"Of course not, Sweetie. Never too busy for you. What's up?"

Kate smiled and shook her head at Ian indicating that all was ok, and then took the phone into her bedroom and closed the door for privacy behind her.

"I screwed up big time at work, Kate."

"What happened?"

"I missed a pre-trial deadline. I was supposed to send some documents to the other side's attorney. Huge mistake. I was summoned into the lead partner's office for a how-could-you-let-this-happen session, the likes of which I never want to experience again. It was nearly impossible not to cry. But I muscled through. I would have died before I would cry at the office. I tried to be as contrite as possible, without being a doormat. It was horrible. Just horrible. I just left the office now, after drafting countless motion papers to try to fix my mistake. Turns out it is quite difficult to draft affidavits that admit, but don't really admit, your own incompetence. I'm on my way home now in the office car service."

Benton's (and Rob's) white shoe law firm was known for its perks. Gourmet lunches of dill salmon and beef wellington for the associates when they took time to sit down for lunch, which was discouraged, and car service home after late nights in the office, which *were* encouraged. In return, all that was asked was 24/7 availability and complete and utter devotion to the firm. Kate thought about how missing-in-action Rob was subject to the same pressures, demands, and schedule. Kate had a hard time seeing Benton last there much longer, not because she wasn't smart enough, but because she was much too smart.

"Benton. It was just a mistake. You're only human. What's

the worst that can happen?"

"Well, let's make a list. Lawsuits with my name on them. Getting fired from this job. Total humiliation for the rest of my life."

"Which partner was it?"

"Shawn."

"Gross. Did he ogle you while he was yelling at you?"

First laugh of the conversation.

"Actually he did sort of."

"He probably loved the opportunity of having you alone in his office."

Shawn had had a pretty open crush on Benton. Of course he was married with two kids, and of course Benton didn't return the attention. But he was pretty renowned for alternately yelling mercilessly at—and then flirting ridiculously with—his young female associates. Benton had been on his radar screen for a few months now and she had confided in Kate about a number of questionable emails he had sent recently. Kate had warned her to report him, but Benton disagreed fiercely with Kate's recommendations.

"As I see it, this is a total win for you, Benton."

"Hunh?"

"Shawn will move on to the next associate, now that he's mad at you. And if he tries to fire you, you simply march yourself into human resources with all the emails he's sent to you in the middle of the night."

"Oh, Kate. Those emails are harmless to the outside observer."

"No way, Benton. They're disgusting. 'Stick with me, kid, if you want to go places in this firm.' 'I need you to be available to me every night whether there are deadlines or not.' He's a louse. I've been telling you to report him for months."

"I hear you. But I don't want to be *that* associate, you know.

Most days, I rely on people at the office to forget I'm a woman. That way, I get the good cases, the good assignments. A little harassment from that weasel, Shawn, seems a small price to pay."

"You're too good for them, Benton. You're smart *and* you are a woman. You shouldn't have to hide that fact so Shawn doesn't hit on you."

"But I screwed up."

"Yes, you screwed up. Oh well. So did Shawn. No one died. It'll pass over eventually. You just have to wait it out. And in the meantime, why don't you think about what it is you *really* want to do. When you're through playing cat and mouse with Shawn."

"You know what I want to do."

"Exactly. Sounds like a good time for an exit strategy. That's what I would do if I were you."

"What you would do."

"Un-hunh."

"Well, that's good advice then. I miss you."

"I miss you, too."

Kate glanced behind her at the bedroom door, which had swung back open.

Oops. I guess Ian overheard our conversation after all.

"Let's get together soon. When I come up for air from this catastrophe."

"Of course, Benton. I'll see you soon."

When Kate came out of her room, she gave an unnecessary explanation to a quiet Ian: "Benton. She's having some problems at the office. Just needed an ear. Back to work for me."

Ian sleepily pulled her down next to him on the couch.

"Hey, Kate Monroe. Can I kiss you?"

❧

When classes ended the third week of May, Kate officially

had the rest of May and June off.

There was a brief graduation ceremony near the end of May, and her parents came into the city, announcing big plans to spend the day shopping and eating. But Kate was so wrapped up in Ian that she actually told her parents she wasn't feeling well after the ceremony and photo ops, and that she would take a raincheck on the day's festivities.

She didn't tell them that she didn't plan on cashing the raincheck until the end of June, so reluctant was she to spend one of Ian's diminishing days in the States away from him.

As luck would have it, Kate's teaching position was not scheduled to begin until late June, a week after Ian was planning to leave for Africa. And so, following graduation, Kate spent all of her free time alternately hand in hand with Ian on the New York City streets and tangled up with him in his midtown sublet.

Kate even avoided Benton, wondering if she was ever going to bring up Rob, or ask about Ian. When Benton called to congratulate Kate on her graduation, and offered to take her out to a celebratory dinner, Kate told her she was swamped getting ready for her new teaching position, and that she'd call when things calmed down. When Kate asked how things were at work, Benton said dismissively, "Fine, fine. Shawn has calmed down. I'm forming my exit strategy, just like you suggested. You always give me the best advice. You always know just what road to take."

Benton didn't mention Rob.

And Kate didn't mention Ian.

❧

Kate answered the phone wearing yellow cleaning gloves.

It was a Wednesday afternoon, and Ian and she had sepa-rated for an unusual but brief afternoon to get some errands/cleaning done before dinner and an outdoor concert in Central Park. Up to her elbows in bleach and glass cleaner, Kate could almost hear Ian's mischievous smile in the tone of his voice on the other end. "I'm actually going to meet you at five instead of six. I changed our dinner plans."

"I thought we were going to that café across the street from the park so we could walk over to the park at dusk."

"Nope. I have other plans. We're going to a place a bit more out of the way. So we're going to have to get an earlier start. Skip the primping and meet me downstairs in 45 minutes."

"As you wish." She laughed as she peeled off the cleaning gloves without finishing and jumped into the shower. With Ian in town for only a few more weeks, it usually felt like there wasn't a moment to waste.

Kate hopped into the cab with a wet head and a little lip gloss and she slid close to Ian.

"I love you like this. Unretouched." Ian tousled her hair.

Kate kissed him then pulled away reluctantly. "Where are we going?"

"It's a surprise," Ian said as the cab headed toward midtown, and Kate tried to think of places she might have mentioned to Ian that she'd like to try out with him. One passing reference to a favorite spot would often land the two of them there the next evening. She couldn't remember ever mentioning any midtown locales however.

The cab stopped suddenly in front of a small familiar neon sign, and Kate leaned back into the cab seat and laughed.

"Oh Ian, Rocco's? Really?"

"Yes, really." Ian paid the driver quickly and grabbed her hand, pulling her out to the curb.

Kate had ditched the Rocco's waitressing gig months ago and had mentioned casually to Ian one night that she had never actually eaten there as a patron instead of as hired help.

Ian was always raving about the food and was still more

than a little upset that she couldn't quite remember him from their first real encounter there, the night he had showed up with Benton.

He gave his name to the hostess, a face Kate didn't recognize, as turnover at those midtown restaurants was frequent. Ian was right. Most of the waitresses and waiters were indeed starving actresses and actors and Kate had been an exception among them, although it had been just a temporary stop for her as well.

They took a quiet table in the corner and after Ian ordered for them both, he narrated his first glimpse of Kate like he was acting out a scene.

Kate sipped her wine, red for a change, and listened to Ian's production.

"And right in the middle of Benton complaining about one of her arrogant law firm colleagues, and me nodding empathetically like a good friend, I saw her. The most stunning wanna be actress I had ever laid my eyes on. Why she was still starving I could not decide. And then I saw her making eyes at the old man across the room who looked so positively boring I could not mask my disdain."

"Ian!" Kate put her wine glass down so that she could punch Ian's shoulder with righteous indignation. "I was *not* making eyes at him. He was my professor. My mentor."

Ian raised his eyebrows and pretended to massage his injured shoulder. "Sure, sure. But then, I heard her." He continued on with his one-man play.

"She was discussing history. In the middle of this midtown Italian tourist restaurant. In the middle of the singing waiters and waitresses, she was discussing European history with this wholly unattractive man and his overly bleached and equally plump dining companion and I was wondering how I could ever get such a lovely creature to discuss European history. With me."

Suddenly, Kate could hear her own pulse, and nothing else. The smoke from the nearby smoking section combined with the scent of rare steak and garlic, was making a sour attack on her olfactory nerve. The whirring noise emanating from her own body ramped up from a minor distraction to a fearsome bellowing in her brain. She stood up tentatively, trying to escape her own senses.

"Kate?"

"I need a little air, I think." Kate exhaled slowly through her words, and walked out of the restaurant quickly. She sat on the curb between two parked cars with her head between her knees, her dress slowly riding up her bare legs. She could feel cool beads of sweat dripping from her temples to her thighs, as the whirring noise quelled. Gradually, it was replaced by the sounds of the city in front and in back of her and around her, and by the soft sound of Ian's hand as it rubbed comfortingly on the fabric of her dress on her back. "Sweetheart. What happened?"

"You. You happened. You have some kind of crazy effect on me, Ian."

Kate lifted her head and pushed the dark fabric of her dress back down her legs, to cover and absorb the streaky lines of sweat she had been too ill to care about just moments ago, but now was feeling very self-conscious about.

"It's a good thing I didn't notice you that night at Rocco's with Benton. I probably would have fainted in the middle of the restaurant. How embarrassing. I'm sorry. I didn't mean to ruin the night. Let's go back in." Kate tried to stand up, but Ian pulled her back down onto the curb. He put his arms around her and held her there for few more minutes. The sounds of the city disappeared and she focused only on his heartbeat under hers. He tucked her hair behind her ear and whispered, "You haven't ruined anything. Don't you know the effect you have on *me*, Kate? I love you. I've loved you since that first day I saw you *here*."

Kate could only kiss him in response.

She couldn't say the words. She couldn't even think the words without feeling her heart begin to break in two.

∽

Kate and Ian spent one of their last days together in Bryant Park.

Near the spot where Kate had met Benton right next to the Bryant Park carousel. They were sharing the paper and drinking iced coffee on a park bench. Kate's feet were draped in Ian's lap, when suddenly, he scooted her legs off his and announced, "I'll be right back."

When Ian returned, he had two pink tickets in hand. He had bought tickets for the carousel.

Kate laughed. "You are such a tourist."

"After you, Madame," Ian waved his arm toward the empty carousel. It was a hot June Sunday afternoon, and the park was practically deserted. The city was already starting to empty itself as it would for every summer weekend from here on out. The city dwellers would begin their long weekend sojourns to the Hamptons' beaches, and the tourists would soon be left to their own devices. The Bryant Park carousel had just opened for the season, and so that particular day, Kate and Ian were its lone travelers.

They walked past the glossy animals, chose a bench seat on the carousel and Kate rested her head on Ian's shoulder the way she had done the night of their first date, in the cab. She was tempted to give in to the sadness she had been fighting for the last month, as the weight of Ian's looming departure finally settled over her. She started to cry, but tried not to let Ian see. She tearfully watched the ride operator take his hand off the levers, seemingly allowing extra go-rounds for the un-merry couple.

She wanted to yell out to him. *It's enough. We've had enough. Please stop the ride. Please.*

But the words stuck in her throat as the carousel continued its sickening revolutions.

When they got off the extra long ride, sad and dizzy, Ian suggested they go to the nearby Bryant Park Café for lunch, but Kate's only response was to blurt out, "Oh, Ian, I am going to miss you so much."

Ian put his hands on both sides of Kate's face to steady her. "We'll find each other again."

She shook her head. "Ian, I love—"

Ian looked at her expectantly, but she did not reward him. "I love your optimism, Ian. But six months is a long time. We'll be different people when you come back. *If* you come back."

"But we keep finding each other. It's like—I don't know— divine intervention or something."

"Ian, you're too smart to believe in anything like that."

"What do you mean?" He looked stumped.

"Just forget it. Let's go grab lunch."

"No, wait. Where *do* you stand on God? That's actually one topic that's never come up."

Kate shook her head again.

"No God for me. I hate the way people use God. I believe in goodness. In people. But God? Throughout history, people have simply used 'God' as a way to achieve power, enslave the masses, and validate their personal agendas. No thank you."

"So no higher being setting our destinies in motion?"

"Now that's the very *last* reason I would *ever* believe in God. Destiny? Fate? Divine Intervention? Do you really want to live in a world where you have absolutely no control over any of this?"

"Well, the Christians believe in a God who allows for choice. Free choice."

"And yet, *He* knows everything they are going to choose anyway. Some free choice," Kate chuckled and continued on.

"No, I like to be in control of my own life. Thank you very much. *I* make the choices that shape and affect my journey. *I* am in charge of my little corner of the universe and *I* find that reality very reassuring and very comforting. In that way, I don't need a false comfort brought on by believing in a 'God' of some sort. Oh my—"

"There's more?" Ian looked startled.

"This is a very serious conversation to have just outside the Bryant Park carousel."

Ian nodded. "True. Well, I think it's great that you have it all figured out. You make your choices. Conscious deliberate choices. Like the night we met. Like the night *you* claim we met. On Cinco de Mayo. You came to meet the man of your dreams and look at what happened."

"Oh, Ian, stop. Now, you're just teasing me."

"I'm not teasing you. I'm just challenging you, Kate. I'm not discounting your theory about choice. I don't rule out the possibility that there is something more as well. And you shouldn't, either."

Ian took her hand and led her into the café where the topic of God and goodbyes turned to avocado and turkey and how they should spend every one of their last Manhattan evenings together.

As the June date approached, Kate and Ian ignored the fact of Ian's imminent departure.

Until one day.

They were each lying on opposite ends of the sofa in Ian's sublet on a lazy New York morning. The air conditioning units were working at half-strength given the unusually warm June temperatures covering the city.

They were watching a documentary about a revolutionary urban schoolteacher on cable television in the muggy apartment, when Kate started talking over the on-screen narrator.

"Oh, this guy reminds me so much of my dad. That urban schoolteacher philosophy about having to be creative and determined if there is any hope of shaking up the otherwise pre-determined destinies for these inner city school kids."

"Is that why you are going into teaching?"

"Well, let's face it. I'm not exactly heading into an urban school to try to shake things up and change the world like my dad. I'll be teaching over-privileged college kids. Still, it feels right. Feels like where I'm supposed to be. For now, at least."

"I had such a strange phone conversation with my parents last night," Ian transitioned quietly.

"About what?"

"About my trip to Botswana."

Kate flinched a little at the word, and its implications.

"What did you talk about?"

"They don't really understand why I'm going back. They'd like me to start staying put a bit more. I tried to explain it to them, but I found myself flailing for words. It was odd. Not like me at all."

"I understand why you're going, Ian."

"I know."

"I'm hungry." Kate jumped up and headed into the kitchen, trying to stave off the tears that were brimming, burning her eyes with the effort to keep them from streaming down her face.

She opened and closed cabinet doors mindlessly. Then she stood in front of the open refrigerator letting the cold air blast her face. It helped to push back the tears and the burning sensation she was starting to feel in her chest.

Kate leaned out of the refrigerator to call to Ian, "Well, my darling. It looks like we are going to have to eat mustard and cold beer for breakfast, or actually venture out of this apartment into the heat for bagels and coffee. Iced coffee today, I think."

"That sounds like a plan," Ian said barely audibly, but stayed right where he was on the sofa.

Kate returned to the living room and collapsed back into the sofa in her former spot. She wrapped her legs around Ian's, and started to watch the documentary again. Ian interrupted a few minutes later.

"What would happen if I didn't go?"

"To get bagels?"

That is not what he means.

"What would happen if I didn't go to Botswana?"

"I don't know, Ian. What would happen?"

They laid there with their legs wrapped around each other in a silent duel, until finally, Ian was the one who spoke first.

"Let's go get bagels."

"Yes, I think that's a good idea."

❧

There should be fireworks. More fanfare. It feels like any other night with him.

On the last night, Kate and Ian went back to their Indian restaurant to end the romance the way it had begun—over shared curry, generous goblets of wine, and comfortable conversation.

In the cab ride back to Kate's apartment after dinner, she rested her head on Ian's shoulder just the way she had done that first night, coming home from their first date. And Ian said quietly, "I'm not going to ask you to come with me. But I want you to know that I would like to ask you to come with me."

Kate took a sharp breath. "I know. And I'm not going to ask you to stay, but I would like to ask you to stay."

Ian kissed the top of her head. "I know."

When they kissed goodbye outside her building for the last time, Kate struggled with whether to invite him up one last time.

You have just said goodbye to a wonderful and charming and romantic man who seems to enjoy having no permanent address and who is on his way back to Botswana for who knows how long. To write about time travel and marula fruit liquor. It was beautiful while it lasted.

But, it's time to let go.

It's time.

Kate stood on the corner wrapped in his embrace one last time.

She didn't cry, and she didn't say "I love you."

She simply let the unspoken words settle in her brain like a dormant seed.

"ROB SUTTON. WHERE HAVE YOU BEEN?"

As if on cue, Rob called the morning after Ian left. And listening to Rob's rambling excuses about deadlines and a six-week trial that had kept him buried unexpectedly at work ever since Cinco de Mayo, Kate found herself feeling grateful instead of angry.

Grateful that Rob had been too busy to interrupt her days and nights with Ian, and that he had showed up again today, on the day after Ian had left for Botswana.

Just when she needed him most.

She accepted his invitation to a SOHO rooftop barbeque and headed downtown.

Benton was at the SOHO party, too. She smiled when Kate walked in with Rob and said, "Oh, Kate! It's been weeks! I've missed you so much. Where have you been hiding?" And as she leaned in to kiss Kate hello, Benton whispered, "Didn't I spot you a few times in my lobby, darling, at odd hours of the day and night?"

"I don't know what you're talking about." Kate had forgotten that Benton kept bizarre hours at work—particularly so after the whole Shawn debacle. Kate had foolishly been thinking that no one ever saw her coming or going on trips to see Ian at his sublet.

"Well, anyway, now Ian is off on some exotic trip as usual, and you're here with Rob. I'm thrilled. He's lovely. Much more for you, darling. You'll have me to thank if this all works out." Benton squeezed Kate's hand and swirled around the room to mingle, leaving Kate to wonder why Rob was "much more *for*" Kate and what Benton's definition of "working out" would really mean.

❧

"I know it sounds corny, but I've always wanted to be a lawyer."

"I don't think that sounds corny at all. I've always wanted to be a teacher, even though I almost went into banking after college."

"Banking? You don't exactly seem the banking type." Rob laughed a little as he poured wine into Kate's plastic cup. He had grabbed a bottle from the bar in his friend's apartment and two plastic tumblers and led her up to the rooftop.

Before she took a sip, Kate reached out and took the wine bottle from Rob, examined it, and handed it back without explanation.

Chardonnay. Thank God. Kate spontaneously and involuntarily prayed as she drank her wine, ignoring the irony.

"Yeah, I know. But I had a job offer my senior year of college and I thought for a short time that it was the practical thing to do. I have been accused of being a bit too practical. To a fault, really."

"Well, practical isn't so bad." Rob clinked her tumbler. "You just have to balance practical with knowing when to throw caution to the wind a little bit, too." He smiled. "I've been accused of being a bit too practical as well. Law is not exactly a creative profession, let's be honest. But you—"

Kate looked at him inquisitively.

"You didn't choose banking. So, I'm thinking maybe you are not quite as practical as you think. I have this feeling that we could make a pretty good team, you and I."

"A pretty good team. I like that. Like we could run a

marathon together or invent something. Go team."

"Well, practical or not, I haven't been able to get you out of my mind, Kate Monroe."

They talked and laughed over Chardonnay and enjoyed the rooftop view. Rob kissed her without asking, and not one thing seemed familiar.

1998

"BENTON, WHY DID YOU and Ian Campton never get together?"

Kate and Benton were sitting in their favorite spot in Bryant Park on a warm May Saturday nearly a year after Ian's departure, eyes closed, faces turned upward like hungry plant leaves soaking in the sunlight. They were trading war stories from the week. Kate about her no-longer-new teaching gig and Benton about her real-life law firm drama, most of which Kate already knew from Rob, whom she was dating seriously by then.

Rob hadn't gotten the job she had been helping him prepare for in the coffee shop several months earlier, so he and Benton still worked together, and were both still planning exit strategies.

Kate and Benton were waiting for Rob and Benton's then-boyfriend, Sam, to come meet them in the park for a brunch date.

"Ian and me? Oh lord, Kate. Don't tell me you're still pining for Ian?"

Kate snapped too quickly. "Of course not. I just wonder why you two never tried out dating, that's all."

"Well, he never asked, for one thing." It sounded as ludicrous out loud as it must have sounded in Benton's head as well. "But, really, I've always known that Ian wasn't serious boyfriend material. Certainly not husband material. That's why I was glad your 'fling' was just a temporary one." Kate winced at the flimsy characterization of their love affair.

"So what makes Ian non-husband material in Benton Daly's book?" Kate tried to sound casual, eyes still closed, holding back tears with an effort that surprised her all this time later, knowing she would certainly have surprised Benton had she let them flow.

"Well, darling, for one thing, he has no plan for the future. He lives in the present—and in the past. It's a lovely, romantic way to live, but completely unrealistic for maintaining a relationship. Plus he always admitted that he isn't sure at all that he ever wants to settle down, or have kids. He's too much of a gypsy."

"Hmm. Do you think that's the kind of thing a person changes their mind about as they get older? More settled?" Kate asked rhetorically, thinking that she, too, was a little confused about the subject of kids, whether and when to have them. The subject had come up only briefly with Rob to date.

Benton didn't answer. Instead she tapped Kate's shoulder and said, "Oh! Would you look at that?"

Kate opened her teary eyes just in time to see Rob a few yards away jumping and reaching to grab at a balloon that was floating slowly upward as a small boy gasped and cried at his loss, and his mother comforted him.

Rob didn't seem to notice Benton and Kate staring at him as he repeatedly missed the balloon that was floating away, but they watched as he turned and headed past the Bryant Park carousel to the balloon vendor across the park to buy up the rest of his bunch.

Soon after that, Benton and Kate started to see less of each other.

Rob would see Benton every day at his firm, and give Kate

updates on her, and so Kate actually *felt* as though she was seeing her more often.

That's how she justified the gradually increasing distance.

But the simple truth was, Benton reminded Kate of Ian.

Which didn't really make sense, Kate had to acknowledge, because Benton was the one who actually introduced her to *Rob*. Nevertheless, Kate linked Benton with Ian in her mind. And as the months, and eventually years, went by without any word from Ian, Kate had to make peace with Ian's role in her past, and that included seeing less of Benton in her present.

Brunch dates and Saturday afternoon catch-up sessions were replaced by chance meetings on Manhattan street corners and in Bryant Park.

During one such chance meeting in the park, Kate learned from Benton that the Botswana trip had landed Ian a very prestigious and very lucrative gig working as a writer for a national travel magazine. "I just ran into Ian Campton on his way out of town, Kate. He's traveling like crazy, still no signs of ever slowing down. Same old Ian."

Kate physically stifled an audible response at Benton's mention of Ian. By that time, Rob and Kate had been dating for years and were vaguely discussing marriage. Benton had left Rob's firm to (finally!) start her own fashion line, shortly before Rob left the firm for a new position himself. When they said goodbye to each other that day in Bryant Park, Benton embraced Kate warmly. "So great to see you, Kate! Feel free to thank me for introducing you to the great love of your life!" Kate laughed, wondering for a split second who *Benton* thought she was referring to, before responding quickly, "Rob is great—he will be happy to hear that you are doing well, Benton."

Kate walked away, shaking her head, as if physically shaking off the exchange with Benton. She walked quickly and deliberately by the carousel, without stopping, but the memories chased behind her as they did so often, trying hard to catch up.

Long talks with Ian about God and destiny and marula fruit.

Ian asking permission to kiss her.

Being tangled up with Ian in his midtown sublet.

Ian's "I love you" on the curb outside Rocco's.

Ian leaving.

2001

BEFORE KATE GOT PREGNANT the first time, she had to admit motherhood seemed a very strange and confusing concept.

For as much as Kate thought about having a baby sometime down the road, she felt like a foreign exchange student whenever she visited one of her college friends or cousins, all mothers several times over long before Kate. That is to say, she recognized the rituals and appreciated that they were probably perfectly appropriate in the culture in which she was visiting; however, to her, they just seemed so, well . . . strange.

Sippy cups and soggy cheerios littering every surface. Women with disheveled clothes and hair, stopping in mid-sentence to scream absurd directions into the next room, such as "James, stop looking at your sister," before resuming their story or worse—starting the story over again.

And the strange mix of envy and disdain with which she seemed to be regarded by her "mother" friends. After all, Kate had a career. While her days were filled with intellectual rigor, preparing syllabi and lesson plans for college kids, she didn't have homework to do, girl scout carpools, school fundraisers to plan, age-appropriate party favors to buy.

No, she just worked for a living and had no children at all and so she endured the stops and starts in conversations, and the sounds of children screaming over coffee, while her friends ignored them and quoted from the latest parenting books, which sounded quite dreadful and misguided in Kate's opinion, although she never said so.

Interestingly, much like the way key moments of someone's life must flash before their eyes when faced with danger, these strange cultures and rituals all flashed before Kate's mind's eye in the moment she found out she was pregnant in 2001. She was 30 years old, all alone in her bathroom staring at a little urine-covered stick. And she was initially filled with the same mixture of fear and happiness she assumed most newly pregnant women feel.

She wasn't at all sure what Rob would say. She wasn't sure he would view this as good news from the outset, so she kept the news to herself for about three whole weeks, rolling the idea around and around in her brain, picturing the baby growing inside her, imagining his eyes, his nose, his little feet. Kate was certain he was a boy, though she couldn't say why exactly. She simply couldn't believe she was growing anything other than a beautiful little boy with dark hair and dark eyes who would look just like Rob.

And over the course of the three weeks that she cradled her secret inside her, she fell in love, consumed with this little being that no one knew existed except for her.

Sure there were complications. They had not planned for a child so soon, and there were jobs to consider and schedules and just who would stay home with the baby? Rob was climbing a tough partnership ladder at his new law firm, and Kate was settling into her college teaching job—teaching intro to world history to privileged undergrads while studying for her PhD at night.

They were not exactly ready for a baby.

But who is ever really ready for a baby?

Sometimes she would say these words out loud, as if she were practicing what to say to Rob when she told him.

One afternoon at lunchtime, she left the campus where she taught, and wandered into a children's clothing boutique. She strolled the aisles of the small shop, touching the baby things softly, carefully. She smiled at the salesgirl who asked if there was anything she could help Kate find.

"No, I'm just looking," Kate said.

And then, before she could catch herself, "I'm expecting. It's all brand new. But I want to buy a little something."

The salesgirl's face lit up and she took Kate over to the wall of soft newborn sweaters. Kate bought a small almost golden-colored cashmere baby sweater. Before the salesgirl wrapped it up, Kate held it up and admired how small it was.

This is wonderful news, she thought hopefully.

As she walked out of the boutique, Kate called Rob at the office, and asked him to meet her after work at their favorite Italian restaurant downtown.

On her walk back to the college, Kate planned out exactly how she would tell Rob that they were having a baby. She would show him the sweater.

And she would tell him that it was time for them to finally consider getting married.

"YOU'RE WHAT?!"

Sitting in the restaurant, Kate realized with a start that Rob was not even a little bit happy. He was in fact, extremely upset. She acknowledged with a pang that she had known this all along somehow, which was why she had brought him here to tell him. To their favorite restaurant, a public place filled with a mix of familiar and strange faces where Rob would be compelled to put on a good face no matter what.

I'm a coward, Kate nearly answered Rob's question this way.

So clear were the words in her head, that for an instant, Kate thought Rob had actually called her a coward out loud. But no, it was only a knowing voice in her own head. Rob was sitting silently.

Rob ran his fingers through his gorgeous dark hair, the same hair Kate imagined on their firstborn boy, and took a gulp of his wine.

"I'm sorry, Kate. I would really like to be eloquent right now and say something really special so that when we look back on this moment, it won't be so damn unhappy. But I'm just a bit taken aback. This is not what I had planned—well, this is not what I thought *we* had planned anyway."

Kate's heart dropped out of her chest into her lap.

"You think I planned this?"

The words came out weakly. Kate found herself thinking: *Did you plan this? Didn't you? Didn't you know this is what would happen?*

"No, I'm . . . please, Kate. I can't talk about this right now.

I'm afraid of saying all the wrong things. I need to process this. Could we just get the check and skip dinner?"

Kate nodded and flagged down the waiter. They waited for Rob's credit card slip to be returned as he finished his wine in silent gloom and then the couple headed for the door in silence. Kate's eyes were stinging and the small unopened box holding the cashmere baby sweater felt like a lead brick in her oversized handbag, weighing her down.

They did not talk the entire taxi ride back to Kate's apartment. Rob asked the cab driver to turn the music down and Kate fidgeted. She tried to think of some way to break the silence. She wished she could hear Rob's thoughts. But not once did she wish she wasn't pregnant.

By the time they pulled up to Kate's apartment building, Rob looked even paler than he had in the restaurant.

Kate reached for the door handle, stared straight ahead out the windshield, and said calmly, "Rob, I love you. And I'm sorry that you are upset. But I am having a baby. And you can either choose to be happy about that news or not. I choose to be happy about it. Happy and hopeful that this is the way things are supposed to turn out. I have a good job, and I'm not 18. I am 30 years old and I can have this baby with or without you. That's not a threat—it's just a you're-off-the-hook, ok? So go home, process this news and let's talk in a few days. I really don't know what else to tell you."

The words were unplanned. They were quite different than the speech she had planned as she walked out of the boutique earlier that day.

Kate closed the door and left Rob alone in the cab.

❧

It was 4 am when Rob let himself into Kate's apartment

door. She heard his key in the lock from the couch but she did not move. Kate had known of course that today would be the day he showed up. She had been waiting for him all day. It had been two days since she had left him outside her apartment to "process" the news about the baby. He had left a few messages to call him back but she had ignored them. His voice still sounded like an exhale—no exuberance. As she listened to the key turning and turning for an extraordinarily long time, as if it was the wrong key, or the wrong door, she wondered if she was ready for this.

Because she had begun bleeding this morning.

She was sitting on the couch with her feet up. Waiting. Her doctor had told her over the phone that it was the only thing to be done.

"Kate, I'll be honest with you. Some doctors will tell you to stay off your feet, to rest. We could act like there's something to actually do right now. But truly, there's nothing to do. A healthy pregnancy can survive a lot. And if this is a healthy pregnancy, then you can stay off your feet, or stay on your feet, and it won't matter. But if this is not a healthy pregnancy—well, it's just a waiting game, you'll know soon enough."

So, Kate had called in sick to work and was sitting by the TV, flipping through channels mindlessly, the hope literally draining out of her. As the bleeding got heavier, she began deleting Rob's messages without listening to them.

And when Rob showed up at 4 am, Kate was not surprised. She was still awake, still flipping through the TV, still losing the baby.

Kate did not get up when she heard him come in the door. She was reluctant to stand even though she knew. She knew how this would all end. She wanted to stay on the couch and continue to squeeze her insides—to save the baby who was desperately trying to leave her.

Please let things be different, she prayed silently.

To whom she was praying she couldn't be sure. She still didn't believe blindly in God. Although, she was beginning to admit she was on the fence.

Of course things won't be different. They can't be.

She exhaled as Rob walked in and saw her, sad-faced and unshowered on the corner of the couch.

He rushed over and wrapped her in a tight hug and began talking incessantly.

"Kate, I am so sorry. I was such an ass. I should have jumped up and down when you told me about the baby. I should have done everything differently. Kate, I love you. You know that. I want to marry you. Hell, I wanted to marry you long before the baby and I would want to marry you even if there was no baby. We are meant to be together and I don't know what I thought I was waiting for. This baby is just a wake-up call."

Kate pulled away from Rob, put her face in her hands and sobbed.

So much for praying.

"Kate, I'm saying this all wrong. I don't mean that this baby is not wonderful news. It's a baby. Not a wake-up call. This is all coming out wrong."

On he went. Misinterpreting why she was sitting here like this. Talking, talking, talking. He kept going. Kate thought she was going to be sick.

"I mean in a good way. I mean, Kate, I want this baby. I want you and this baby and I *am* happy. Like you are. Really happy. Please, Kate. Please marry me, Kate."

Rob popped down off the couch onto one knee and held up an open ring box. Kate stopped crying and closed the ring box before she could even look at it.

"Rob, I'm losing the baby. There's not going to be a baby by tomorrow. Your timing is perfect. Just perfect. You're not going to be a father right now, after all. You can go home now."

And as Kate got up to show Rob out—the first time she had stood in hours, she felt the warm flow of blood rush down her leg. She reached out for Rob who grabbed her, and through her light-headed and hopeless haze, she could not tell if it was her imagination playing tricks on her or not, but she could have sworn that she saw a passing twinge of relief on Rob's face.

∽

Rob proposed for the second time later that same morning in the emergency room.

"Kate. Marry me. Please, Kate."

Kate wondered if she should wait, and take time to heal.

But no, she thought. *He has a choice. This time he has a choice.*

There was no baby, nothing forcing Rob to propose in the emergency room.

He loves me, and I love him.

Hadn't he arrived just when she needed him most? Hadn't he said he wanted to marry her, baby or no baby? Kate thought about the way she had felt when her pregnancy test first came back positive. Confused, yet hopeful. She just knew that somehow this was all meant to be.

But she had to know. Had to know about the look of relief she saw on Rob's face earlier.

"Rob. Do you *want* to have babies? With me?"

"Kate, of course I do. In the future. I'm so sorry that this baby wasn't meant to be. But we are. Marry me. I know we'll have the family we are supposed to have down the road."

Rob.

Always living in the future.

But that's better than the alternative.

Isn't it?

A few hours later, Kate was headed home from the

emergency room, with discharge instructions and an engage-ment ring. She went to bed at 2 pm and slept straight through the night.

Rob stayed by her side. When she woke, she was lying next to him and he was awake, stroking her dirty hair lovingly, a look of concern and determination on his face. His expression reminded her of something then. She remembered the day she and Benton had watched Rob trying in vain to save the child's balloon in Bryant Park before buying out the balloon vendor's inventory for the anguished child.

"How do you feel, beautiful?" He leaned in and kissed her forehead as she stretched and massaged her crampy stomach. She brushed away some tears and as she did so, she caught a glimpse of her engagement ring. She held her hand out in front of her and smiled up at Rob.

"Good Morning, Fiance."

She cuddled into him. "Thank you."

"Thank you for saying yes," Rob brushed away a few tears of his own.

Fresh start. Kate thought, and then—

It's time.

"I DON'T WANT TO SHARE YOU. I love you."

When they were newlyweds in Rob's midtown Manhattan apartment, Kate loved hearing these words. Every time Kate insisted she had to go to a department dinner or visit an old friend, Rob would playfully wrestle her back into bed and murmur in her ear, "Don't go, I can't share you. Stay here with me."

They didn't talk babies or miscarriages or emergency rooms. They talked about far off places they would travel to in the future. About growing old together. About how much they loved each other.

End of story.

Kate poured herself into her roles as wife and professor. She embraced her teaching position, and worked hard to finish her doctorate. She listened to Rob tell perplexing and complicated stories about his clients at the law firm.

She cheered him on and reassured him that he was on the right career path.

She waited patiently for him to be ready to discuss having a family.

Kate kept only in erratic contact with Benton, who was still single, while their other friends had long since married and moved to the various New York suburbs which might as well have been other countries, the lifestyles were so different from those in Manhattan. As Kate lost touch over time with most of the women she had known in her 20s, she began to feel as though that former life was just a distant memory, a dream really.

And it was hard for Kate to make new friends in her 30s in part because Kate was not entirely sure where Rob's career path would take him, and whether they would be staying in the city or not; so she was generally unsure how much effort she should put into the women she met.

Plus, the simple truth was that it was difficult to meet women friends in your 30s.

This she had learned gradually and regrettably. Margaret Dyer was the only other female professor in Kate's department under the age of 50 and she was not exactly what Kate's mother would have referred to as "the friendly sort." There were female professors in other departments, of course, but any who were close to Kate's age were either starting their families or diving into their careers full speed ahead and Kate fit neither profile. She had little in common with these or any women she met in any venue who were her age. They were all choosing at the proverbial fork of the road, digging into careers or leaving to bear babies. And it seemed sometimes that Kate was the only one straddling the fork, waiting for some mysterious moment when the time would be right.

When she would know what she was supposed to do.

By 2004, Rob and Kate had been married three years and Rob was working seven days a week at law firm number three since graduating law school. This time, he promised, the hours and the schedule were all necessary as the words "partnership track," if not exactly promised at his interview dinner for Parker & Hall, were murmured over winks and nods. He was being given his own cases and his own team to manage. All the while, Kate worked at sorting out her own career path, finishing her doctorate thesis, taking on additional classes, and court- ing the department head with her ideas for the department and the university and trying to decide if this was the place for her.

But in her quietest, darkest moments, Kate gave in to the loneliness and uncertainty and allowed herself to wonder, albeit fleetingly, whether her marriage was even going to last.

∾

"His. Story."

Kate looked up questioningly. "What was that?"

"History. I've always hated that word because it sounds like His. Story. What about us?"

Kate and Rob were out to dinner with one of Rob's law firm colleagues and his very pregnant wife. Kate had just told the couple that she was a history professor and this was the wife's response.

Kate looked at Rob to see whether he could tell how much she was bothered by this exchange or by the woman's bulging belly and constant pronouncements about all that she *could* or could *not* eat or drink because "I'm expecting!"

Yes, we know.

But Rob was locked in conversation with his colleague, and Kate was left to defend her childless status and sexist profession alone. She ordered another glass of wine as the waiter stopped by their table.

"Sauvignon blanc. A New Zealand wine, if you have it. Please," Kate pleaded before turning back to her insufferable dinner companion. "Yes, well—history is very much about men. But I try to focus my students on how we can learn from history to shape our own futures. My male *and* female students."

"That's nice. I'm very conscious of shaping tomorrow's generation of women. I'm having a girl. Did I mention that already?"

What? You're expecting? Who would know?

Kate gulped her wine to quiet her snarkiness.

"Congratulations."

Rob looked over then during a pause in his conversation with his colleague.

"So, what are you ladies talking about? Fill us in."

❧

"What if I quit my job?" Kate asked that night when they arrived back home after dinner with the colleague and his bore of a pregnant wife.

"Why on earth would you do that? Until I make partner, we *need* your salary to stay in Manhattan. Besides, what would you do all day? I know you, Kate. You'd be bored senseless."

I could have a baby.

Kate thought the words, but could not say them out loud.

She thought about bringing up the topic constantly but never really knew how to, given the way the baby topic had gone so disastrously awry last time.

In truth, the pain of the miscarried baby still caught up with her at unsuspecting moments. She would go days, weeks even, without thinking about the miscarriage and then suddenly the excruciating memory would wash over her, stopping her in her tracks, forcing her to reach out and grab the wall or a chair to keep her knees from buckling.

But Rob never mentioned the miscarriage and so Kate didn't either. She just endured the episodic pain and the constant loneliness. And she waited for things to change.

❧

"Do you think I am optimistic, Rob?"

"You are ever the optimist, Kate. It's one of the things I love most about you."

They had this discussion often on Sunday afternoons when they slept in late and reconnected for a short time between legal briefs and course syllabi. They made love and laid together for hours afterward talking about their careers, whose turn it was to check in on their parents, their favorite take-out restaurants, what they should make for dinner that night, and who had time to pick up the dry-cleaning on Wednesday.

And while they seemed largely unconnected most of the time, on those occasions, they seemed so in sync that Kate would relax about the likelihood that things would sort themselves out down the road.

After Rob made partner. After Kate had more career flexibility. After her paycheck was no longer imperative in the household financial calculations.

After. After.

But the reassurances from Sunday afternoons were always gone by Monday morning. Kate would wake in the morning and say to herself, "You are happy. You have a wonderful life and a wonderful husband." But she felt ridiculous for all the convincing she had to do.

If you have to convince yourself you are happy, you are probably not, she heard herself say out loud on more than one occasion.

2011

"You are such a damn pessimist, Kate. It's one of the things I hate most about you."

Kate gripped the counter under her. For support, yes. But also to keep from throwing her coffee mug at Rob, as he headed past her on his way out the door to work.

A few weeks before the Superbowl party, Rob had come home late again, exhausted, and smelling faintly of cigarettes and white wine. In the morning, she had ignored the hour and the stale odors, choosing to believe his story of late night client meetings and appeal briefs, and instead asked Rob while he was getting ready in the bathroom if he thought he was going to make it to the boys' school concert the next day.

"I will certainly do my best, Kate. I do work for a living you know."

The words had stung, obviously intended to distinguish Rob from Kate in her new role at home.

Kate barely hid her pain as she zapped back. "Well the boys are going to be very disappointed if you cannot make it."

"Kate, I said I would be there. Stop being such a nag." Rob spat out the words as he was shaving and Kate responded by heading to the kitchen to make a one-cup pot of coffee. She had been sipping her coffee and eating a cup of yogurt in a silently aggressive display of selfishness. The boys were still sleeping and she let them sleep so as to miss the (all too familiar) hostility between their parents this morning.

Draining the last of the coffee from the pot, Kate decided she would not be asking Rob if he wanted a cup of coffee or some breakfast, and she was in that moment, both satisfied and embarrassed by how a simple thing like being impolite was her best retort these days.

But Rob had the last laugh, when he had breezed through the kitchen on his way out the door to accuse her of the thing she most feared—becoming a hopeless pessimist.

"You're right. I am a pessimist." Kate conceded in spite of herself. "I've known all along that, no matter how hard I wish it to be so, I am *not* an optimist," Kate murmured, defeated as Rob stormed out.

"Ian was always the optimist."

Kate clamped her hand over her mouth, surprised by the words that had come out just as Rob slammed the door behind him.

For a moment, Kate wondered, *if no one is here to hear them—is it ok? To say the words out loud?*

"Ian was the optimist, not me." Kate repeated the words more loudly, more defiantly—before resuming her grip on the kitchen counter, this time to hold herself up as the pain of so many memories overwhelmed her.

INTERESTINGLY ENOUGH, when Kate had finally asked Rob for a baby, it didn't go nearly as badly as she had anticipated all those years. Kate had been standing in the bathroom, washing her face when Rob came in one evening after work.

"What a nightmare day. The client wants us to file an interlocutory appeal in the Fifth Circuit by tomorrow morning and we had about four hours of conference calls to discuss why we have absolutely no chance of winning and why filing the losing motion only diminishes our settlement position. But no, they want to file in the morning, anyway. So, I have some poor second-year pulling an all-nighter on the stupid thing. And now I have to go in at 7 am to review and probably rewrite the entire brief by 10 am Texas time."

Kate stood frozen, staring at him. She had no idea what he was saying, and worse, had no idea what to say back. She didn't plan it, but she blurted her words out anyway, "I think it's time we think about having a baby."

Rob stood frozen, staring at her from the bathroom doorway, but she was even more surprised by the words herself. She heard a ringing noise in her ears as she stared at Rob who started to visibly un-freeze, walking over to her at the bathroom mirror.

Kate reached out to Rob with her sudsy face. "Really, Rob, I'd like to try again to have a baby."

She prepared herself for a fight. She steeled herself for the inevitable argument she felt was on its way. But it didn't come. Rob looked resigned. As if he had known this day would come but had not yet decided how he felt about it.

"Well, let's think about what that would mean. As a practical matter."

It was very lawyerly and on any other evening, Kate might have found it sexy; today she found it incredibly arrogant. She began to say things like, "We're not getting any younger you know." Clichés that she was actually embarrassed to be repeating but there they were. Rob looked flustered and interrupted her to say, "Well, you can't just spring this on me all of a sudden. I'm not saying no. I'm just saying give me a few days to think about it." To which Kate could think of no other response, as a few days was quite inconsequential to a couple who rarely saw each other outside of Sunday afternoons anyway.

The next day, as Rob woke at 5 am to head off to his waiting legal brief without saying a word about the discussions of the prior night, Kate pretended to be asleep but was still wrestling— as she had all night—with the two thoughts that remained stuck in her head. First, that Rob might not actually want a baby at all. Not now. Not ever. And second, that even if he did, making a baby would be quite tricky on this schedule indeed.

But Kate was wrong on both counts.

Rob came home the night he filed his interlocutory appeal in Texas—whatever that meant—with a bouquet of pink and blue carnations and handed them to her with a flourish. "Let's do it." He answered her questioning look with a wide smile and wrapped her in a hug.

"Thank God for you, Kate. I know I'm always focused on the future. And sometimes, I just need a little perspective about what we're doing here. I mean, I would hate to share you." Rob held her away so she could see him wink at her. "But, I would *love* to have a baby. With you. Right now."

Kate buried her nose in the carnations. "Well, it's going to take a little while, you know." Rob kissed her head and, taking her hand to lead her into their bedroom, said, "Better get started then."

Once Rob adjusted to the baby idea, he cooperated fully on task. He even came home early when Kate (and her drugstore ovulation kit) told him to, and six weeks after Kate's sudsy-faced "baby" conversation in the bathroom, Kate held up the positive pregnancy stick to Rob in the bathroom. Rob wrapped her in a bear hug, all but erasing the bad memories associated with the first time she had told him she was pregnant.

When it was time to disclose the pregnancy, after Kate white-knuckled her way through the first three months, she relaxed and told her family and colleagues, "It's funny how things just work out." She was due in June, such an ideal time as she could take the summer off without recourse to her position at the college.

And Rob was doing so well at the new firm. At a review shortly after Kate found out she was pregnant, Rob was told that partnership would be a realistic three-year goal, news that he relayed to Kate exuberantly when he got home with a bouquet of flowers and a baby bib that said, "I just pulled an all-nighter."

It seemed to Kate that she was meant to have this baby, this year. She spent much of her pregnancy congratulating herself on getting Rob to come around to the idea at such an ideal time.

❧

That June was the first carefree, blissful June she could remember in a long time.

In such a long time.

Since that June with Ian, really.

Rob was busy with his job spending less and less time at home, but Kate didn't mind. She was so caught up in the newness of motherhood and she was enjoying being home with Michael. Every day she took long walks with Michael in his stroller or in his baby carrier and took millions of pictures of him in every mood, in every little outfit. She counted his fingers and toes all day, and read to him incessantly, loving his expressions that she could not help but interpret as adoration, even when he was only four weeks old.

The prospect of returning to work in the fall loomed over her otherwise magical summer. In July, as she started interviewing nannies, she also began researching mommy and me music and sign language classes that she could squeeze into her fall schedule when she returned to her teaching post.

Over the summer, Kate noticed peripherally a distance growing between her and Rob that she only barely acknowledged. She slept on the couch most nights, falling asleep while nursing Michael. She would slowly lower Michael into his crib and return to her empty bed after Rob left for work in the early hours of the morning.

They survived like this mostly in silence it seemed, until one night in late August when Michael was barely two months old, Rob turned to Kate in the bathroom on a rare occasion where they both found themselves in the same room at the same time, and said something jarring. "I think it will be good for you to go back to work, Kate. You need to do something other than cater to Michael's every whim around here. It'll be just what the two of you—the three of us, really—need."

Kate said nothing but kept flossing and staring straight ahead in the mirror. It was hard to floss, of course, because her teeth were gritted and she was trying not to throw her bottle of moisturizer at Rob's smug face. How did he know absolutely nothing about her? How did he not know how wary she was to return to work and how that was the absolute worst thing he could have said to her at that exact moment? She smiled fakely at him and left the bathroom to head into Michael's room where she pulled her whimpering baby onto her breast to nurse and doze in the rocker in the nursery.

❧

On Kate's first day back at the college, Professor Dyer asked her approximately ten times whether she wasn't "so happy" to be back at school with "the kids." Kate kept nodding and blinking back tears.

It didn't get any better the next day. Or the next.

And so, it wasn't long after she returned to work that fall that Kate began to daydream about another baby. She was anxious to get back home to Michael.

"What a strange reason to wish for another baby. Maternity leave?" Kate's mother looked at Kate questioningly as she cradled Michael during a weekend visit, just after Kate had mumbled something about Rob working through the weekend, yet again, and how she couldn't wait to take another maternity leave.

As the fall gave way to winter and a new year beckoned, Kate grew more sure that another baby was exactly what she was supposed to have.

But how to convince Rob?

Truth be told, Kate knew Rob was distracted by his job and the partnership track. They had been off birth control since trying for Michael. With Rob's erratic hours, and Kate's night-time nursing schedule, sex was as careless these days as it was infrequent.

Kate knew that eventually Rob would be a bit more vigilant. So, this time, she didn't have any conversation before the fact.

And one night when Michael was about 11 months old, after Rob arrived home late from work and headed over to kiss Michael's head lovingly in his highchair, Kate turned from the sink and announced: "Well, I have some news. Turns out, we are having another baby."

Rob looked from Kate to Michael playing in his highchair with cheerios, and smiled. "Well, that *is* good news."

And Kate turned back to washing the dishes, so proud of herself for choosing just how this should all happen.

❧

David was born in the winter of 2007. Kate had let herself exhale a bit in the hospital room, as she looked over and saw Rob caress his new son's head. She leaned back into her pillow and felt optimism and hope settle all over her like a warm, welcome blanket.

This is right.

This is where we are supposed to be.

It's working.

❧

"I think I need to start looking for a new job."

Uh oh. Kate thought. *Here we go again.*

Rob was sitting on the side of their bed at 5 am, about to leave for an early morning at the office. Kate was nursing David in bed. In a familiar motion of running his fingers through his thick (well, to be honest, these days it was just thick-ish) dark hair, Rob continued, "I've been working for this client for over two years now and I don't see any progression. No partnership whisperings anymore. No sign that it's going to lead to anything more than headaches.

"I've been talking to Matt about moving over to Larter & Gold."

Kate said nothing as she nursed David and tried to piece together the players in this story. Matt had been Rob's law school buddy and a colleague at his first law firm. Kate vaguely recalled that Matt had headed off to a smaller firm, Larter & Gold, while Rob had moved from large firm to larger firm, pinning all his hopes for partnership on one white-shoe firm after another. Kate had met Matt only a handful of times, and apparently he had left very little impression on Kate. As she tried to summon up a picture of him in her mind, she was left only with a hazy face in a dark lawyer suit.

Could have been anyone.

Could have been Rob, for that matter.

Despite her calm façade, inside, Kate was frustrated at the seeming regression. She really did not want Rob to start over, now that their second baby was here, especially since Kate was so anxious to leave her career—no, her job, really—that's how she felt about it these days—so she could create a real home for this family. Then again, perhaps the only way to the financial security that would allow Kate the choice to leave her teaching position, was to encourage Rob to follow this new path. Kate felt desperate to change the trajectory of what she feared would happen if they all continued on the track they seemed to be on.

Just the day before, in fact, Kate had been on the phone with her department head, discussing the possibility of an extended 7-8 month maternity leave, in which she would hold off returning to teaching until after the summer class schedule had ended. Kate was surreptitiously trying out a life without a career just when Rob announced to Kate that he really thought he should switch jobs yet again. A groan escaped Kate.

If Rob heard Kate groan while he was sitting there on the edge of the bed that morning, he didn't let on. He just sat in silence for a few moments, before getting up and announcing. "It's what's best for me, Kate. For us. I'm going to schedule a lunch meeting with Matt and his partners at Larter next week. Cross your fingers for me."

"Good luck Honey. I'm sure it will all work out," Kate said. And Rob looked over his shoulder at her, almost as if he was expecting—no hoping—for her to say something more. But Kate just rolled over to get a little sleep before her Michael would awaken early and demand breakfast and Mommy.

IN THE END, it wasn't Rob who convinced Kate it was time to go back to work after David was born.

Actually, it was the urban book club fiasco.

The same day that Rob was having his luncheon meeting with Larter & Gold, Kate was out walking the boys, alone despite the crowded Manhattan sidewalk. Frustrated, lonely, and a bit lost, as she had not yet settled into a comfortable routine with the boys, Kate was wishing for some girlfriends. She thought about all those years of sharing stories and dreams with Benton a lifetime ago, and wished she had found someone smart and fun to dream with in *this* life.

So it was fortuitous that, while pushing Michael and David in their double stroller, Kate saw a flyer at the corner bookstore about a local mother's group that was starting monthly book clubs.

The first meeting was just four days away. Kate had never been away from David since his birth, but she steeled herself and called one of her former college students to babysit the kids. She bought the book the same morning she saw the flyer and read it while sitting up with David for midnight feedings over the next few nights.

The night Book Club arrived, Rob was working late, of course. Michael was nearly two and was usually in bed by 7:30. David generally nodded off after his 7 pm feeding and was good for at least 4-5 hours until his next feeding. So Kate got the boys in bed, left her babysitter with the chips and the remote and dashed off into the night with her paperback, exhilarated by the promise of the evening.

When she arrived at her hostess's apartment, she found eight women in a circle in the comfortable living room of a woman named Rita. Some sat cross-legged on the floor; some on a couch and others on chairs that had been brought in from the adjacent dining room. They discussed the book for about 15 minutes and then they digressed and sipped wine and ate homemade guacamole. It was divine. They covered choices, careers, family, and faith. They avoided whiny discussions of husbands and children. The guacamole led to a discussion of sustainable gardening. They discussed religion but it was non-judgmental.

Kate confessed that she was starting to believe in God for the first time in her life.

Since my children were born.

The women all nodded. Even though some of them had just confessed the opposite conclusion. It was a reverent and respectful atmosphere.

The group announced their plan to read a book a month and on the third month Kate invited the women to her own home.

Rob was gone most nights these days with the new job at Larter & Gold and Michael was a good sleeper. David was easy, spending most of his time on the breast, alternately suckling and sleeping. It would be lovely to have a group of women in her home to discuss a new book and new motherhood and current events and who knows what else.

She had such high hopes.

Kate bought organic wine and made bruschetta and laid out a dish of cheese and waited. The women arrived. Her old couches, covered with slip covers were soft and welcoming and the women said so. But the conversations were stilted somehow. They were stuck on the book for a while and Kate tried to discuss the organic wine but it led to nothing except more drinking and then the wine was gone and the women looked ready to leave but it was only 8:30.

Kate was mystified.

Where was the discussion? The substance? The intellectual vigor?

When one of the women named Margot got up to leave, she asked, gazing at the living room windows, "So how long have you been in this apartment?"

"Ages. Since before the kids. It was my husband's apartment when he was still single, actually."

"Ah. That explains it. You never really settled in, right? No window treatments even."

No window treatments.

They could not believe she had lived there for years and did not have a single window treatment or new piece of furniture that hadn't seen her through graduate school or Rob through law school. They were confused. Apparently, it clouded their minds. Clouded the discussions.

"Well, I've always worked. I'm a college professor. I spend very little time actually *in* the apartment. When I'm not on maternity leave, like I am now."

"Oh, a full-time job!" Rita exclaimed. "Really, I don't know how you do it."

Kate winced. In her experience, that phrase was usually code for "you don't really *do it*, now do you?" reinforced in this setting by the constant glances up at her unadorned windows.

Sitting there, Kate was suddenly embarrassed that she had believed having babies, leaving her job, and settling into the world of stay-at-home moms would somehow bring her the contentment she was lacking.

"We can help you out with decorating ideas if you'd like. We should meet over coffee later this month. I'll bring some fabric swatches with me." A crunchy woman named Laura with a long graying braid patted Kate's knee, and Kate wondered briefly what bohemian oasis Laura would turn her apartment into before blurting out a decision she had just made on the spot.

"Thanks, but I'm actually going back to work later this month."

She would go back to work in time for the summer class schedule.

Because, really, she wasn't ready to leave her job.

Besides, she needed to save for window treatments.

∾

By the time Kate got her window treatments a year after the urban book club fiasco, they were hung in her new suburban home, after she and Rob moved out of the city, a few months after Rob joined Larter & Gold.

They had moved out of their Manhattan apartment into a spacious four bedroom home in the suburbs, not too far from Kate's parents.

Kate continued commuting, working, teaching, and mothering.

We have arrived, window treatments and all, Kate repeated often, as she had begun the somewhat uncomfortable habit again of talking herself into being happy.

∾

It was nearly two years after the trip to Paradise Resort that Kate left her position at the college. A move that actually seemed to surprise Rob, when, in fact, it was Rob's reaction that surprised Kate.

After all, David had been barely two years old when Kate had first blurted the news out to Rob, shortly after they got back from their trip to Paradise Resort.

True, she had let it slip in a moment of weakness. But still, she would have expected Rob to remember.

One night in the middle of putting the kids to bed, she found Rob laying on the couch watching TV, and she had entered the room exasperated. "Rob, a little help please? I had a hard day today too, you know, at a job I don't even want anymore."

He had turned to her, startled by her outburst. And she had looked at him sheepishly. But he had gotten up and cleaned up the dinner dishes and started a load of laundry while she was putting the kids to bed and stomping around cleaning up the kids' toys and Legos and thinking about the papers she had to read that night and feeling so very sorry for herself.

She was tired. Tired of faking it, and tired of trying so hard. She had snapped at Rob without even realizing it. Without warning, and without any specific trigger.

"What's going on with your job?" Rob asked when he finished the dishes.

"Never mind. Forget I even said anything."

Rob walked over to her. He knelt down on the floor and started sorting Legos into their respective bins. For a moment, Kate found herself warmed by the realization that he actually knew which ones went where.

But the moment passed quickly, as she thought about how tomorrow he would likely stay at work late with clients, without giving her a passing thought or concern. Or how he would most likely make plans with his colleagues this weekend without including her. Or worse yet, he would decide he needed to start his career over at some new law firm.

He would disappoint her again somehow, tomorrow and the day after that, just like he had so many times before, and a few well-placed Legos would not change that fact. She continued slamming toys into bins.

"You drive me crazy, Kate. You never tell me anything. You

never talk to me about anything. Anything other than Legos and kids. Don't you want to know about my job? Don't you want to know anything about what's going on with me?"

"Oh by all means, Rob. I want to hear every little detail of your glamorous life at your ridiculously overpaid job. I want to hear about your colleagues and the witty tales of last-minute briefs and petitions. Right after I get done cooking, and cleaning, and caring for our two children. The two people who live with us. Remember them? They are my full-time job. Oh wait, no—that's right, I have an actual full-time job teaching arrogant teenagers about life since their parents were way too busy to do the job. You know, probably important lawyers or some such profession."

Rob clapped mockingly for a moment, exclaiming, "Nice performance, Professor."

Then he fell back into the couch, grabbing the remote. What had passed as interest in his expression a few moments ago had evaporated, replaced by a glazed disinterest. And Kate found herself more comfortable with this expression as it was the one she was so used to lately.

Rob gave one last retort as Kate continued sorting Legos. "Yes, Kate, by all means, you are the noble one in this equation. I am the one who has sold my soul to the devil. I am the one for whom there is no hope left."

After that night, Kate stopped bringing up her job and most importantly, stopped complaining about it. Instead, she mapped out an exit strategy that involved saving and strategizing. One of the many steps along the way was supporting Rob's ever needy career goals. Kate saw no way to leave her career until Rob was safely settled into a firm—any firm—for the long term.

And so when Rob made partner finally at his fourth law firm, she had toasted him the night of the partnership announcement dinner ("four's a charm!"), and Rob had leaned down and kissed her warmly in front of all his colleagues.

Their boys were six and four then, and Kate convinced Rob that it was either time to have another baby or time for Kate to stay at home and focus on the ones she had.

"Time is slipping away, Rob. I've missed so much already. I've lost so much. I can't keep on at this pace any longer."

Rob didn't want another baby, so he gave his blessing to her decision to leave her college post. Permanently. Which was what she wanted him to say all along. "I'm just surprised, that's all," Rob had said while Kate looked at him incredulously. "I thought you liked having a career. I thought you liked teaching. It's what you've always wanted to do. Ever since I've known you."

Kate ignored him as she sat down to pen her official resignation letter.

"We'll celebrate with a party. I'll host a Superbowl party," Kate said as she sealed the envelope.

AFTER KATE FINALLY FOUND A HOME for the acrylic rice pudding bakery bowl in her re-arranged refrigerator, she stood stoically at the kitchen counter, stuffing goody bags complete with football erasers for the boys and pom-pom pens for the girls.

And while she stuffed, instead of talking herself into being happy, she recited the facts.

You live in the suburbs.

You have window treatments and plenty of choices.

Rob made partner finally, and now look at how it's all turned out.

Ten years of waiting for this moment.

All those choices made, and goodbyes said.

And yet here we are.

⤳

"Kate?"

"Yes?"

"Kate, It's Celeste. Celeste Morrison."

"Hello, Celeste. Rob's not here—he's at the office."

"Kate, I know that. I'm calling to talk to you."

Celeste sounded off when she had called a few days before the Superbowl party, her words slurred. *Drunk,* Kate thought dismissively.

And then in an instant, she had known why Celeste was calling, although why or how Kate knew, she couldn't be sure.

Kate had met Celeste at several firm functions. She was pretty in an obvious way, and Kate had of course noticed her. Had hugged her goodbye at Rob's partnership announcement dinner.

Had Rob hugged her? Kate could not remember. She had been trying to remember this all-important detail ever since that phone call.

In truth, while Kate had not given Celeste a single thought since that dinner, Celeste now lived in every single one of Kate's waking moments.

A stupid move, that phone call, Kate had thought almost instantly after she hung up the phone. Didn't Celeste realize that when Rob found out she had given him up and embarrassed him that way, he'd cast her aside? Celeste likely thought she was speeding things along. After too many late-night promises and too many glasses of wine, she thought calling Rob's wife would force his hand.

But Kate knew better.

Strangely, she comforted herself with that thought. *Rob would not stay with the mistress who betrayed him. He'd find another one and now they would both lose him.*

While folding laundry and putting away dishes in the days after Celeste's phone call, Kate tried in vain to put thoughts of Rob's girlfriend out of her head. When that didn't work, she'd shake her head and say out loud, "I know him better than his mistress does."

And it was these thoughts that kept her from going crazy while she tried to figure out just what to do. *I know him,* she kept thinking. Strange thoughts for a woman who had just found out that her husband was cheating. Strange to think that you know your husband truly under these circumstances. Kate would think about this anomaly as well as she folded tee shirts and tried to figure out which color dinosaur underwear were her four-year-old son's and which were her six-year-old's as she juggled laundry baskets in the hallway, and folded Rob's socks just the way he liked them for the billionth time in their marriage.

"I knew this day would come." She said it out loud to no one but herself just to hear the words in the empty house. "I knew all along." She said it almost triumphantly.

What now?

There were rare moments when Kate was not certain at all she would tell Rob about the phone call. In those moments, Kate told herself that Celeste and Rob deserved each other and she did not want to stand in the way of what was obviously a perfect match of narcissists. *I'll watch them self-destruct from afar,* Kate thought at odd times, strangely empowered.

But in all the other remaining moments, Kate was angry and sad and embarrassed—especially given the fact that Rob would risk his family, his children, and his future, for a woman who did not know him well enough to know that he would not stay with a woman who had called to betray him to his wife.

This morning she had one glorious moment just as she woke up, when her mind had forgotten what it knew and she felt hopeful again. Just before the crashing of the waves of sadness as she fully awakened. When she knew. Rob was not home. He never came home last night. A 3 am text that he was stuck at the office.

Sorry. Luv u. Kiss kids. See u tomorrow.

He always spelled everything else out. But not Love. Or You. It was as if he did not consider it a lie if he didn't spell out the words.

Every day since he had proposed to her in the middle of her miscarriage, she had *wanted* to believe that things could be different, could work out. She had willed herself to be optimistic—had tried so hard to be optimistic, but the reality was that she had always been waiting for this day to happen. And in her few honest moments, she felt like a fool for sitting around letting it happen to her after all.

❧

The phone rang on Superbowl Sunday just as Kate was finishing up the kids' goody bags. Kate picked up to hear her mother on the other line.

"Hi, Dear."

Kate snapped out of her Celeste-stupor for a moment as she realized that her parents, who had said they would stop by before the game to help her get ready, should really have been here by now. So punctual they were. So reliable. Kate was beginning to assess the whole world now in terms of the reliables versus the not reliables.

"So, we aren't going to make it tonight after all."

"What's wrong, Mom?"

"Nothing, dear. Your father just had a long lunch with the District Superintendent and now is popping TUMS like they're breath mints. He isn't up for it so we'll just check in tomorrow. Ok?"

"Sure, Mom. I'll call you tomorrow. Why don't you plan to come over for coffee?"

Kate hung up with a sense of relief. She couldn't face her parents tonight anyway. Couldn't watch her dad slap Rob on the back with male camaraderie and discuss sports plays like her whole life wasn't falling apart.

There would be a time to tell her parents, and everyone else, just as soon as she confronted Rob.

So, when to confront Rob?

Kate was still trying to answer this nagging question when the dinner guests began arriving.

PAM AND GREG ARRIVED FIRST with their girls, Rebecca and Sara, in tow. Rebecca and Sara were older than Michael and David, but they were kind enough to treat Michael and David as peers and it made evenings with Pam and Greg a treat for Kate. Pam was a friend of Kate's from Pilates class and a few years ago, while Kate was still working, they had started a small suburban book club together as well. The book club was really Kate's idea. A mulligan. A re-do of the urban book club that had affected Kate so greatly the year David was born.

Greg was Pam's husband, which was to say, he was not an actual friend of either Kate or Rob. But Greg was good company and Rob in a word "tolerated" Greg's jokes, which were not always politically correct or funny. In return, Greg was not intimidated by Rob's lawyer demeanor which often found him devouring dinner companions who failed to see his way on some issue or another.

Pam and Greg arrived effortlessly with kisses and hugs and encouraged the girls to "go find the boys" and to "be nice" and looked completely non-plussed when Kate reported that Rob was still at the office and would likely be home by the half-time show but they were in no way to wait for him. Kate opened a beer for Greg and directed him to the sofa while she stirred sangria.

"I have something to tell you. But later. Later." Pam said to Kate, just as the doorbell rang, leaving Kate to wonder why Pam was saying these words to Kate instead of the other way around.

Lex and Ryan had a new baby named Sophia. They would let you know this about them instantly when you met them whether or not the baby was in the room as well. Although she always was. In the room.

They seemed certain that they were the first people in the world to have had a baby and they seemed equal parts exhilarated and dismayed by the fact. Kate invited them three times before they agreed to come to the dinner party. Too many kids. Too many germs. Too much noise. The baby's "schedule" was referred to approximately twelve times without clarification but Kate kept at it.

She remained convinced that Lex had to get out with the baby or she'd become so overwhelmed that she would never have another.

Or that she'd give away the one she had.

Kate held out promises of Rebecca and Sara watching over the baby. She explained that babies need to sleep through noise or they'd never learn to sleep properly. She promised organic food and wine, and when Lex protested about breast-feeding, Kate promised that she would personally feed the baby bottles of expressed milk while Lex diligently pumped and dumped her wine-filled milk at the end of the evening. For right or for wrong, Kate secretly held out hope that she'd convince Lex to nurse the baby after a half glass of wine and that the baby would in turn reward everyone by sleeping quietly in the corner so that Lex could let her hair down for just one night.

Kate knew Lex from her grad school days even before her years of friendship with Benton. Lex was also a history student but had quit grad school early on to see the world, chronicling her modern-day journeys from a historian's point of view, juxtaposing the ancient worlds of Greece, Turkey, Rome, and Morocco to her modern experiences traveling in each locale. Her travels lasted several years. Polishing the book lasted several more. Shopping the book—countless more. By the time Lex became an award-winning published author, she was in her mid-30s and had missed quite a bit of the dating scene. She had no idea how to meet men her equal at that point. She dug her heels into her newly landed college teaching job, and though she and Kate had lost touch somewhat during the travel years, they had reconnected a few years earlier over their shared experiences of teaching. When Lex met Ryan, an older widowed childless TV journalist, Kate was not at all sure they would have children. And the fact that Kate did have children, two to be exact, more than somewhat strained the newly rekindled relationship she had with Lex.

Having been on the other side for a number of years—that is, the childless friend—Kate was well aware of what Lex would like most when they got together. Thus, they talked around the children, which was to say, they met for coffee when Kate was working or had a babysitter, and they basically pretended that Kate did not have children at home waiting for her.

At Kate's insistence, Lex joined the book club, adding her unique flair to the discussions on her monthly trips into the suburbs from the city. Kate liked to pretend that she and Lex were peers in the truest sense of the word. And Kate enjoyed the escape she found in those times she spent with Lex. Pretending she was a carefree woman of the world, instead of a suburban mom.

In fact, as Kate began to consider actually leaving her college position, she found herself (albeit embarrassedly) weighing the factor of whether or not she and Lex could continue their friendship, which was a relationship Kate considered to be an invaluable one in her current life, if and when Kate was no longer a professional woman and her status as mom could no longer be ignored.

So when Lex announced that she was pregnant at 40, Kate

was thrilled for her (and for herself!) knowing that only now would the two women have an authentic friendship again, as they could freely acknowledge that Kate, too, was a mom.

And when Lex asked Kate for the name of her suburban realtor, the deal was sealed. They would be neighbors and moms together. The friendship would happily survive.

On Superbowl night, Kate greeted Lex who arrived with two diaper bags overflowing with baby paraphernalia, by removing the infant carrier from Lex's arm and directing Ryan to the couch with a lager where he and Greg could forge out some companionable discussion about football. And beer. And whatever else they could think of. Men were easy. It was usually just that easy.

Lex was out of breath from her day with the baby, which as far as Kate could gather involved a host of issues that were simply not on the baby's schedule, all in an effort to get here on time, which was going to put the baby "so off her schedule for the night." Kate found this part of her friendship with Lex greatly satisfying because she had true, genuine, first-hand expertise to impart. She nuzzled Lex's baby daughter's head. "Sophia, you sweet child. Life does not go according to plan, no matter what your mother tells you. And Sophia, I know how you feel. Really, I do. Lex, dear, have a glass of wine."

ROB SAILED IN JUST AFTER HALF TIME during the Superbowl. In all the obvious ways, it was just an ordinary night. Kate was exasperated by the way he breezed past her and the boys, kissing the boys' heads casually and grunting a "hey" at Kate as he cracked open a beer and headed to the TV. But of course, it wasn't truly an ordinary night. Nothing had been ordinary for Kate in almost a week, now.

The last quarter of the game found the men pitted against the women, not choosing teams, or point spreads, but simply arguing the philosophical merit of the losing team's coach calling the same play he had called in the final minutes of the first half. It was a risky play in the first half, the men said, and he was a fool to do it then.

"He's even more a fool if he does it now," Greg proclaimed.

But it paid off, the women argued. His team had scored seconds before ending the first half.

Even more reason not to call it again, according to the men.

"It simply cannot work two times in a row. And the element of surprise is gone. And it is simply foolish," Greg voiced on behalf of the men.

"Or hopeful," Pam had said over her bruschetta.

The men shook their heads. But Kate put her arm around Pam as she tried to hide the tears in her eyes. It felt so wonderful to have an optimist in the room, even if the only thing at stake was a football game.

"Well," said Rob, "we'll see who's right because it looks like he's about to try it again, the fool." Rob pointed to the screen and the group stopped arguing long enough to watch the last play of the game.

❧

"You don't have to stay to clean up." Kate said the words but continued handing Pam plates to dry in an assembly line fashion. Rob and Greg were watching post-game replays. Lex and Ryan had made a quick departure with the baby. Pam's girls and Kate's boys were asleep on the L-shaped family room couches, still clutching their various favors and trinkets from Kate's Superbowl goodie bags.

"I wanted to tell you something—ask you something really." Pam was a bit flustered, which was unlike her, and for a moment Kate feared the question would be "do you know Rob is cheating on you?" But Kate was immediately ashamed of her self-centeredness as the question came out of Pam finally, like an exhale. "Will you go with me to the doctor on Tuesday?"

Words continued spilling out.

"I need to have a biopsy. I found a lump. I'm sure it'll be fine, but I really need some company on the trip to and from the doctor's office. It's a lot to ask I know, but—"

Kate stopped handing plates and stepped toward Pam with arms open. "Of course I will—when did you find the lump?"

"Two weeks ago. A lump. Then an exam. Then a mammogram. Something showed up on the mammogram and I'm going for a biopsy on Tuesday. It's just that I don't want to go alone and I can't tell Greg."

"Oh, honey, are you sure?"

Pam nodded. "I'm sure. I could say I don't want to worry him, but it's more selfish than that. I don't want him to worry me. I want to go in there thinking I don't have cancer and if I have cancer I want to start out thinking I'll beat it. He won't let me do that. You will."

"Tuesday, it is," Kate said before she began handing plates again. She stopped suddenly. "Oh that's good news."

Pam looked up suddenly, and for a minute, looked confused. Kate continued lightly, "It's good you could get an appointment Tuesday, because Thursday is the Sample Sale on Westmoreland Avenue and we do *not* want to miss that." She winked at Pam.

"Yep. That's why I want *you* there on Tuesday." The two women continued clanging dishes, lost in their own thoughts.

∾

After Pam left, Kate continued cleaning up the downstairs and Rob carried the sleeping boys from the couches up to their beds. Kate studied the boys' expressions as Rob moved with each boy past her.

Contentment.

She was surprised she could even identify the expression, since it was such an elusive emotion in their marriage.

How long had it been missing?

And whose fault was it that it was gone?

Kate thought back to when she had first returned to work after David was born. The contentedness had almost completely ebbed from her marriage by then, she knew.

Rob had become less and less a part of their lives, spending so much time at the office and focusing on his always imminent partnership that he hardly had time for the day-to-day details like which preschool Michael was going to attend in the fall or whether or not the babysitter was following Kate's instructions to feed the baby only organic grapes cut in half.

Over lunch hours and coffee breaks, Kate had called the babysitter for reports on the boys and relished the little details like how long of a nap each had taken and what toys they were enjoying that day.

Some days, when Kate hung up with the babysitter, she

would think briefly about calling Rob to share some of the details, but she quickly thought better of it. *He'll be bored by these details,* she would think. Although she really had no basis for thinking that. She'd never even tried to tell him.

One day, she couldn't help it. The babysitter had told her that the baby was being so cute playing with Michael, and reaching over to hand him toys. *"A great sharer that little one is going to be."*

Kate was so proud, taking it as such a source of joy that the boys were getting along well, and then, in the next moment, feeling so nostalgic thinking that the following year Michael would be headed off to preschool. Tinged with her joy, she was also feeling a sadness for David who was just getting used to a full-time playmate in time for that playmate to be leaving him behind.

She was feeling so sentimental and weepy over the boys that Kate picked up the phone to tell Rob about the sharing story, eager for empathy from someone.

I should call Rob more during the day, Kate had thought as she dialed. *I am doing him a disservice not sharing these little details with him. I should be discussing the little day-to-day aspects of the boys' lives with him. With Rob. Someone who is on my team. Someone who is not the babysitter. Someone who is not paid to act like she cares what I say and do. I should call Rob more often in the middle of the day. I need to stop being so pessimistic about him.*

Stop assuming things are going to fail.

But that particular day when she called him, Rob was distracted at work and curt. His short tone put Kate off right away, and instead of telling Rob she loved him or the conflict she was feeling about David losing his brother and playmate, she simply blurted out:

"I just wanted to tell you that Michael and David were sharing today."

"Ohh—kayyyyy."

"Forget it."

"Kate, I just . . . it's busy here, and I'm not quite sure what you want me to say—"

"Nothing. Nothing. I want you to say nothing." Kate had hung up. And she never called Rob in the middle of the day at work again.

∾

By the time she was done cleaning up the Superbowl dishes, and Rob had finished taking the boys up to bed and come back down to turn off the TV, Kate was vulnerable from worry over Pam.

Exhausted by the weight of Pam's news and the knowledge of Rob's affair, she felt her tight grip on control loosen. As Rob was heading soundlessly up the stairs to bed like he did so many nights, Kate stood at the bottom of the steps, looking up at Rob walking away from her. She thought about her few countable impulse decisions, when she had let her guard down.

The day she had finally blurted out to Rob that she wanted to try again to have a child, despite having wanted a baby ever since that excruciating day in the emergency room before they got married. The day she decided to get pregnant again without consulting Rob.

And yes, Ian. Ian floated through her brain, even at that moment, ever so briefly.

Some of my finest moments have not been properly planned.

"Rob, are you cheating on me with Celeste?" He looked over his shoulder to face her and his face transformed itself in an instant. He was unrecognizable to Kate. And she gripped her chest as if literally grabbing for her heart, realizing that it was of course true. Because, while in some fleeting moments over the last few days, she had allowed herself the luxury of hoping that it was *not* true, she was not foolish. She had known all along.

Kate looked hard at Rob, memorizing his transformed features. She didn't know what else to do in this unfamiliar moment.

He looked relieved, something she had not necessarily played out in the list of scenarios in her head. It was an expression that reminded her unwittingly of the night of her miscarriage. Rob turned on his heel, came down the steps, and for a moment, Kate thought, *he's going to leave, before I have a chance to say a word.* But then, Rob put his arms around her and sobbed, "I'm so sorry."

Kate pulled away, horrified. She backed away. She put her hand up and quieted him wordlessly.

Then she said things that sounded foggy in her own ears.

"I need you to stop talking. Right now. I need you to leave. Right now."

He left quietly and tearfully a few minutes later—to go to Celeste's, she assumed.

22

"Lemongrass."

"What are you talking about, Mom?"

Kate's mom, Sandra, was looking over Kate's head at the TV screen. The two women were sitting at the kitchen table, but in the other room, the TV had been left on. A documentary was flashing on high def, showing First Ladies over the years. A parade of inaugural day dresses and evening gowns. Just now, pictures of Michelle Obama in her 2009 inaugural day dress and coat had appeared on the screen.

"Lemongrass," Sandra repeated. "That's what they all called the unique color of that dress back then. It's supposed to be the color of hope, of optimism. New days, a change, and all that." Sandra kept looking over Kate's head at the screen.

Kate wasn't sure what her mother was trying to say or if she was, quite simply, just commenting on the First Lady's wardrobe. They had made small talk about her dad's indigestion from the night before and Kate's mother had assured Kate that her father was "fine, just fine." Then Kate had very matter-of-factly told her mother that she and Rob were having some pretty stark troubles and were likely getting separated. Kate was not sure what she had been expecting from her mother. But this was not it.

They sat together in silence with the documentary flashing images of dresses in the background, until Kate finally broke the silence.

"Lemongrass," Kate repeated, finished her coffee, and

placed her mug deliberately down in front of her on the kitchen table. "And to think, all along, I've just been calling it gold."

23

On Tuesday, Kate and Pam drove home mostly in silence from the radiologist's office. Kate tried to keep the conversation light and the music upbeat. No country music today. Kate settled on a hip hop channel, unable to decipher a single word and certain that no one was singing about death or cancer or other sad topics that would exacerbate the tension in the car.

The radiologist had been "cautiously optimistic." He had actually said those words to them. "We can be cautiously optimistic." And Kate had thought she would like to take those words out into the world and wear them the rest of her days.

"It is a mass," he said definitively. "But it looks contained and benign. Only pathology will tell for sure."

"So when?" Kate asked for Pam who was still sitting quietly, covering herself only with the doctor's cloak of cautious optimism.

"Tomorrow morning," he said. "We'll know for sure tomorrow morning."

Twenty-four hours is an excruciatingly long time, Kate thought. But what she said was, "Ok, we'll know more tomorrow. That's good."

Pam looked stricken. Kate knew that she was only thinking about how long the next 24 hours would be.

Kate quickly began making plans in her head as they walked together to the elevator bank. "Why don't you guys have dinner with us tonight? We'll order pizza and make sundaes. And tomorrow we'll go shopping while we wait together for the doctor to call."

Pam nodded, but Kate knew that she was making some quick calculations in her mind and knowing that she'd still be alone with her worries for at least half of the next 24 hours. The girls would want to go home to their beds to sleep, after all. It was a school night, and there was likely homework and showers and all the other little nighttime rituals that were so easy to take for granted until something like cancer came along.

When they arrived back at Pam's house, Pam looked over at Kate and said solemnly, "I really appreciate your going today, but I just realized I need to be alone with all of this. I need to act like nothing is strange, nothing is abnormal, or I will probably spin out of control even before I get the results. I'll call you tomorrow after the doctor calls me."

Kate said she understood of course, but she was disappointed. And she realized with a pang of embarrassment that she was actually trying to distract herself as much as Pam. The night before, Rob had come to get the boys, who knew nothing of their parents' trials and drama, for a dinner outing, and while they were gone, Kate had started researching divorce lawyers and two bedroom apartments.

∽

Kate woke up Wednesday morning slowly, with a gradual, queasy feeling washing over her as her consciousness first began to form its thoughts.

Something's wrong.

What's wrong?

Rob's wrong.

She sighed, rolled over and breathed deeply, preparing herself for the day. Today she had the extra anxiety of Pam's looming test results, and since she couldn't exactly call Pam for a pick-me-up call, she called Lex after she dropped the boys off at school.

"Meet me for coffee today. Please."

Kate steeled herself for a barrage of excuses from Lex about why she couldn't. But instead, Lex surprised her with an upbeat response. "Great idea. I'm trying out a new babysitter today. I'm hoping she'll free me up to start working on my next book. I can be at the diner by 9 am if that works for you."

Kate couldn't believe it. She was relieved and saddened at the same time. Lex was starting to adjust to motherhood finally and soon would realize that despite Kate's outer self-assuredness, Kate had very few answers after all. The fact that Pam didn't even want Kate around to wait for her news was making Kate worry that her own heaviness must be too obvious. And Rob was right now waking up with a younger, prettier, and freer version of Kate altogether. It was as if Kate was obsolete in all aspects of her life.

Kate dressed up for coffee and put lip gloss on. She grabbed a designer bag from the top shelf of her closet. She wanted to appear put together and ok when she delivered her news to Lex. Well really, she wanted to *be* put together and ok, but the appearance of same would have to do for now.

࿐

Lex was going on and on about her new book. Coffee hadn't even arrived at the table but she was animated and alert in a way Kate could not recall having seen in quite some time.

"It's about the evolution of motherhood.

"Mothers, it seems, defy the typical Darwin theories of evolution. It is not at all about the survival of the fittest. In fact, we've become more frail, more crippled as time has gone on. Our ancestors used to give birth in the fields for heaven sake. Now we cannot give birth unless we are situated in a room with the proper birth plan, complete with Mozart symphonies, mood lighting, and a focal point."

Kate smiled. This was how Lex had wanted to give birth. Of course in the end, she had given in to drugs. Lots of them. But Kate didn't interject. Clearly Lex was on a roll. And her exuberance was a welcome distraction.

"And then when they come out? My lord, we become even more crippled. As if that's possible. Lost to their schedules. Confused about breastfeeding. I mean, really, when did breastfeeding become so hard? It's supposed to be the most natural thing on the planet but now you have to invest hundreds of dollars in a breast pump and nipple crème before you can even think about this process working.

"And what does that mean? Working? They are your breasts! That is what they do. You shouldn't have to prime them first!"

Lex looked triumphant as she poured another bag of sweetener into her coffee, and Kate glanced around to see if anyone had been watching Lex as she banged her fist on the table yelling out the word "breasts."

As Kate listened to Lex she felt something like admiration tinged with a bit of judgment. She was happy for Lex's newfound confidence, but Kate couldn't help but think Lex sounded hypocritical coming to all of these realizations just as her newborn had finally begun to sleep through the night.

Kate smiled on the outside, while inside thinking how easy it was for "veteran" mothers to forget how insecure new mothers are. How vulnerable. Kate had tried very hard *not* to forget while dealing with Lex's innumerable vulnerabilities all these months. But Lex was sounding like she had little memory about just how difficult life is for new moms.

And how wonderful.

Lex seemed to have turned a corner, a corner Kate in many ways had resisted turning these last few years—the one where you actually think you have it all figured out.

Kate continued nodding and smiling quietly while her inner

voice clucked on and on.

I would feel like even more of an ass right now had I actually ever turned that corner.

No, I never turned any corner.

I always thought this just might happen.

That the bubble would burst at some inopportune time.

I always suspected, let's face it.

Lex continued on, selling her book idea like she was delivering a persuasive sales pitch, and eventually Kate succeeded in ignoring her embarrassment, judgment, and inner voice. By the time the egg white omelets arrived, Kate had been safely lulled into a superficial state of happiness. She was, despite some moments of cynicism, generally happy about Lex's new book and thrilled for her that she had found a project so engaging.

So when Lex finally took a breath and asked Kate, "Well, what's new with you?" Kate was disarmed. Totally disarmed. Which led her to blurt out her news over a forkful of egg white and feta in a way she did not plan at all. "Rob is having an affair."

Lex put her fork down and stared at Kate for what seemed like a long time. Kate nodded. She kept eating but she didn't look away. She knew Lex was trying to think of what to say and Kate didn't feel like helping her. Didn't feel like saying, "I'm fine, really. It'll all be fine. I just need to sort out what to do." All the things Kate imagined she'd later say to people to let them off the hook of feeling horrified.

Later she'd say those things.

To other people. But not now. Not to Lex.

Lex was one of her oldest and dearest friends, and Kate knew she would see right through any lies. So Kate didn't say "I will be fine." She said, "I really have no idea what I'm going to do, to tell the truth."

And then she waited a few more moments to see what Lex

could come up with.

"That. Sucks."

Kate liked that this is what Lex had come up with. So she smiled and nodded again. "Yes. Yes, it does.

"And the crazy thing is, I think he would like to put the affair behind him and stay with me. That's what he told me the other night after he took our children out to dinner without me. 'Think about it,' he said as he helped carry them up to their beds asleep. And I genuinely think he means it. No harm, no foul. Do over."

"Do you even want to stay?"

"Honestly? I don't know. I just found out a week ago, and I just told him on Sunday night that I knew."

"Sunday night?" Lex started putting pieces together. "You mean when we were there?"

"No, when you were there I had not yet told him that I knew about it."

"But you knew Sunday night?"

"Yep, I knew. His mistress called me last week. She's a little bit pathetic. I actually feel sorry for her. The little we've talked over the last few days, Rob talks about her like she is nothing. And I'm so mad at myself, because I actually feel, well, *grateful* that he feels that way. I mean, it's just so sad. I'm holding onto the fact that he actually talks *badly* about his mistress. What does that even say about me?"

More egg whites. More feta. More silence. Then Kate said out loud what she hadn't admitted yet even to herself.

"But you know, given a choice, I don't know how I would actually leave. I can't stand the idea of breaking up the kids' home. Their lives. It's like the affair was his choice but now breaking up the home would be on *me*. I don't know if I can live with that. It would *destroy* the kids. Destroy everything I thought we were creating for them. I don't know that that would be better than just staying and trying to get past all this—for the kids' sakes."

Staying for the kids.

It was so damn cliché and yet so true. There would be no reason to stay if there were no kids. There was no love affair left to cultivate. There was no longer a dream of a future with him. There was nothing but the kids and a fervent desire to see them through this.

How could Rob have put me in this position?

Like she had in so many moments since Celeste had called, Kate felt guilty for having brought the boys into the world with this man. For having forced him to have children she was never wholly sure he wanted. For having tricked him, really.

But, looking at them sleeping in their beds last night, Kate had felt this overwhelming sense of peace, as she had thought a silent prayer that came from some internal place she didn't even recognize.

Thank God I talked him into all of this because they were meant to be. This was meant to be. It just has to be. Look at them.

Which was confusing because that just meant that she and Rob were meant to be.

Also confusing since she still wasn't sure about all this God stuff.

Kate was lost in her inner stream of consciousness when Lex brought her out of it rather abruptly.

"See, now that's bullshit. And that is exactly what I'm talking about. We are crippled by motherhood. Why can't we evolve, dammit?"

Kate felt certain that she had missed a point that Lex was making that had nothing to do with Kate and Rob, but Lex continued on unmistakably accusing Kate of something nefarious.

"We are supposed to be such strong, powerful, independent

women. We make our own money, own our own retirement plans. But we *refuse* to be happy. We pour everything into our children. We hover over them to ensure that they are twice as talented and twice as ambitious and twice as successful as us even though we were pretty damn talented, ambitious, and successful until *they came along.*"

"But then to add insult to injury, we stay with men who aren't worthy of us. For what? For our children? To show our children what? What cost? What lesson? I'll tell you the lesson. That women get cheated on by men. That women do not deserve happiness or love or fulfillment. In this way, Kate, we are exactly like our mothers and grandmothers. We refuse to break the cycle and create stronger versions of ourselves. The weakest do not die out. They keep churning out women just as weak."

Kate was wounded by these words, realizing at once that Lex was in many ways the best—and the worst—first person to share her news with.

"Lex, that's not fair. And with all due respect, ask yourself if your husband was cheating what would you do? What would you *really* do? Do you actually think it would be that easy to just kick him out and leave Sophia with a broken home, half a college fund, and a weekend town home? Worse yet, would you be able to give up half your holidays and weekends and an entire summer with your daughter each year to that same man who cheated on you? I guess you're a better woman than I, because I would rather wake up every day with Rob, spend the day not talking about anything other than schoolwork and sports activities than send my children to stay with him every other weekend while I organize closets and attend meetings for the recently divorced and abandoned."

Kate was a bit out of breath when she finished. And flushed. And crying. But she did not regret her outburst.

Because she realized as she heard herself saying these words out loud that she did not want to leave Rob.

Kate would be punished. Kate would be the one kissing the boys goodbye each summer when they headed off to their paternal grandparents' home in Florida where there would be not one picture of Kate, let alone a good word spoken about her. Kate had spent countless hours creating an illusion of perfection and a happy home, and now Kate would forever be the one who destroyed that happy home by leaving their father.

Kate would be the villain in her sons' stories, which she had tried to write and rewrite over and over again, in vain.

On her way home from coffee and omelettes with Lex, Kate realized with a start that Pam had not yet called her. She kept checking her cell phone and briefly considered going home to wait it out. But that was undesirable for many reasons.

Kate turned off Chestnut Road and headed to the West Street Deli where she picked up a lunch salad for Pam and two organic green iced teas and headed for Pam's house around the corner.

Pam answered the door with a tired smile. "I brought grub." Kate waved the bag of salad like a peace flag hoping against hope that Pam was happy she was here and that she hadn't overstepped boundaries. It was hard to know. They were navigating this new road together—what to do and say and what not to do and say to a friend who might or might not have cancer.

Later they'd navigate the road of what to do and say and what not to do and say to a friend whose husband was an adulterer.

But that day would wait.

"I heard from the doctor," Pam said. Kate felt her heart catch in her throat and her arms and fingers started tingling. Pam continued, "I have good news and bad news.

"The good news is I don't have cancer. Yet. The bad news is I don't have cancer. Yet."

Kate was still trying to wrap her brain around what Pam had just said and had not even had a chance to hug her when Pam turned around abruptly and walked toward the kitchen. Kate followed her, the bag of salad and tea a sudden albatross she had no idea how to unload.

"Honey, you don't have cancer. That's wonderful. But why don't *you* think that's wonderful?"

Pam sat down at the kitchen table and motioned for Kate to join her. "I do think it's wonderful that I don't have cancer.

"But. I stayed up all night last night, first planning a course of action in case I had cancer. Next planning the course of action in case I don't have cancer. This is my third scare in four years. And I'm 44, Kate."

Kate was speechless.

"My mom was diagnosed with breast cancer at 46 and she died when it recurred and metastasized at age 51. I feel like a ticking time bomb. The truth is, I actually spend more time lately planning for my inevitable breast cancer than I spend living. I actually mapped out a timetable last night for chemo and surgery so I could plan to be cancer-free by Sara's First Communion next May. For beach vacations in July."

Pam looked up. Kate was still looking at her breathless. Trying to think of something comforting to say. Instead, Kate handed Pam the salad, and Pam began digging into it. Kate exhaled in relief that Pam was eating something she had brought, and waited patiently for more from Pam in this moment settling heavily between the two women.

After a few seconds, Pam put her fork down and looked Kate in the eye.

"There's something I haven't told you. There's something I haven't told anyone, not even Greg."

In the few moments that Pam sat chewing in a pregnant suspense, Kate was left wondering whether Pam was cheating on Greg. Kate's subconscious betrayed her even now.

"I was tested last year for the breast cancer gene. And I have it." Pam paused, waiting for Kate to catch up.

"That. Sucks," Kate borrowed.

Pam looked at Kate with something that resembled a faint smile and then it faded.

But still Kate was silently grateful to Lex for helping her out with just the right sentiment in this moment.

"Yes. So you can imagine my surprise now that this time wasn't actually cancer but some crazy fibrous cysts. Around 3 am this morning, I said to myself, *even if I don't actually have cancer, I swear I'm never going through this again.* Walking around the dark, quiet house planning my illness and possible death. Walking in and out of the girls' rooms, covering and re-covering them. Wondering how many more nights I could actually have that privilege. Lying next to Greg and wondering how I could ever do this to him. He has his career, his life. He'd give up everything to stay home and take care of his sick wife—I can't let him do that. I love him much too much."

Kate was still trying to think of something—anything—reassuring to say, when Pam announced, "It's done. It's over. There's just no other answer."

"Oh my God, Pam." Kate got up and walked over to Pam and put her arms around her. "Pam, you cannot talk like this. We'll get you someone. You need a support group. Someone who can really help. Who's been through what you've been through. Who can offer you something more than cranberry salad and green tea. What was I thinking? I'm so sorry. Pam, your family needs you. We all need you."

Kate was crying now and Pam pulled away dry-eyed and smiling.

"Oh, Sweetie. I'm not going to kill myself or anything like that. I'm having a double mastectomy. No breasts. No breast cancer. It's not that complicated. I'm taking control of this completely uncontrollable situation. I made a pre-op appointment with the surgeon for next month. I need to tell Greg of course. But he won't talk me out of it. Not when I tell him that I have the gene."

Kate felt overwhelmed by her inadequacy at helping Pam—at even understanding an inkling of what was going on in her head in this moment. She sat back down and stared at her.

"That's so drastic. Are you sure?"

"You're not really questioning my logic are you?" Pam was smirking a bit now.

And Kate wasn't sure what the smirk was all about until Pam reminded her. "Remember last year when head lice was going around the kids' school?"

Ugh. Kate felt nauseous at the memory. She had checked and rechecked the kids, pacing countless nights until one day she woke up with the brilliant, easy idea. She took the boys for quarter inch crewcuts, watching their gorgeous waves and curls fall to the floor of the barber. Rob had told her that she was irrational and crazy. *Why would you cut off all their hair when they don't even have lice?*

But when Kate had relayed the story to Pam, including Rob's reaction, Kate had said simply, "No hair, no lice—it's not that complicated."

So now while Kate felt a pang of both nausea and embarrassment at the memory, particularly in light of what Pam was facing, Pam was simply smiling serenely at her. So peaceful did Pam look, that for a minute Kate almost thought the double mastectomy was a joke—a belated mocking for her own imaginary head lice drama last year.

But no, Pam was serious and resolute about her decision

already. She was taking control of her own destiny with singular purpose. And she was a heck of a lot more rational than Kate had been last year.

"Pam, you wow me, breasts or none. You are amazing." Then, Kate clinked her green tea bottle on Pam's and smiled. "I'm happy for you. You're taking control of this and I'm so, so happy for you."

"Now, *that* was *exactly* the right thing to say right now," Pam said as she clinked back.

OVER THE NEXT FEW WEEKS, Kate thought about Pam's words of wisdom—delivered unwittingly to a friend who needed them so much—*take control of a completely uncontrollable situation.*

She replayed these words over and over, wondering how to take control of her own uncontrollable situation. She stopped taking Rob's phone calls. He was allegedly staying at a corporate hotel for the time being, and she began keeping communication to bare minimum texts that addressed only when he could come get the boys for dinner each week. An outing to the park each weekend. She continued evading the boys' questioning about why Daddy was working so much lately. She spent her days and nights wondering over and over just how to get control back.

❧

Kate drove by that boutique every day.

It was on the way to and from the kids' school. She never caught the light at that corner which found her staring out the window at the mannequins draped in elaborate dresses that were for special occasions, formal occasions. Occasions that Kate knew nothing about.

But one day, after returning from dropping the kids off at school, and on a morning after Rob had been gone for nearly a month, Kate was thinking about the fact that soon she would have to have a conversation with the kids that went beyond: *Daddy is working a lot. Daddy will be back soon.*

These were the thoughts in her head as she absently looked out the window at the stoplight. These were the thoughts in her head when she first saw the dress in the window of the boutique. She parked the car and waited for the boutique to open for the morning.

Kate was not the type of person to swoon over expensive clothes. She liked pretty things. She had been known to purchase the occasional discounted-perhaps-counterfeit-perhaps-stolen designer goods on online auction websites. But she was not one to pay five hundred dollars for a boutique dress without batting an eye.

But this dress.

It was something special.

The dress was soft and heavy with sequins. The golden silk had a red velvet zipper up the back and a soft, thin, red velvet lining. It was exciting and daring and decidedly impractical. Kate stood in front of the mirror in the boutique asking the salesgirl questions about the dress. The dress that fit her like a glove.

How long had it been there?

Who was the designer?

The salesgirl knew very little. She knew that her boss had ordered the dress at a trunk show a few months ago and had been lamenting that the dress had garnered such little interest from the boutique clientele.

"What do you know about the designer?" Kate asked.

"Not much," the salesgirl replied nonchalantly.

"Were there more where this came from?"

The girl shrugged. "It was handmade by artisans in rural India, apparently. It landed at a Trunk Show in New York City. That's what I've overheard from the owner, anyway."

Kate turned around again in front of the mirror. She rolled the tags around in her hand. The tag showed it had been marked down from $1000 three times to $500. The girl, seemingly sensing that there might be an actual sale evolving here, piped up a bit. "It fits you perfectly. And it is a great color on you, I must say. Such a beautiful shade of gold."

"Lemongrass," Kate said almost curtly. And then caught herself. She added more softly, "They say lemongrass is the color of hope, of optimism." The girls' bright eyes dimmed. She looked apathetic again.

This dress did not belong here.

Kate told the salesgirl she'd be back in 15 minutes. She went to the bank and withdrew five $100 bills and then returned for the dress. She couldn't charge the dress. Rob would see the charge. Besides, she couldn't really afford it.

❧

On the way home from the boutique, with the dress in a garment bag hooked onto a hanger in the back of her car, Kate's cell phone buzzed with her mother's number.

When Kate picked it up, she heard her Aunt Lily's voice instead of Sandra's. A close match, however, so she was a bit startled and confused. "Aunt Lily, I'm sorry. I thought it was Mom calling. I just didn't expect to hear your voice. Are you over there?"

"Kate, where are you?"

"I'm on Beechwood Avenue. I just got coffee. What's going on?"

Kate was nervous but didn't know why. Something had happened. Something bad had happened and she steeled herself for whatever it was. Lily seemed to realize she was doing this and paused for a moment before she replied.

"Your father has had a heart attack, Kate. I'm at your parents' home. Kate, you need to come here right now."

Kate did not say goodbye. She did not even hang up the phone. She just dropped it on the seat next to her and drove to her parents' home on autopilot, knowing of course that the fact that she had been summoned there instead of to the hospital meant that her father was not at the hospital. There was only one reason her father would not be at the hospital after having a heart attack.

She tried to say it out loud but could not say the words.

She tried to think the thought, but her brain could not finish it.

When Kate pulled up to her mother's home, there were several cars already there. Dark cars. That's what struck her as unusual. The cars were unfamiliar and certainly did not belong to anyone she knew. But her mind obsessed on the simple fact that the cars were dark, and therefore ominous.

Kate walked into the house and saw her mother sitting at the table with papers in front of her. Lily was helping her fill out something. Sandra looked at Kate and immediately came across the room to embrace her.

"Kate. Your father is gone, Kate."

There was a loud buzzing noise in Kate's ears and she reached for the arm of the sofa and sat down in it while her mother made her way across the room to her.

Sandra was talking and Kate watched her lips move while the buzzing made the words nearly impossible to hear. Still, she strained to hear them.

Heart attack . . . in his sleep this morning.

He is still here. . .

. . .Bathed and dressed . . . and he is in our room.

We'll go up there together . . . When you're ready, Kate.

Sandra sat next to Kate and held her. Kate put her hands to her ears and tried to get the buzzing noise to stop. She tried to think of something to say. After her mother stopped talking, her mind continued talking to her.

Your father is not here. He is. Gone. This is your mother hugging you. Right now she is all business. She is practical. She made sure your father's body was presentable before Lily called you. She is filling out the requisite paperwork—probably promising away his corneas right here in the living room. Her entire life is over as she knows it. She is now a young widow, yet she's comforting you, hugging you, supporting you. You must pull yourself together. For her. That is what she needs now. That is what you can do for her.

Kate was trying not to dissolve into tears. Her mother's bravery was so inspiring and so endearing. So like her. When the buzzing subsided a little, Kate thought a familiar thought, *I want to be my mother's daughter. I want to be like her.* Kate practiced being her practical mother as she climbed the steps solemnly and slowly with her. But in Sandra's bedroom, as Kate and Sandra dissolved into tears, saying goodbye together to Kate's father, the pain gripped Kate fiercely in its jaws and she thought to herself,

I am not truly brave or practical.

And I will never survive any of this.

❧

At the funeral, Kate stood alone with her mother.

Pam took the boys for the afternoon.

Pre-op consults and testing done, Pam's double mastectomy surgery was scheduled in a few weeks, but still she stepped outside of her own worries and fears to offer to take the boys when Kate repeatedly told her, "No, I will hire a sitter."

"The boys are too little to see their grandfather's body laid out at my mom's church and I don't want them to see their mother or grandmother wracked with grief. Frankly, it's really too much for me to see my own mother swallowed up in grief. How can I do that to the boys?" Kate was telling Pam on the day before the funeral when Pam interrupted to insist she would watch the boys.

Kate had been coming over most mornings to have coffee

with Pam and just to be with her in the days leading up to her surgery. But on this morning, the women had switched roles in a familiar female dance as the scales of trauma and need had shifted ever so slightly in Kate's favor.

And even though Kate had no intention of telling Pam about Rob while Pam's surgery loomed over her own distracted mind, she matter-of-factly told Pam about that situation as well. "You see, Rob has been cheating on me and isn't even living at home now. We are trying to work things out but it's very awkward. So, you know, he could just stay with the boys and skip the funeral, but—"

Pam rubbed Kate's hand. Kate wondered briefly whether Pam already knew, or whether she just knew this was all the "Rob's affair" conversation Kate could handle right now, as she looked neither surprised, nor prodded Kate for more information.

"Rob really wants to come to the funeral and while I don't want him there, I certainly don't have the energy to explain to people why my husband is not at my father's funeral," Kate went on, and Pam nodded.

"Kate. Let me watch the boys tomorrow."

"Yes. Thanks, Pam."

At the funeral, Rob stood near the front of the church but enough out of Kate's viewpoint, so that she could stand with Sandra and focus on her mother's and her own grief instead of Rob's betrayal.

But Kate could not help but see Rob when she and Sandra followed Kate's father's casket out of the church. He smiled helplessly at Kate when he got her eye. Kate looked away quickly. She looked over instead at her mother and sighed. Sandra's face was contorted with tears, and her expression was so pained. Kate looked at her and felt just one thing.

25

"JEALOUS? You felt jealous?"

Kate was startled by the harsh tone that had invaded Pam's voice. She had only confided this emotion in her because she thought Pam would be the one nonjudgmental ear she could count on. So empathetic and comforting had Pam been in the days leading up to the funeral despite her own worries and fears, even after Kate's disclosure about Rob's adultery the day before, Kate mistakenly thought she would understand even this strange emotion confession.

The girls were entertaining the boys in the basement and Kate and Pam were having a cup of tea while Kate debriefed her on the funeral service. Kate was going to take the boys back to her mother's home for refreshments, but Pam offered her a quiet cup of tea before she headed back to the crowd.

"You felt jealous of your mother as they were carrying her husband out of the church?"

Kate nodded, truthfully.

"I did. I felt jealous."

But then Kate realized something.

"Oh! But not because she has a dead husband. Is that what you thought I meant?"

Pam nodded a little over her mug and Kate laughed a bit sardonically. "No, no."

"It's just that she loved my dad so much. They had such a great life together and she is in such pain. I can't imagine. I can't picture feeling that way if Rob died. It made me feel jealous—envious for having missed out on a true life partner the likes of my dad."

Kate remembered feeling this way before. Before she knew about Rob's affair. Years before, in fact. Kate had been sitting in her university office drinking coffee and reading the newspaper when she had stumbled upon a story of a decorated local policeman's funeral. Kate had sat there, tears streaming down her face, when a colleague knocked on the door jamb and came in, catching her streaky and teary with the tragic headline and photo face up on her desk.

"Yes, I know," Professor Myer had said. "What a terrible story. What a tragedy." Kate had nodded and sniffed and wiped her eyes. But all she was thinking about when she stared at the widow and her raw grief was that she could not imagine feeling like that at Rob's funeral. Or that Rob would feel even an inkling of that raw emotion at her funeral. That was the state of things. Of their marriage. Even then.

Kate was brought back to the present day by Pam.

Pam was still business-like as she patted Kate's hand, and Kate cringed a bit as though scolded, as Pam said, "Kate, my dear, you still have your boys and you have tomorrow. So really, there is nothing to be jealous about."

And then, her tone changed a bit as she said, "You know, marriage is not for the weak, Kate. There have been many, many times I have thought about leaving Greg."

"You and Greg?" Kate was shocked.

Pam ignored her shock as she nodded. "But marriage is about waiting those times out. When you get to other side, you say, well, that was terrible, but I'm glad I didn't throw in the towel."

"This isn't just a fight about how much quality time Rob spends with me and the kids or the division of household labor. He cheated on me, Pam. For months, maybe longer."

Kate looked up in time to see the fleeting look on Pam's

face which was something between wounded and angry. It faded quickly but it was very shocking for a moment.

"Greg and I have had real problems too, Kate. Cheating is not the only terrible thing that can happen in a marriage."

Kate was not at all sure they were on the same page here. But Pam continued on, lowering her voice for effect and Kate felt certain that Pam had said the next sentence out loud only as many times as Kate had said out loud that Rob had had sex with another woman.

"Greg once told me he was sorry he ever married me. Terribly sorry."

"Oh," Kate said very ineloquently.

"So did he mean it?" Kate asked.

"Well, I think he may very well have meant it when he said it, which was years ago. But I know for a fact he doesn't mean it anymore. That's what matters. Today. Now. Not years ago."

Kate rubbed her eyebrows and shook her head. "I don't know, Pam. I am having a very hard time seeing how I could land on the other side of this. I mean aren't there certain deal-breakers in a marriage? Cheating? Abuse?"

Pam shook her head violently. "No, no, Kate. Those two things are not the same at all. Look, Kate, what Rob did was terrible, but it didn't involve you. It was about problems and insecurities that *he* was facing. It's terrible, but it's not the same as abusing you. Not by a long shot."

Kate was still looking down at the coffee table, thinking *this is going nowhere.* Pam did not at all seem to understand the fact that Rob had had sex with another woman—and Kate realized on this day, the day she was burying her father, there really wasn't any point to discussing the whole sordid matter any further.

She doesn't get it. Kate thought disappointedly, feeling certain that the thought must be painted across her face. And as she looked up reluctantly at Pam, Kate realized Pam was looking at Kate with an expression that said exactly the same thing.

∽

Back at Kate's parents' home, Kate paraded the boys through the house, introducing them to people who had never met them before, and reintroducing them to older relatives who hadn't seen the boys since they were babies.

Rob's parents had not made the trip north for the funeral, sending flowers instead. Rob had politely declined Kate's equally polite invitation back to the house. "Tell everyone I'm not feeling well, and don't want to get anyone sick." Kate had rolled her eyes at his feeble excuse, but decided to use it anyway, as she moved through the post-funeral crowd, answering questions including how old the boys were now and how was Rob, and relieved that neither Rob nor his parents were present to add to her grief.

The boys were a welcome distraction especially to Sandra, who pulled them into the kitchen to feed them brownies and milk and show them off to her childhood friend, Liz, who had made the trip in from the West Coast to comfort her grieving friend.

With the boys and her mother distracted, Kate meandered through the house. Lex was talking to a neighbor across the room and smiled warmly and then gave a questioning look to Kate. Kate returned Lex's smile and nodded to let her know in silent code that she was holding up ok as she kept moving through the crowd.

After a few minutes, despite the people and body heat, Kate felt an unmistakable chill, and decided to head upstairs for a sweater.

At the top of the steps, she hugged an older woman standing in line for the bathroom whom Kate didn't quite recognize but who seemed to know her and who asked for Rob. "Well, he's really sick, I sent him home so he wouldn't infect anyone," Kate responded tensely, before slipping quickly into her old bedroom and closing and locking the door behind her.

Kate sat on her bed and looked around. The room was still decorated as if a 17-year-old girl lived there. Cheerleading pictures, and certificates of achievement and other academic awards decorated the walls in cheap plastic frames. *A shrine*, she had always called it to her parents, who never redecorated the room, leaving it just the way their only child had left it more than 20 years earlier.

Kate had always loved being an only child—until today. Today she had the thought that it would be so much easier to go through this day and every day that was about to come next, if she had someone in her life who understood her, truly understood how it felt to lose *this* father.

∾

"I feel like I'm fighting against destiny, Dad."

Kate had been sitting on this bed, in this very spot. Home on a break during her senior year of college, she was in turmoil about whether she should go to graduate school or start working. She had a job offer from a bank that she felt she should jump on. On the other hand, she had gotten into two graduate schools and was trying to figure out if she should pursue her love of history and a teaching career.

Bill Monroe had always tried to hide how much he wanted Kate to become a teacher. He was not very good at it. A career high school history teacher, he had become a High School Principal in a tough urban New Jersey neighborhood not too far from New York City in Kate's teen years, and Kate had idolized him—something she had never been good at hiding, either.

"It's a great job, Dad. My friends—heck, my college advisor—

all tell me I'd be a fool not to take it. But who am I kidding? All my life, I have thought that I'm probably meant to be a history teacher. How can I buck my destiny, right?"

Kate smiled at her Dad as she searched his face for something. Something that would tell her what to do. Yet, she knew he would not tell her what to do. They had never had that kind of relationship.

"Well, I don't really believe that our destiny is something that we have no control over. That's a bit of a cop-out, don't you think?"

Kate was confused. Was her Dad actually telling her not to pursue teaching?

He continued.

"Teachers—good teachers—don't believe in blind destiny. Otherwise, why would we do what we do? We believe we can help the kids we come in contact with to make decisions that affect—sometimes change even—their destiny. We don't let our students cop out with 'Well it's just what's meant to be.' Otherwise, every inner city, underprivileged kid would stay put.

"And history teachers? Well, we study history—we *teach* history so that we can learn from it. No. Blind destiny has no place for history teachers. We have a choice. You have a choice."

Kate laughed and made her decision on the spot. "Yes. I have a choice, Dad. Because I am a history student—and a history teacher in the making. You're right. I'm going to go to grad school. To hell with that banking job. Sorry." She covered her mouth, embarrassed by the rare swear in her dad's presence.

"Well, if that's your decision, you know I will fully support it, of course. Your mother and I will both support it." He had stood up and kissed her head, his pride transparent.

And long after he left her room, as Kate had lain in this bed thinking about how to gracefully turn down the bank job, she wasn't sure if blind destiny had talked her into grad school or not.

History teachers don't believe in blind destiny, she thought. Still, she had had the unmistakable feeling that she had only one possible choice and that her dad had known that even before she had.

∽

The only other time Kate and her father had talked about "destiny" had been the morning of Kate's wedding. She had sat in this room again, after coming home to get married to Rob. Even though she had not lived here in years, she had slept in her childhood bed for one more symbolic night before beginning her new life as Rob Sutton's wife. Her last night as Kate Monroe.

Her hair done up with a flowered veil after a morning at the local salon, Kate was sitting in her bathrobe procrastinating getting dressed. He mother was smoothing and admiring her white dress on the hanger when her father had come in to talk to her.

"Cold feet?" he had teased.

Kate had never told him, or anyone for that matter, about the miscarriage or the emergency room proposal. She thought about confiding in her mom and dad that morning, but changed her mind quickly.

"No way. Following my destiny," she smiled.

"Destiny? I think that's just a fancy word for making the right choice." Kate's Dad kissed her head. "And I know one person today who is making the absolutely right choice."

"Thanks, Dad."

"Rob." Kate's Dad smiled over his shoulder as he left Kate and her mother to dress Kate for her wedding day.

AFTER THE FUNERAL, Pam started planning for her surgery, and Lex started working in earnest on her book, and Kate was left alone with her grief.

Rob was still allegedly sleeping at a corporate hotel, taking the boys on outings a few days a week, and Kate sunk back into a depression. She had wanted to invite Rob back home, but her father's death and her mother's grief had jarred her.

Clearly, she and Rob would never have that kind of marriage. Could she accept that fact and move on? The uncertainty was oppressive.

She found herself dropping the boys off at school and then sleeping all day.

And Kate *hated* napping.

It was such a concession of defeat.

She would lie on the bed, all the will power and energy zapped from her body, knowing that she had laundry and dinner and shopping and the weight of a hundred other errands over her head. But she lay there. Shielding her eyes from the light that shone in through the windows but lacking the energy to get up and close the blinds. Besides, to get up and close the blinds would be to admit she was going to nap which she never did admit.

Instead, the ritual started with telling herself five minutes of quiet was needed. She dozed on and off, waking with a start, panicking that she would be late to pick up the kids. Willing herself to stay awake so she wouldn't miss pickups but refusing to set an alarm in case she fell asleep, because she could not admit to herself that she was even thinking about sleep.

This went on for days, then a week, and the napping or pretend-to-not-be-napping depressed her even more. Consequently, Kate also grew increasingly unable to sleep at night. One night she lay in bed tossing and turning for hours before coming downstairs where she turned on a soft light in the living room.

A movement across the room startled her when she turned on the light.

It was a moth.

Kate sat on the couch and watched the moth dance in the corner of the living room, and a new ritual had begun.

The moth came out nearly every night for a week and Kate grew amazed at his resilience. She could hardly believe that anything living could thrive in this house. The air seemed so thick and so toxic.

Each night, she would emerge from her sleeplessness in the bedroom, and turn the light on in the living room. She would read a few hours. She watched a little TV. But mostly she watched the moth dance in and out of the room looking for light but hiding from the movement Kate made with the remote, or her book, or her drink.

The moth disappeared after a week.

Kate stopped sleeping all day, and forced herself to start sleeping nights again.

She had to get things back under control.

～

One night, after she had started sleeping at night again, Kate dreamed about a conversation she had had with Rob, just a few years before. A conversation that had actually taken place.

"I always wanted a best friend," Kate had lamented.

"You have lots of friends."

"No, a best friend. One friend. The one go-to person when your world is caving in around you. I don't have that. I guess I hoped I wouldn't need one once I got married. But here I am, marriage in upheaval, world caving in and no one best friend. Lots of well-meaning friends, but no one person to just talk it through and make it all go away."

She had seen something then in Rob's face. Confusion and then something else. Empathy? Anger? It went away quickly and Kate had looked away.

"My mom always had her friend, Liz. I just wanted that. But it's not the kind of thing you can create in your life. I think it's like love. It either happens or it doesn't. You can't force it.

"And I don't think you can have a best friend when you are always unhappy. Because you have to be a best friend to have a best friend. And that means you have to be everything to someone at some moment in time. When you're 3 or 13 or 33. And then they'll be your best friend. Forever. But if you're always the one in need of a best friend, well, you are not likely to find a match."

In her dream, as in reality, Kate had looked up for a moment to see if Rob was still listening. And in her dream, as in reality, he wasn't.

He was texting. He was nodding—to Kate or the phone, she couldn't tell. But in her dream, she did the one thing she had wanted to do in reality, but hadn't. She picked up her shoe and threw it at him across the room. It missed by a mile. Rob barely ducked; he didn't have to.

She walked out of the room, out of the house, without a soul to call.

And then she woke up.

27

THE NIGHT BEFORE PAM was scheduled for surgery, Kate took Pam's girls for the night. Greg dropped the kids off alone. Pam had said her goodbyes to the girls at home and was feeling emotional and uncharacteristically unsocial, Greg explained.

"Greg, it's quite all right. Pam certainly doesn't need to come talk to me before her surgery. I just want her to know I'm here for her."

"I know. Thank you so much. Thank you for all you and Rob are doing for us."

Kate jumped a bit at the mention of Rob's name.

"It's a hell of thing. Watching your wife go through anything like this. Well, watching your spouse go through anything hard. You know what I mean? I just feel so helpless."

Kate tried not to let the fuzzy realization that Greg knew nothing about her separation distract her from the fact that Greg was the one who needed comforting and empathy in this moment.

"I know, Greg. But she is one tough cookie. And this is her way of taking charge of things. She is going to do great and come out of this stronger than ever."

"Yes. I believe that. I do. It's just that—well, I wish she had told me. Wish she had done this when she first found out instead of living with so much fear. I'm not sure why she thinks I'm the one who needs protecting. That's supposed to be my job. I feel like I've failed her somehow. I really have to fix that. I guess we all get a second chance after this surgery." Greg looked defeated somehow and Kate patted his hand.

"Second chance. That's a wonderful way to look at this all. A second chance for everyone. Now get home to your wife. Be strong for her."

As Kate closed the door, she thought about how nice it was to pretend not to be separated from Rob for a few moments. Greg obviously didn't know and while he was there, she could pretend it wasn't true. That her whole life wasn't falling apart at the seams. It *did* feel nice to have a second chance. Just like Greg had said.

After Pam's surgery the next day, Greg came to get the girls to bring them home. Even though Pam would be in the hospital for a few more days—or maybe because she would be—he wanted the girls home with him. Kate was sorry to see them go. The presence of a few more kids in the house was a welcome distraction from her own sorrows. Her mother had been stopping by daily but was largely unable to share her own grief with Kate, maintaining a stoic disposition.

So like her.

Kate was equal parts inspired by her mother's stoicism and defeated by it. She wanted to emulate her mother. She wanted to have that strength, that life, that marriage.

But of course, all that was impossible, Kate reminded herself daily as she watched her mother. As they both inevitably discussed her father, Kate found it exhausting trying to be strong for her mother. Be strong *like* her mother. She had the sense that her mother was likewise trying to be strong for Kate. Which must have been exhausting as well.

Kate started to think it might be good for her mother—for everyone—if Kate could just get away for a few days.

28

A FEW NIGHTS AFTER PAM RETURNED home from having surgery, Kate went to visit her. The boys were having dinner with Rob, and so she headed over with a casserole tray and some activity books and scented markers for the girls.

When she arrived, Kate told Greg to go take a nap or a walk or run an errand. He looked exhausted and Kate knew instantly that Pam could use a break from Greg's caregiving just as much as Greg could.

"I'm going to wait until I heal to schedule the reconstructive surgery," Pam told her as Kate set the table so they could eat. The girls were distracted with their goodies and Kate thought it would be nice for the two women to eat dinner while it was still hot. Later she'd microwave food for Greg and the girls before she left.

"Ultimately, the theory is that the body will do better with the reconstruction when you let your body heal first. From the double mastectomy. That's what my doctors said anyway. So I have to live like this for a few weeks." Pam waved her hands vaguely over her chest and smiled wanly before she winced with physical and other pain.

"How *do* you feel?" Kate asked.

"Deformed. But relieved. No regrets. I'm glad I took my time. Prepared myself. Prepared Greg. Doesn't he just look awful?"

Pam laughed a small laugh at first, that strengthened within seconds. Kate nodded.

"Oh my word. Terrible. Has he even showered in days?"

And the women erupted into familiar, breathless, happy laughter that mingled with weepy eyes and running noses. As she wiped her tears and nose, Kate swelled with gratitude at the sound of Pam's laughing tears. The two women ate the rest of their dinner in a comfortable peace punctuated occasionally by fits of sudden laughter, so that when Greg came home an hour later, they had to both quickly put their forks down, for fear they might choke at the laughing marathon that ensued for a good five minutes after his entrance.

When Kate got home that evening, she pulled into the driveway just moments before Rob pulled up with the boys.

They jumped out of Rob's car, arms overflowing with cheap plush figures, excitedly talking about dinner with Daddy at the diner.

"Daddy let us play on the claw machine and he got *all* these animals for us, Mommy."

"You should have *seen* him. He was so good at it! He's like an *expert* at claw machines! Can we *please* skip baths. We are *so* tired, Mommy."

Kate bent down and hugged them and looked over their heads at Rob, who shrugged and smiled impishly before reaching over and ruffling David's thick black head of hair. The gesture sent her careening for a moment back to her first pregnancy.

At that time I imagined Rob's dark-haired mane appearing on my first born. Our first born. But no, it didn't arrive until David.

Kate squeezed the boys harder before standing back up.

"Come on guys. Sounds like you had so much fun. Let's get you to bed. Yes, you can skip baths if you promise to go *right* to sleep."

Kate and Rob took the boys up to their respective rooms, moving through the nighttime rituals of pajama changing and teeth brushing and tucking in endless quantities of claw machine emigrants.

After the boys fell asleep, Rob lingered a bit, until Kate yawned and said she'd walk him out.

As he drove away, Kate thought about how she would like to have Rob move back in, but still felt she had healing to do from the initial blow. *Ultimately, the theory is that the body will do better with the reconstruction when you let your body heal first.*

She went to her closet and took out the lemongrass gown. She hung it on a hook on the front of her closet door and thought how nice it would be to have somewhere to wear it.

To heal.

Over the next few weeks, Kate looked at the dress every morning and in spite of her overwhelming grief over her father and her marriage, there was no mistaking the feeling.

The dress made her *happy*.

She showed Lex and her mother the dress on two separate occasions.

What they likely thought, she knew, was that she was crazy but no one said it out loud. They said "oh, how pretty" and "where will you wear it?" and "how's Rob?" But no one said, "Kate, have you lost your mind?" She wondered why they did not ask that but she showed it to them anyway.

One day, Kate logged onto her computer to check emails and scroll through the latest Facebook updates in an attempt to both catch up on lost friends and distract herself. Over the last few years, she had found herself so hopelessly out of touch with so many people. She liked these periodic updates. She also liked the superficiality of Facebook—the way you could post a status about the beautiful weather when in reality your husband had cheated on you and your marriage was in a state of constant disarray.

She was thinking about posting a picture of the dress. She felt childish and silly for even thinking about it but still, she did not dismiss the idea as she scrolled down the page.

And then she saw it.

A familiar, though long absent, face popped up next to an intriguing status: "Just booked a cruise to the Bahamas to cure a bad case of heartbreak . . . It's been 10 years since the last one—(cruise, not heartbreak)—anyone want to join me?"

Benton Daly's face smiled up from the computer screen like an invitation.

It had been such a long, long time.

Kate recalled that ten years earlier, Benton had reached out and invited Kate on a cruise she had also dubbed "a heartbreak cruise" but Kate wasn't feeling very heartbroken at that time. It was months before her miscarriage. She had been dating Rob at the time, and things were progressing along nicely. Slowly but nicely. Ten years ago, she had briefly entertained the notion of going along on the cruise to catch up with Benton, but decided against it at the last minute.

How strange that Benton was now organizing a new cruise at this particular time in Kate's life. A time when getting away from things could be so very healing.

Kate thought for a moment about what it would be like to still be friends with Benton Daly. About the interesting life Benton must be leading now where a heartbreak was simply a motivation for a tropical vacation. And she couldn't help herself. Kate wondered if *he'd* be there.

She turned and looked at the lemongrass gown hanging on the closet door. *Ultimately, the theory is that the body will do better with the reconstruction when you let your body heal first.* She paused for just one more nanosecond before clicking quickly on the "Like" button.

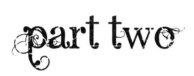

part two

I WAS EXCITED AND ANXIOUS as I drove to the cruise ship pier but still I could not stop thinking about how I left Rob.

He had shown up at 11 pm the night before, overnight bag in hand, long after I had put the boys to bed. They had needed bedtime stories, so many bedtime stories, along with so many answers last night. They were wary about me leaving them for the first time ever, which made me feel guilty, of course.

"How long is a week, Mama?"

"Why can't we go?"

"But why can't you tell the school we will come back next week?"

"Do you promise to bring us soup and ears?" (This from David who understood the *concept* of souvenirs but not the pronunciation.)

"And Daddy is really taking off the whole week to play with us?"

I nodded enthusiastically to that question. They were so excited about the promise of Daddy to themselves for the whole week that I felt my heart would burst. It was the one thing that alleviated my guilt for leaving them for the first time ever in their little lives.

To be honest, I was still wondering how I had convinced Rob to take a week off—or at least to work from home for the week—so I could go "gallivanting."

His word.

But he said it with a smile and a wink and I didn't take offense. And he said, "Yes," immediately.

I was still packing at 11 when I heard his key in the door. I chided myself for jumping a bit when I heard the door open. After all, I was expecting him and after all, it was still *his* house, too.

"Up here, Rob," I called downstairs in a loud whisper, hoping not to wake the boys. I couldn't bear to say goodbye again. I wanted to leave cleanly at 5 am. With my cherubs asleep in their beds and Rob safely asleep in the guest room.

I heard Rob stop in the guest room, and put his bag down loudly. I cringed. Was he *trying* to wake the boys? Moments later he arrived in my bedroom doorway.

"I come in peace," he waved a white tee shirt before tugging it on over his Ralph Lauren pajama bottoms as he walked into the bedroom, and I smiled in spite of myself. *Ever the disarming charmer, that one*, I thought before I could catch myself.

"Come on in, I'm packing. You can help me."

Rob sat quietly on a chair next to my bed, our bed, and I continued folding clothes and pressing toiletries into my suitcase. I had already zipped up my garment bag with a few dresses and the lemongrass gown. I did not want Rob to see it. I felt uncomfortable to have bought such a thing and to be even thinking about wearing such a thing without Rob nearby.

After a little while, Rob ran his fingers through his hair in that familiar way and leaned forward with his elbows on his knees.

"You know, Kate, it *is* over."

I looked up, startled for a moment. *Was our marriage over? Really? Did I have no say in this whatsoever?*

Rob looked stricken by my expression and then said quickly, "No. I mean, with Celeste." Rob shifted uncomfortably in his chair while saying her name, and I was likewise uncomfortable by the fact that I took some brief solace in that fact.

"It's been over for some time which is why she called you.

You know, that day. I really *have* been staying at the corporate hotel I told you I was staying in."

I kept folding. It had occurred to me many times over the last several months that maybe it was over with Celeste, and moreover, that maybe there was some hope left for us.

"I had thought that was a possibility. But really Rob, that's somewhat irrelevant here. You do realize that, right?"

Silence.

I sat down on the bed across from his chair and looked him in the eye and asked him the question I had been wanting to ask for some time now. "How long did it go on, Rob?"

I saw him waver between lies and truth and I believed his answer because it was just so, well, hurtful.

"About a year."

"A year. That's a relationship, Rob, not an affair."

And I believed him again, because he said, "Yes, in a way it was."

And so we sat together in complete honesty for the next hour or so, discussing his affair in a way we had not been ready to do up until that moment.

I did not ask, "Did you ever love her?" I did not care to hear the answer to that question. But I did want to know something else. So I asked, "*Do* you love her?"

"No."

"Do you regret it?"

"Absolutely."

"Why did you stay with her so long?"

"Why? Well, to be honest, because of the guilt."

It was an extraordinary answer, even for Rob.

"What are you talking about? If you felt guilty, how could you keep it up? I cannot even imagine how you juggled all the lying, all the games."

"I was so riddled with guilt, Kate. The first time, it was such a ridiculous lapse in—in everything. I just gave in out of selfishness and then I felt so lousy, so disgusting, it was as if I had to stay with her just to prove it wasn't a one-time thing, that it was something more. By the time it was clear to me that it was not, in fact, anything more, I was drowning in disgust and sadness, and the short-term physical satisfaction helped me forget. She was like a substitute for a tequila shot, or heroin or something. I didn't love her but I hated myself, and she helped me forget that, for short periods of time at least."

"Hunh." I understood this in some crazy way. This made sense to me and I found myself feeling sorry for him. He must have sensed this because he said, "I miss us, Kate. I miss our family. I really want to come back home. When you're ready."

As I drove to the ship the next morning, I was thinking about how happy the boys were knowing Daddy was going to be home again for the week.

I wasn't sure how I felt about Rob anymore, but to be fair, that confusion had settled in long before Celeste came into our lives, long before the lies. In a way, it wasn't logical to ban Rob from moving back in just because of Celeste. Which is why as I drove to the pier the morning of the cruise, I was thinking that when I got back home, I would ask Rob to move out of that corporate hotel. At least to move back into the guest room. And see how things went from there.

I NOTICED HER RIGHT AWAY. It was hard not to. She was everything I was not.

A graceful gazelle.

She had one lovely chic carry-on and was not struggling for one moment to navigate the ramp to get onto the cruise ship.

In contrast, my attempt to cram all necessities into one lovely and too-small Lilly Pulitzer bag that I had bought online a week earlier from the "Resort Collection" link while suffering from moth-less insomnia, was competing with my inability to ever pack lightly.

It's a pervasive problem in my life, my inability to pack. On our honeymoon, Rob had chided me for over-packing. "No way, Kate." He had shaken his head when he stopped by my apartment—the one I would be moving out of shortly—just a week before the wedding. "I am not lugging all of that on our trip to Hawaii."

I had smiled sweetly and promised to reduce the bags to a more manageable amount; but of course, I never did. And Rob overlooked the bags on our honeymoon night. Actually did not mention the bags at all when our limo driver piled them high in his trunk. I loved that he did not say a word about my over-packing that night. I remember thinking, "See? A simple thing like *silence* starts our life together on a good note."

I couldn't help thinking about the irony of calling silence a *good* thing in our marriage, as I unpacked my car at the parking garage at Chelsea Pier and headed to check my luggage.

And so, as I watched the gazelle from my spot on the cruise

ship ramp, I was lugging one lovely Resort Collection floral bag that couldn't zip properly (the zipper may or may not have actually broken in my latest attempt to jam it closed), and two plastic grocery store bags with some rarely worn shoes and belts that I had decided at the last minute I absolutely had to have on this trip.

Because really, if I didn't break them out on this trip, when else was I ever going to use them?

I was also juggling one reusable grocery bag I had crammed full with the huge pile of magazines sitting on the kitchen island that I had sworn to make time to read every Saturday morning for the last 14 months.

But not the gazelle. She had one very practical looking and yet stunning burlap bag with red beaded embroidery. The zipper was closed and there was not a single grocery store bag draped on her arm. She looked . . . unencumbered. She was talking with another lovely woman who seemed to be her traveling companion and whom I recognized suddenly as my old friend, Benton. I did not call out from my spot in line as I wanted to see Benton after I had a chance to get on board and freshen up. Benton and I had exchanged a few brief emails in which I told her only that Rob and I were separated and that I, too, needed a "get away" trip. I wondered as I watched Benton and the gazelle, what creatures like this would ever need to get away from.

∾

Benton and the gazelle were just saying goodbye to the attractive couple with whom they had been walking along the boarding line. The couple was adjusting themselves to pose in front of a fake backdrop of a boat that looked nothing like the one we were actually boarding for their "Welcome Aboard" photo.

From a distance, I could hear the gazelle saying things like, "Well, I'm sure I'll see you around. Have a wonderful anniversary trip." And she wasn't turning to look for anyone. She was just smiling. She looked marvelously happy and I suddenly found myself wanting to catch up and talk to her despite my earlier idea of freshening up before reuniting with Benton.

I could not stop myself from hoping that perhaps some of that lovely unencumbered happiness would drip off her graceful shoulders into my now permanently open resort bag.

I was just about to finally call out to Benton as I saw her talking to the pimply blonde photographer. Apparently she was telling him that she and the gazelle would just go ahead and skip the Welcome Aboard photo, as they sashayed past him. He clicked his camera at the group of silver-haired ladies in various colored pastel capris who had gathered themselves into a group formation in front of the fake backdrop, clucking and giggling.

I decided to skip the photo op, too, in an effort to catch up to Benton and the gazelle.

But the gazelle boarded the ship just then by reaching effortlessly into a front pocket of her embroidered burlap bag, apparently reserved just for important information required at that exact second. I, on the other hand, had to stop on the ship ramp, drop my grocery bags and begin the frustrating process of digging through my bag for my passport and boarding information. By the time I stood up victorious, with passport in hand, and overflowing bags perched precariously on my hips, I could only see that the gazelle and Benton were gone and that the pastel-clad ladies were ready to board ahead of me, their IDs ready and open.

WHILE I WAS UNPACKING in my cabin, I texted Rob to let him know that I was on board and that communication from here on out would be spotty as we had discussed. I sent a photo of my cabin, complete with a towel folded into a dog, and asked him to show the boys and tell them I missed them already.

When my cell pinged a moment later, I thought it was Rob's reply, but was surprisingly disappointed instead to see that it was Benton—telling me she had boarded but was going to take a quick "siesta" and that the plan was to all meet up in the main lounge before dinner at six.

Left with a free afternoon on my own, I changed into my swimsuit and cover-up and headed out to the deck with my stack of magazines, to relax and grab a drink while the ship was still in port.

~

"Catch you daydreaming?"

I shielded my eyes from the sun and looked up under my thick and oversized black prescription sunglasses—"rock star" sunglasses Rob used to call them. "Hey, rock star!" he'd yell out to me whenever I wore them, although in recent years, his tone had gone from charming to mocking.

The waiter was decidedly not mocking me, however, as he stood over me with a drink tray, temporarily distracting me from my thoughts of Rob and the boys as I sat by the pool. I felt as if he was trying to help me out of my daydream for good. I had made it. I was alone. The kids were with Rob. My mother knew where I was and there truly was nothing to do for the next seven days but enjoy myself. Be by myself.

Heal.

I had chosen a chaise lounge near the pool in a crowded area where I could sit by myself and not be quite so alone. The truth was, I was very unused to traveling alone. The discomfort I had felt seeking out a lounge chair was a brand new sensation. It had been so long since I went anywhere without the kids, let alone by myself.

My chosen seat was close to, but not right next to, two younger girls and I immediately regretted my choice and the self-consciousness that had led me there. My respite with my stack of magazines was intermittently interrupted by cigarette smoke and 20-year-old conversation which ranged from trite to absurd.

I had been trying to block out their voices by closing my eyes under my sunglasses, when the waiter interrupted me.

Taking a watermelon drink from his tray, I closed my eyes again, trying not to overhear the nearby conversation or accidentally inhale the smoke circles billowing my way.

"I just don't know if I can trust him. I met him when he was dating another woman. He left *her* for me after dating her for an entire year. What if Spike finds another younger, prettier version of *me* in another year?"

You can count on it, I almost said aloud.

Also almost uttered out loud: *Are you really dating a guy named Spike? Good lord.*

Spike's girlfriend took a long drag on her cigarette before asking brutally:

"How's your divorce going?"

I opened my eyes with a start, afraid she was talking to me, until I heard the companion mumble a response.

"Oh—it's all so stupid."

Shielding my eyes, I looked over at the girls. They couldn't be more than 25. How could one of them be divorcing already? It pained me strangely. I did not even know them. But then the divorcee piped up.

"My lawyer says just another six months."

"Do you hear from him?"

"Not a word. He has all he wants. Citizenship. He's moved on. I feel foolish. But I have to get over that. I knew that was his sole reason for getting married in the first place. I hoped once we got married he would fall hopelessly in love with me. I guess that was crazy."

"No, of course not."

Yes, of course it was.

Such choices people make.

I spent my whole life making what I thought were logical, rational, *right* choices, And yet here I was unemployed, with a cheating husband, and in little better straits than the boyfriend stealer and the green-card wife lounging next to me.

I ordered another watermelon juice drink right off the waiter's tray when he came back around, which I nearly spilled on myself as a couple plopped themselves down right next to me and began an amorous display that included phrases like "not if I have anything to do with it" and "our room is waiting."

Great.

Now I had to try to ignore both the 20-something-year-old girls *and* the canoodling couple. I was almost successful, until the pretty blonde woman called her partner "Rob" and I actually looked up startled, half-expecting to see Rob and Celeste making out next to me on the chaise lounge. It was not them, of course, but the couple had now made themselves irksome nonetheless in my eyes.

They weren't kids. They were 40-something-year-olds, albeit nubile and in love. And when the man named "Rob" said in the same loud whisper my boys used in occasional church visits with my mother during the quietest moments, "No one is paying attention to us, don't worry," I sighed a little too loudly. They were lovers. Probably philanderers.

I reluctantly turned my attention away from Spike's girl-friend and her companion and watched the couple over my watermelon juice and tabloid magazine. Total abandon. Total narcissism. Before I could stop myself, I imagined my Rob with Celeste and how they must have behaved the same way. Reckless. Carefree. Wasn't that really what the affair was all about? Throwing off the stifling mantle of being the children's father. Of being my husband? Tears welled up in my eyes as I watched the careless couple and thought about the people each of them was sick of. Exhausted by this Rob and his partner, and the smoke clouds, I took my leave of the pool and headed back to my cabin to dress for dinner.

BY DINNER TIME, I had collected myself and dressed in my favorite black maxi dress with a thick gold costume necklace draped around my neck and a cocktail ring on my wedding band finger. I had stopped wearing my wedding and diamond bands when I was pregnant with David. So bloated and uncomfortable, I had slipped the rings off and tucked them away in a safe, never bringing them back out again.

Strangely foreboding in hindsight, I thought briefly as I dressed.

And now the cocktail ring felt heavy and weighted on a finger that had been bare for so long.

But after I dressed, I felt more myself. Well, more of my old self. A self that had been gone since finding out about Rob's affair. No, a self that had been gone longer than that.

The self that was once happy and hopeful and didn't have to talk herself into any of that.

I headed to the main bar and lounge on the ship. A jazz trio was playing softly and I headed over, intending to grab a glass of wine and wait a bit until it was time to meet Benton. It was then that I spotted the gazelle. She was sitting on a sofa in a lounge area near the bar. She was alone but without a book or a magazine, or even a phone or other texting device to distract her from being alone. She was sipping what appeared to be bourbon or a Manhattan. She was smiling. And staring directly at me.

I smiled back, and then as if she was waiting for me, the gazelle motioned me over. I was flustered as I headed her way. I am sure I even stammered a bit as I asked, "Me? Were you talking to me?"

But quickly I realized with embarrassment that the gazelle was not talking to me at all, but rather to the tall man whose profile passed me while I was still focused in on the gazelle, a man who, in my unfocused side vision, pulled up another lounge chair to sit closer to her.

Without missing a beat, the gazelle patted the sofa next to her and looked up at me, "Well, of course you're welcome to join us too, Sweetheart." She tapped the seat again and I sat down, hypnotized by the gazelle's assurance and kindness in the middle of what should have been such an awkward moment. "I'm sorry," I apologized. "Obviously, I'm not used to traveling alone. First time in a while actually. I've forgotten all proper protocol. I did, however, bring the requisite reading material, so I'll be just fine." I held up and tapped my unopened book first, then held out my hand. "I'm Kate, by the way."

"I'm Brie. Spelled like the Cheese." The gazelle smiled.

Of course you are. Likely the love child of a celebrity socialite and a Vogue model. A fitting custom-made name for such a creature.

"I'm waiting for some more friends—oh, here is Benton now." The gazelle waved to my Benton and as she did I turned to look at the gentleman who had breezed past me in my embarrassed distraction, and who was now seated next to the gazelle. He was smiling, smirking really. Waiting for me to turn and notice him. I nodded as the gazelle began to introduce us, "And this is my friend—"

"Ian."

It came from me. I had wondered if he'd be here, of course. I had never asked Benton in all those email exchanges; but yet, I had wondered.

And so when he stood up out of his seat to step over to me, I was already standing, waiting for him to put his arms around me, as if not one moment had passed since the last time we had stood like this, nearly fifteen years ago.

Now Brie jumped up to hug me. "Oh how lovely! You are the famous Kate I hear so much about. Benton told us you might be joining and how thick I am not to recognize you from your pictures. You are even more beautiful in person."

"I am so looking forward to this week," Benton exclaimed as she joined the group and hugged me like no time had passed at all before hugging the others. As I sat back down, Ian said, "I'm looking forward to catching up, Kate. You look gorgeous as ever." And then he hugged Benton hello and took up a seat on the couch next to me. Right next to me. Almost as close as Benton had seated herself that day in Bryant Park. We shared a knowing smile. I wondered if he was doing it on purpose. I wondered if he was recalling that old story, too.

What do you remember, Ian? After all this time, how do you remember us?

"So Kate," Benton reached over and patted my hand, "I am so thrilled at your spontaneity. I felt certain that life would get in the way and you'd never be able to join us on our little heart-break cruise."

"Yep. Life got in the way all right," I murmured. I recovered quickly. "But, this came at exactly the right time for me. So glad you invited me. Well, via Facebook, you know." I was beginning to feel pink all over as Benton, Brie, and Ian seemed to all be laughing a bit at me. It felt awkward to be admitting to Ian that I was meeting him again while heartbroken. As if I was meeting him again at a desperate hour.

And as if it might seem strange to him that anyone other than him could break my heart.

But Brie chimed in, dissolving the awkwardness. "Well, I just think it was so convenient that Benton and I were suffering dramatic breakups at exactly the right time so we could convince everyone to come and cheer us up." She patted Ian's arm and she smiled as he waved down a waitress.

Suddenly I felt like a third wheel.

But of course. Brie and Ian. How convenient. Brie recruits a handsome man to get over her heartbreak and I am left with Benton and a ballgown to help me get over Rob's adultery.

I turned to order an overdue glass of wine, but heard Ian ordering for me. "Do you have a nice sauvignon blanc by the glass for my friend? New Zealand, preferably?" I shivered a bit and smiled at him.

"Still?" Ian asked me after ordering.

"Yes. Still," I replied. Although it wasn't exactly clear he was asking about the wine, nor that I was responding about it, either.

Waiting for my wine, I was a bit distracted by my thoughts about Ian, when I realized that Brie was talking, and apparently, talking to me. I turned to her and said, "I'm sorry—you were saying?"

"Just that my ex, Gia, and Ian and I all met many years ago while rooming together in grad school. But I have heard that you and Ian go back nearly as far as he and I do." She winked now. But it seemed to be directed at Ian. Not me. Or maybe me. Who knows? I felt quite confused then and wasn't sure at all if Brie was laughing at me.

Or, given the interesting disclosure about a certain Miss Gia, hitting on me.

"Now," Benton said, as she tapped Ian on the knee. "Doesn't he look wonderful, Kate. How about our Ian?"

SITTING IN THE CRUISE SHIP lounge before dinner, I was aware peripherally that our group made small talk, and sipped, and laughed. But I was transported back to those days with Ian before he left for Botswana. I found myself looking at his bare ring finger before pulling myself out of a daydream to join a conversation between Benton and Brie.

Ian must have caught my gaze, because he moved his hand (uncomfortably?) as I watched and then reached his hand over to my knee to get my attention while I vaguely engaged in conversation with Benton and Brie about the merits of taking excursions in the Bahamas versus sitting quietly and decadently on the beach.

"Kate, it really is wonderful to see you again. You look—the same." He was mirroring my thoughts. And also looking at me that way again. I had forgotten what it felt like. To have someone search your face so genuinely, and love what he saw there.

"You too, Ian. You've come a long way from your days at Time Travel, Inc., I take it?"

Ian nodded. "Yes. What about you? You married that Rob, right?"

"Yes." I thought about not adding any more. But I couldn't help myself. "Well, my marriage is in a bit of upheaval right now. That's why I'm here. Heartbreak cruise—right?"

I smiled wryly up at Ian. I felt a little dishonest leaving out the part that until I had seen Ian a moment ago I had been certain I would be returning to my adulterous husband and working on forgiving his philandering ways. But not so dishonest, because like I said, I had felt that way up *until* I saw Ian. Until I saw Ian looking at me in that familiar searching way, all over again.

I wondered what had brought Ian on this cruise, and I wondered selfishly if I really wanted to know about *his* heart-break. Then I blurted it out.

"You never came back, Ian. After Botswana. You never—"

Strange to be there already. But there it was. We had cut through all the niceties in five minutes flat.

Our conversation was interrupted, however, because just then, a new companion joined us, taking up the chair Ian had originally occupied before he had moved closer to me. An elegant and beautiful woman who looked a lot like the gazelle, except—

"Mother!" Brie leaned over and folded the woman in a hug and I thought, *but of course.*

Brie introduced her mother to me. "This is Max, my mother. I invited Max to help us nurse all our wounds. She knows a thing or two about healing broken hearts, having healed every last one for me since I was 13 years old."

"Ah yes, well, you can't get to my age without learning a thing or two about love and loss. But believe me. Life goes on, my beautiful souls." Max said it casually, looking behind her for the waitress and waving her down for a drink, before turning to me and locking eyes with me warmly.

I felt her gaze settle over me. As I looked at Max, beautiful and without a single visible scar, I couldn't help but wonder what sort of loss Max had endured. Had it been a cheating husband and a failed marriage? I suddenly felt a strange connection to this woman I had just met a moment ago, and I was anxious to talk more to Max.

But only after I got a chance to catch up a bit more with Ian.

～

Our group huddled noisily around a long table in the ship's dining room that found Ian and I separated. I took up a seat across from Benton at one end, and Ian sat at the other end with Max alongside two empty seats we were apparently saving for two more traveling companions. I heard Benton ask our waiter to save the seats but not to wait for them before serving our entrees. But before I could ask who was joining us, Brie took up the seat next to me and interrupted my thoughts.

"So Kate, it's such a treat to finally meet you. Benton has always talked so fondly of you and Rob. Ugh. I'm sorry—"

I must have looked a little sad at the mention of Rob's name, because Brie turned immediately sorry that she had said his name out loud and she didn't look like someone who was comfortable being sorry.

I patted her hand the way I would one of my boys to comfort them. "It's ok. I'm fine. This cruise is already doing wonders for my damaged soul." I turned to glance down at the other end of the table, and then quickly turned my attention back to Brie.

"Tell me about you. What brought you on this cruise, Brie?"

I sipped my wine and settled into a tale about Brie and Gia, and love gone awry, happy for the distraction of comforting someone other than myself for a change.

When the waiter came around offering entrees, he stopped silently at me. I looked up startled. I had been so engrossed in conversation with Brie who had just now said, "You know, I loved her. But it's over. I accept that and I'm willing to move on. Instead of grieving the loss, I'm really trying to figure out what I learned from our time together. My mother always told me that every time I broke up with someone—from the time I was 13—I had to ask myself 'what have I learned?'"

I glanced over at Max who was smiling back at Brie having

heard part of her conversation and it was then that I noticed that the waiter was still standing next to me for my order. I had not heard his litany of offered choices, so I was a little embarrassed as I asked, "I'm sorry. I didn't hear the choices. Could you please repeat them?"

The waiter smiled kindly. "Sea scallops wrapped in bacon, fillet, or we have a vegetarian option."

"Um, sea scallops, please." I turned to resume my conversation with Brie, but Benton interrupted.

"Oh dear, now I feel like I should change my order."

"Why?" Brie asked her.

"I don't know. It's like a little game I've played over the years. What would Kate do? I like to emulate Kate in lots of things."

Benton turned to Max on her side. "I've always admired Kate so much. Since the day I met her, she's always been captivating. Always so sure of herself. Always making the right choices."

I blushed under Benton's praise. I remembered that she had always been so heavy-handed with her compliments, and yet always made me feel somehow that she meant them. I had loved her thick admiration during our friendship, and it was always mutual.

But tonight, it was a heavy burden. I wanted to say of course, that despite having always believed I had made all the right choices, I now found myself desperately unhappy. That I was constantly talking myself into a happiness I might never know. Sitting across from Benton and seated next to the light and breezy gazelle named Brie, who seemed so sure of herself, and adamant that her recent breakup should be some sort of cosmic learning experience rather than a soul-crushing experience, I was feeling very unhappy about a great many choices I had made. I also wondered if my days of "faking" it had expanded way back to my days of being friends with Benton, an uncomfortable realization as I had always thought those were some of my most authentic years—the years I had been trying to reclaim for so long.

"Benton, you are so sweet as usual. But really, it's been a long and winding road for me. Tell me, how is the organic fashion business?"

"Oh, fine, fine. But please, I want you to tell us all about your professorial career. Is it wonderful? What classes are you teaching this semester?"

"Well. Actually this is my first semester off," I confessed quietly, realizing I had conveniently left that information out of my numerous superficial email conversations with Benton leading up to the cruise.

"A sabbatical?" Brie looked interested. "Are you writing? Oh! Are you writing about us?" Brie looked delighted at that possibility.

"No," I laughed at Brie's earnestness.

Benton chimed in again. "No, silly. Kate's not a sociology professor. She teaches history. She's brilliant. Gorgeous and brilliant. A killer combination." Benton nodded at me and held her wine glass out in a fake toast.

"I'll never forget the day I met her. Well, *we* met her. Ian and I met her at a restaurant where she was working at the time, and we had a vicious argument about whether she was a starving actress or a closet intellectual. I won." She glanced down the table at Ian, who was listening and nodding a little concession to Benton. I blushed, then stammered a response to Benton and Brie's questioning.

"Well, it's not really a sabbatical. I've resigned from my teaching post, actually." The silence from Benton and Brie was deafening.

"Well, darling, why ever would you do such a thing?" The question came from Benton and it was pointed.

I looked down the table at Ian, unsure how much of this conversation he could make out. He was in conversation now with Max, so I continued on a bit self-consciously. "Well, it just wasn't very fulfilling. And now that I have young kids—it's just a struggle, that's all. I had to make some tough choices this year. One of them was to resign from my teaching post."

Benton eyed me curiously, and I noticed that she did not change her dinner order.

Then something caught her eye over my shoulder and all talk about my time-off-that-was-not-a-sabbatical ceased as Benton said, "Well, look. Here's Rob and his new girlfriend."

I'M CERTAIN THAT THE CLANGING and breaking of my wine glass was very loud.

Very loud indeed.

I could not hear a thing over the buzzing in my ears, but I could see everyone in the dining room looking in my direction to assess the damage, as I looked down and saw the shards of glass all over my bread plate, my hand remained poised in the air where it had just been holding an unbroken wine goblet seconds before.

I looked up at Benton, who was mouthing a word that looked like "sorry." I couldn't tell if the words were audible or not. I couldn't hear a thing, actually, over the buzzing noise.

While I was still staring incredulously at the shards of glass, two people took the reserved seats across from Ian and Max. I saw Ian look at me with a concerned expression as the waiter swooped in to clean up the glass and spilled wine at my place. He handed me a dark cocktail napkin and I used it to dab at the spilled wine in my lap as I saw the canoodling couple that had annoyed me earlier in the day take their seats next to each other. The woman and the man she had called "Rob."

It was Benton's brother, Rob.

As if in slow motion, as I recognized him, and recognized my error, the buzzing noise started to subside and now I could hear that Benton was actually apologizing out loud for startling me. "Sorry, Kate. Oh my goodness. Didn't you know my brother and his girlfriend were joining us on our little heartbreak cruise?"

She rolled her eyes laboriously at me and stage whispered now. "Of course, they don't really seem like they need any healing. They're the happiest couple I know. Both left their spouses last year for each other and you'd think they didn't have a care in the world now."

I remembered Rob—this Rob—only vaguely from our New York City days. Benton had always kept me far away from him, declaring me much too good for her older brother. When Ted and I had broken up, I had asked Benton half-jokingly if she was ever going to introduce me properly to her brother. She had looked so concerned and had announced on the spot that she would find me a much more suitable new boyfriend.

Apparently, my Rob was the one she eventually deemed "much more suitable."

The arrival of Benton's brother and girlfriend injected a new energy into the group's loud dinner discussion and seemed to soothe over my embarrassing gaffe. I settled back into a warm conversation with Brie, who really was so easy to talk to and finished another glass of wine with my sea scallops.

After dinner, my clutch purse vibrated on the table in front of me. Apparently, we still had cell service since we were in port, and gradually I realized that my phone was ringing inside my purse. I pondered for a moment whether I should answer it, wondering whether it was Rob and whether any exchanges with him would be awkward in that moment. But, thinking maybe my boys wanted one more goodbye, I put aside my qualms about talking to Rob at this dinner table, and reached inside for my phone.

A number I didn't recognize was flashing on the screen so I held the phone for a moment waiting for the vibrating to stop and for a voicemail message to flash on the screen.

I happened to glance down at the other end of the table to see Ian tapping on his phone. I looked at him questioningly. My phone buzzed again a few seconds later. This time with a text.

"You still have the same number."

I looked up at Ian and blushed, smiling.

Just before he put his phone back in his pocket, I tapped a reply text on my phone.

"Still."

Shortly after his text, I was grateful when Ian got up from the table, came over to me and leaned in. "I'm heading to get some air on an upper deck. You in?"

I nodded, and excused myself from Brie and the table. Benton gave me a smile, but her eyes looked a little strange as I left with Ian. I wasn't sure if I was imagining it or not, but I thought I saw disappointment.

Ian and I headed comfortably to one of the ship's upper decks. The ship was departing from the port and everyone, including the rest of our group apparently, was gathered to watch on the uppermost deck. So the one we had chosen was quiet and peaceful.

"This is like heaven." Ian sipped his drink and looked out toward the lights on shore. The view was marvelous. But still, I had a hard time losing myself as easily as Ian had obviously done. He must have noticed something on my face and misinterpreted it.

"That's right," he said. "I remember you were struggling with religion in the old days. Used to hate all references to an afterlife or divine intervention."

I rolled my eyes. "Was that me? Yes, well that was a long time ago. I'm done with the angst—the complete devotion to philosophical agnosticism."

"So now you believe in God? Divine intervention even?"

I couldn't be sure it was even a serious question. The dark eyes, the glass poised just right, one, and only one, eyebrow turned upward. He was looking at me with something that could be "I'm interested in you" or just as easily "I'm making fun of you." And I was struck by conflicting and equally powerful feelings of wanting him to still like me and realizing how much more complicated everything could be if he did.

Rob was like this when we first met. The thought danced through my subconscious, as I remembered that day on the SOHO rooftop with pain. In the beginning, Rob was confusing, ambiguous, and thought-provoking. He had waited over a month to call me back after we first met, and had assumed I would be right where he left me. That we would reconnect and fall deliriously in love. And we had.

Yet, I hadn't been right where he had left me.

Because in the meantime, I had had this all-consuming love affair with the man sitting next to me on a cruise ship headed for the Bahamas.

Seemingly wondering if I was also right where he had left me.

"Ian, you never came back. You never even tried to find me."

Ian turned away from me and back to the view.

"That's not true. I came back. And I saw you."

"Where?"

"In a coffee shop in the city. I walked in and there you were. I had been back in town less than 48 hours. And for a moment, I thought, "See. I knew we'd find each other again."

"I don't remember running into you in any coffee shop."

"No. You didn't see me. You were with Rob. You reached across the table and you took his hands. And I saw in an instant that you had moved forward. And that I would have to do the same. I really wanted to turn the hands of time back in that moment. I really did. It was excruciating. But I turned around and walked out."

Ian winced, like the memory itself still stung, all these years later.

I remembered suddenly that day, helping Rob get ready for his law firm interview. Warming my hands in his from the cold chill of the constantly opening door in the coffee shop.

What would have happened if I had looked up and seen Ian that day?

What would I have done?

Ian turned to face me now. "So what do you think, Professor? Do you believe in Divine Intervention or not?"

We'll find each other again.

That's what Ian had told me that dizzy day outside the Bryant Park carousel. And I hadn't believed him. Well, I hadn't let myself believe him, at any rate.

I thought about letting Ian's Divine Intervention question go unanswered. Sipping my wine, nodding and laughing, perhaps. But while I now believed in God, I did not believe in rhetorical questions.

"Well, of course, I believe in God now. Otherwise, what on earth is the point?"

Ian was laughing.

"That's funny. You're clever. What on earth? Very theological of you. I had no idea."

And then I was incensed. He *was* making fun of me.

"Do you have children?" I asked him boldly.

He shook his head.

"Well, I do. I have two little boys. They are six and four. And I have realized that there is really no point to going through all the pains and tribulations of raising children if not for a higher power."

Ian didn't look amused. I searched his face, trying to discern his emotion. What was that? It was unfamiliar. Was it sad? Was it bored?

I was annoyed at him in that instant as I imagined Ian finding me boring. My worst nightmare was coming true: Ian was realizing that I was not nearly as fascinating as he had once found me to be.

Annoyance quickly became anger—anger that Ian thought I was making some cosmic and utterly predictable argument that children give you immortality, divinity somehow.

He thinks I have tired ideas stemming from years of bearing children and caring for them at all hours of the night. He believes that the fatigue of never sleeping through the night and incessant worrying about children who are sick, who are bullied at school, who are just unhappy for unidentifiable reasons, have twisted my mind and made me a cliché. A housewife. An unhappy housewife.

He is thinking that this is why my marriage has failed. That my husband has clearly grown tired of me. Because I am unoriginal. Uninteresting. Not at all as he may have remembered me.

Not as I used to be.

Not as he left me.

I was emboldened by these thoughts. Inspired and angry at Ian's unspoken words ringing in my ears, I decided to set the record straight. I was adamant that Ian would not condescend to me wordlessly after all these years.

"I mean that's the whole point. I have evolved. I no longer do the things I do so that some other person, some mere human, will think better of me."

"Very noble," Ian interrupted.

"No, no. You're missing my point. It's not noble at all. It's practical.

"Children are hope. They are like reincarnations of ourselves. The chance to get it right once and for all and if there is no divine being judging at the end whether you in fact 'got it right' well, then what the hell is the point?

"Ugh. That sounds terrible." I sat back in my chair, annoyed that I could not get the words out in the order I wanted to.

I was frustrated by Ian's voice in my head, saying the things

I feared most about myself. That I had gotten this all wrong. That the decisions I had made had been the wrong ones. I continued to defend myself.

"But you know what. I *am* doing this to win. It's like a cosmic board game and I did not make it up in my head, believe me. The goal is to raise the best, most well-adjusted, happiest kids on the planet. It's a game and I *am* trying to win. And I am certain, as I lie in bed at night rehashing the day's successes and victories, that there must be a prize. Judgment day, or whatever you want to call it. At the end of my life, I want someone to say I did it right. I did good. And since it's not likely to be the kids or Rob, well, lately, I'm counting on God."

I leaned back in my seat. "Oh for heaven's sake. Listen to me. No wonder Lex thinks we're all paralyzed by motherhood. I sound completely deranged."

Ian didn't correct my assessment of my sanity. Instead, he asked, "Who is Lex?"

"One of my dearest friends. She's brilliant and a new mother. She's writing a book on—oh, it's a long story. The bottom line is that she believes that I—that we—have become frail with motherhood. I didn't really believe her when she first told me her theory, but now that I'm listening to myself out loud, I'm starting to wonder."

"You never struck me as frail, Kate. And you certainly don't seem to have changed in that regard now." Ian's voice was calming and reassured me that I wasn't deranged even though he hadn't exactly argued with me about that minor point.

"No. I don't feel frail. I feel like—"

I stopped in mid-sentence, thinking about Pam and her courage and bravery. "I feel like I am not the bravest person I know, but certainly not the frailest either."

"Who is braver than you? Who were you thinking about just now?"

In an instant, I felt grateful to Ian, and grateful that the connection we once shared had resumed so easily. That he was asking questions. The right questions. And that he was listening to the answers.

"My friend, Pam."

I told him about Pam, from the evening she asked me to accompany her for the tests, through her decision about her surgery.

Ian looked at me warmly. "Kate. You are just as I remember. The kind of person someone would want by their side when they are facing down a decision of that magnitude. Not frail at all.

"You don't sound like you have been paralyzed by motherhood at all, Kate. You sound like you have been empowered by it. You radiate hope. I love—"

I looked at him quickly and drew in my breath.

He paused and finished, "I love your optimistic view of motherhood, Kate. I would expect nothing less from that girl I used to know."

I nodded, realizing that what I had been defending against were not Ian's wordless accusations at all. I was still the same in Ian's eyes. It was my own view of myself that needed tweaking.

"Yes, I am hopeful about motherhood. They are like little reincarnations of ourselves. That's what kids are, but they come with a real chance to get it right. I love that about them."

I nodded, finally satisfied that it had come out right, even if only with Ian's help and intervention.

I looked over at Ian. He didn't look bored or cynical.

He nodded, reached over, and clinked his glass on mine.

"So, Professor, 'little reincarnations' is it? You're a Buddhist, now?"

I laughed and stopped being mad at him.

As I leaned back into my seat, Ian didn't seem to want to let it go.

"Seriously, Buddhism or Christianity, do you think?"

Ian's either/or question transported me to Michael's Question Game, the one I had always assumed Ian would hate.

"Oh, no either/ors, please. I have enough of that at home."

I explained the game to Ian, complete with the hiatus imposed as a punishment for me, and how Michael continued to play it every so often in the car, and how I never knew exactly when or where I would be tested, but I was always prepared.

I worried that Ian might think it silly, not having kids of his own, but instead he laughed. "That is so endearing. Your boys sound exactly like the children I would expect you to be raising. Interesting. Curious. Challenging."

"Oh, Ian."

Ian had always seen me as I had hoped to be seen. And now, without ever having met them, he had assessed my children exactly as I would have them be seen as well.

"Yes, that's a wonderful description of them. You hit the nail right on the head."

I closed my eyes for a moment and saw my boys in my mind's eye.

Ian interrupted my thoughts.

"I don't think you should be embarrassed about leaving your teaching position to be home with your boys, Kate."

Ah, so he *had* heard my conversation with Benton and Brie.

"Do you think I'm embarrassed?"

"I think you haven't really made up your mind how you feel about things. About the new direction your life seems to be taking. I remember how certain you always were about being in charge of your own destiny."

"Yes, indeed."

"Sometimes, you have to let go a little. We're not in charge of everything. Haven't you learned that over the years? I know I have." Ian sipped his drink and stared ahead.

In the background, I heard cheers from the passengers on the uppermost deck as we left port and set sail. I also heard soft music coming from the ship's speakers. Adele was singing "Someone Like You."

I felt a pang in my heart and I felt my eyes burning as they tried to hold back tears. Sitting here with Ian, my emotions were getting the best of me. I decided to go back to my cabin and pull myself together for a better showing next time.

"I'd better go. I'd better call it a night," I said as I stood up and reached for my evening bag and shoes that I had kicked off next to the chaise lounge. Ian nodded but didn't get up to stand. He remained seated in his chair, and out of the corner of my eye, as I reached down for my shoes, I caught Ian wiping his eyes casually. I was jolted for a moment wondering what could be making Ian so sad. Was the song in the background churning up some painful emotions for him as well?

Was his sadness connected to memories of me at all? Of those days in New York City. Of leaving? Of finding me in a coffee shop holding hands with Rob upon his return? Or was his sadness not connected to me at all, but instead to some heartbreak, possibly many heartbreaks, that had intervened for Ian since the last time we left each other on that Manhattan street corner.

I was still distracted by Ian as I nearly bumped smack into Max who was also getting up out of a chaise lounge. I looked from Max to Ian and noted how close Max had been sitting to us. I hadn't seen her there and I wondered if she had overheard my conversation with Ian.

"Hello, Kate, dear. Are you calling it a night?"

"Yes, I'm tired. I want to try to get a good night's sleep and start this trip refreshed tomorrow."

"I hope we will get a chance to talk properly. I've heard so much about you from Benton, and you seem just as mesmerizing as she described."

"Thank you, Max. That is so sweet. I look forward to talking with you, too. I had the most lovely time at dinner chatting with Brie. She's wonderful. You are obviously an amazing mother."

Max nodded a thanks and I headed back to my cabin, thinking again about Ian's casual tears that I had witnessed moments before on the deck, and about Ian's presence here on Benton's so-called "heartbreak cruise."

And of course, I was embarrassed to admit to myself as I headed to my cabin alone, that the idea of Ian heartbroken was painful for many reasons, including the fact that I was probably *not* the cause.

THE NEXT DAY, Max was sitting at the bar when I arrived for a late afternoon drink after a relaxing morning by the pool followed by an hour in the computer lab on the ship.

The ship had docked in Florida, but I had stayed on board, while the other passengers headed en masse to tourist attractions like Port Canaveral and even Disney World. I had taken advantage of a quiet ship to read and collect my thoughts about seeing Ian again.

I found myself in the ship boutique looking for "Soup and Ears" for the boys. After walking around aimlessly, a luxury really, I picked out two matching crystal globes with small replicas of the ship we were on under a cascading snow of glitter and confetti that swam every time the globes moved even a little bit. I had the cashier wrap each globe in bubble wrap, knowing that the bubbles would be just as much fun for the boys to play with as the crystal "snow" globes.

After the ship boutique, I sent Rob an email for the boys and a few pictures of the ship. Service on the ship was spotty but the email seemed to have gone through, and as I found Max, I was feeling happy and peaceful, knowing the boys would enjoy the pictures and the email letter I had sent.

I purposefully sat next to Max knowing I wanted to talk to her but not knowing what I would say. I didn't have to ponder that for long because she obviously wanted to talk, too. She was either better at coming up with conversation starters or she had been thinking about this for a while as well.

"Come here darling—you look as though you want to talk."

I smiled and melted. I was thinking that I could love this woman. I was instantly drawn to Brie's charm and ease, but with this woman, the connection was even stronger. *Well*, I thought to myself, *Max is where it all started. This is the woman who raised Brie, who influenced who she is now. Despite her claim of love and loss, there is nothing broken about this woman. I am studying her like a student. How can I be like you? How can I raise my boys to be ok even if Rob and I are broken in half?*

Max was so warm and cozy like a fireplace. I didn't even wait for my drink to come. Didn't even wait for the warm buzz of alcohol to wash over me before brazenly asking, "So are you here solely to offer comfort to the broken-hearted passengers or are you nursing your own heartache as well?"

Max didn't seem at all surprised at my forwardness. She acted like we were old friends as she said matter-of-factly, "Well. I've had my share of heartache, but I am all healed now. Now. It has taken me a while to get there. You'll get there, too."

I gasped in surprise. She knew about me. About me and Rob. I was embarrassed, but, still, I was glad she knew. Glad I didn't have to say the words. I asked, "How do you know?"

"Because I've been there. Believe me."

My coziness was fading a bit and I was a little uncomfortable but I ventured in anyway.

"Do you know what happened to me?" I paused before adding, "What my husband did to me?"

She laughed, like I was a child, but still the coziness remained. "I don't know the *details*, Sweetie, but I'm just guessing from your eyes and the fact that you're here alone, that you're running away from something bad."

I laughed in return. Of course she didn't know. No one knew. I hardly ever said it out loud. So I said it out loud to Max. "My husband had an affair with his colleague. We have two little boys." I wasn't sure why I put those two sentences together. But

I linked them anyway. Like I was trying to explain why his affair was *really* bad, and not just bad.

"Um-hmm." Max studied me and then asked, "Is it over? The affair, I mean?"

"Apparently so. He would like to move past it and have me forget the whole thing. Start over. I'm not so sure. But I needed to get away and think about it. Thus, I'm here." I smiled wryly while sipping my white wine.

"Well, I can tell you this. It's easier than you think right now."

"What is?"

"Moving past it. Staying. Hard is starting over with little kids and no husband. Moving past it and staying, if he's serious about the staying part, is definitely easier."

"But he slept with another woman. Had sex with her for an entire year." I was instantly shocked by my frankness and coarseness. But I was concerned that I had glossed over this detail. That I had danced around it in some way.

But no, she smiled sympathetically.

"Sweetie, all of our husbands have had sex with other women. I mean, unless you meet them and marry them at 17, in which case you'd have bigger issues than these!" I laughed at her perspective, and was surprised I had never thought about it that way before. I thought back to Rob's girlfriend, Lisa, the one he had recently broken up with before that fateful Cinco de Mayo party. I had never met her, and while her legacy used to plague me a bit when we first started dating, I hadn't thought about her in years. She was just a woman my husband used to have sex with. A long time ago. For a moment, sitting there with Max, I wondered why I had put Celeste on a different plane than Lisa. I pictured the boys. And I wondered, *does their existence really make all of this so different?*

Because it was not just the sex with another woman that

was standing in my way.

It was the look on my mother's face at my father's funeral. The rawness of her grief. That was the image that haunted me. Sitting with Max, I tried to picture Rob's funeral. I closed my eyes. I pictured my black dress. I saw myself standing in the same funeral home in which we laid out my father. I tried to picture friends and relatives holding my hands as they greeted me, as they walked by a coffin. I could picture Rob's mother there, strangely enough. I could even conjure up her grief-stricken face. But I could not imagine anything that felt like heartbreak for myself. I could not relate to a widow's raw emotion and, if truth be told, that emptiness inside me when I tried, hurt more than the fact of Rob cheating.

This was the true heartbreak I was suffering from. This place we had arrived in—Rob and I. Where having sex outside of our marriage was not the problem in our marriage. Where the real problem was that we didn't seem to give a damn about each other anymore.

❦

"Did you ever forgive your husband?"

"For what?" Max looked somewhat confused.

I realized I had drawn a line between some points that might just be incorrect.

"I'm sorry. You just seemed so empathetic about my situation. Like you had been there. Here. Right where I am." I was stumbling through my words—perhaps the sea air and wine combination was making me incoherent. "I just thought that your husband had, you know, also cheated."

Max got the strangest expression on her face. It was as if she was sad for a moment. And I could tell just from my short time knowing her that she was a woman who was very rarely sad.

"Actually, my marriage did suffer because of an affair. But the affair was mine."

My heart sank. I felt certain that Max saw the expression on my face and I tried hard to recover. Until two seconds ago, she had been my moral hero. But now, she was completely different in my eyes. *She* had cheated. *She* had done to someone what Rob had done to me. So really, she couldn't understand how I felt at all. I felt duped, having confided in her, having wrapped myself up in her warm emotional embrace. No wonder she was fine with her failed marriage. It was all her fault.

It must have been a feeling I was getting used to by then—heartbreak—that caused me to blurt out, "How? How could you do that?"

Even I was surprised by how accusatory my tone was. Especially given my complete adoration of this woman a few short moments ago.

And Max smiled at me in a way I can only describe as *kindly.* From someone else, it might even have been described as patronizing, but not from Max. In that moment, I considered forgiving her. I *wanted* to forgive her. And I had a thought that surprised me. A thought flitted through my mind before I could even stop it.

Perhaps Pam was right. Perhaps cheating is not an automatic deal-breaker for a marriage.

I wanted to hear the details from Max. I wanted to understand. I asked her again, but this time more gently. "Tell me. Please. I need to understand. How could you do it?"

And so she told me.

❦

"Allen and I were neighbors and schoolmates. We met when we were six years old, and traveled through the elementary years together. When I was 11 years old, I decided I loved him."

"At 11?"

"Yes, at 11. And he told me he loved me, too. Right before he kissed me on the schoolyard and ran away. My first kiss. My first love."

Max looked a little swoony remembering her schoolyard crush. And I envied her. Envied such a warm memory at a time when all my memories seemed like they were betraying me. But then I remembered. *Max is the villain in this story. How can that be?*

"You think those schoolyard moments at that age are innocent, without consequence?"

I think my expression gave away my answer.

"I'll tell you something. They are not. Those people you grow up with—you grow together, you dream together. You imprint yourselves on each other. You dream about who will grow up to be successful businessmen and women. You imagine who will stay and who will move far away. Who will be the teachers. Who will be the politicians. Who will have large families and who will have no families at all. You do all of this, and you place yourself in the dreams, in various scenarios, and it is a time that tattoos you. That brands you in a certain way."

I didn't need a mirror to know how skeptically I was looking at Max as she spoke. My inner thoughts betrayed me, I was sure of it.

How could I have imagined this woman to be wise and enlightened? These are the ramblings of a madwoman. How could she be talking about love as an 11-year-old child? Who was Allen? Her husband? Her lover?

Either way, this was a ridiculous tale, and I was beginning to be sorry I had asked to hear it.

But Max continued on, either ignoring or missing my obvious skepticism.

"Allen's family moved away when we were 15. I went to his

house to say goodbye. I took him a love letter. I was broken-hearted. If I close my eyes, I can still remember that feeling like it was yesterday. The pain I felt as he kissed me goodbye one last time. Like a burning pain in my chest." Max did not close her eyes, but her hand went up to her chest and she looked actually pained.

"I was sobbing that afternoon on Allen's porch after he kissed me goodbye. After I handed him the letter. But not Allen. He was dry-eyed, and stoic. He said 'See you around.' See you around. Then he turned and went back into the house. Letter in hand, unread. Like he didn't even care. Like he didn't even love me."

I interrupted. I had to interrupt.

"But he was 15 then, right?"

Max laughed wryly. "Yes, he was 15. And I was 15. And he was my first love."

"Yes, you mentioned that."

I had already figured out who Allen was in this scenario. The way Max talked about him, he could not possibly be the husband. He was the lover. I was sure of it.

"So let me guess. You never forgot him, and later you looked him up and started an affair with your first love."

If Max heard the exasperation in my voice, she ignored it. "No. Actually, I forgot him completely. After he went back inside and said, 'See you around,' I wiped my tears, left his porch, and went on with my life. I made a choice to never waste another thought on him again.

"Because, as I mentioned, I was 15." Max winked.

It was my turn to laugh. I did not know whether to be mad at Max or not for this aggravating emotional roller coaster.

"I met my husband in my 20s. We were in graduate school together, and I fell madly, passionately in love with him, and meant every word of 'until death do us part.' He was brilliant and wise and interesting. I honestly could not imagine life without him. When we had Brie, I felt as though my life, my destiny, had been completely fulfilled. She was the most magical little being, extraordinary. I couldn't believe my luck, my good fortune. In those early years of my marriage, I went to sleep every night thanking the cosmos for my life, for my daughter, for my husband, for my love.

"And then about 20 years into the marriage, I woke up one morning and realized it had been a long time since I had talked to the cosmos. I still felt that Brie was magical and extraordinary. I still felt that way about my husband. I was wildly grateful. Passionately in love. But no one seemed to feel the same about me. No one. My husband had become so engrossed in his work, he seemed to have forgotten he even lived with another live person.

"And by then, Brie was an independent teenager who found my love quite boring, quite stifling even. I had raised her to be an independent creature, and she had taken my lessons to heart. I could not blame her. I could not blame anyone, of course, for what came next. But I was exactly ready for a new chapter in my life, as it turned out."

"You looked up Allen? You found him?"

"No darling. I wasn't looking for him. I wasn't looking for anyone. But he found me.

"Allen arrived at my house one day out of the blue. His wife had died recently. Tragically. His children were grown and he was traveling through town—our childhood home where I still lived—where I had never left. He was looking to reconnect with an old friend, for some laughs and drinks and comfort. He had found my address in the phone book and came to see me. And do you know what I did *not* think when I saw him on my porch that afternoon?

"I did not think 'why me?' Why did he look me up—of all

people—a woman he hadn't seen in over 30 years? Not once did I think that. Because I knew why. Because we were connected. Then and still. And even though he hadn't consciously been in my mind all those years that I had been thanking the cosmos, thanking fate for all it had brought me, he was part of my gratitude prayer, too. He was in my soul. Branded, imprinted there. And so you see, despite all my conscious choices about who and when I would love for the rest of my life, there he was."

"So you had an affair."

"Well, I'm not sure what you mean by that, my dear. I'm sure you have certain ideas about what that means given your experience with your husband. And I'm not going to argue with you about semantics. But I'll just say this. What Allen and I experienced wasn't seedy or tawdry in anyway. We loved each other. Truly loved each other. And in an alternative universe, we would have been together. I still believe that. Even all these years later."

Past tense.

"So it ended. You and Allen."

"Of course it ended. After six months, I had to accept that we were not in the alternate universe we wished we were in. We were in this one. And it was time for Allen to go out and find real happiness. A woman to replace what his wife had been. A life partner. Not what I had been. A soul partner.

"I let him go and I went back to my husband. To my marriage. To my life. It was heartbreaking. And yet, in a way, the heartbreak enabled me to be a better mother to Brie. A better wife to my husband. I was more empathetic. More compassionate. Nothing truly bad had ever happened to me before I let go of Allen. The loss changed me, but in most ways, for the better."

"Did your husband ever find out? Did you tell him?"

"No. My husband went to his grave not knowing about Allen.

I decided that I would live with the secret as a sacrifice. It lived in my soul like a grain of sand, rubbing at me and paining me more than a little, I will confess. But I knew there was no need to burden my husband with my secret. In fact, there was no need to burden anyone with my secret. I never told a soul about the love affair with Allen. It was the most painful and absolutely correct decision I ever made. I am sure of it."

I thought it interesting how she qualified "affair" with "love."

"Until now. You, my dear, are the first person I have ever confessed it to." Max clinked her glass on mine and watched me for a reaction as she drank the rest of her martini.

"Oh." In a way I was more stunned by that fact than the confession that had just been made about Max's affair with Allen.

"When did your husband die?"

"Ten years ago. Heart attack." Max sighed. "I miss him."

For a moment, Max's face transformed and she looked like a grieving widow.

I couldn't resist.

"Did you ever look Allen up again? Before or, you know, after your husband died?"

"No. Eventually I heard from mutual childhood friends what had happened to him."

"And?"

"He remarried. He is, even now, living happily with his bride in the Midwest somewhere." Another sigh. "I miss him, too."

Again, Max's face flashed with pain. And again, she resembled a grieving, stricken widow.

And I was overcome by the same emotion I had felt when I had watched my mother grieving for my father.

Jealousy.

"Why me? Why did you tell me this story you have never told anyone. Not even Brie?"

Max shook her head.

"Because you are the first person I have ever met that I felt could be completely open to the possibility."

"The possibility of an affair?"

"No, no, my dear," Max laughed wryly and continued. "To the possibility, that these things are not always exactly black and white. That love is not ruled entirely by the choices we make, no matter how much we pretend it is so."

"You think I believe that?"

"I do."

"*I* don't even know if I believe that."

"I know. But now that you've heard my story, you are questioning the possibility, no?"

"Yes," I answered her reluctantly.

"Then, I was right. To tell you."

Ian arrived at our side and hugged Max and me hello while we were sitting on our bar stools. I could feel my heart in my chest as he hugged me, and worried that Ian felt it, too.

Max stood and said, "Well, I'm heading back to my cabin to dress for dinner. I'll see you two later." She left me with my thoughts. And with Ian.

"So. Here we are." Ian broke the silence first after Max left.

"What did you do all day? Did you go to Port Canaveral?"

"No. I stayed on board to read, relax. I needed some quiet time." Ian paused to order a Manhattan as the bartender approached. "How about you? Did you go to Disney?"

"No," I laughed. "I needed a little quiet time, too. That's the whole reason I came on this trip. To get away from—" I stopped. I don't know what I was trying to get away from. My thoughts. My anger. But how to explain that to Ian without talking about Rob again, a subject I just really didn't want to discuss anymore with him.

What I really wanted to talk to Ian about was—

"So how was Botswana? Did you ever find the marula fruit? Or a time machine?"

Ian took a sip of his drink and met my gaze. "Well. Here's what I discovered about time travel in Botswana." He paused dramatically, and I suddenly found myself wondering if Ian still really believed in time travel.

And hoping that he did.

"I discovered that there are people who believe that when the conditions are right, time can be altered. There are really truly people who believe that. People who are otherwise perfectly sane, rational beings. That's what I discovered."

"Hunh," I said ineloquently. And then before I could help myself. "You made me believe once."

"Did I?"

"Yes. I believed you. The marula fruit, the agate and the Botswanan mystic. All of it. I believed it a little. I was embarrassed to admit that for a long time afterward. But I did. I believed it." I picked up my wine glass.

Ian didn't look too ruffled by my admissions of belief or embarrassment. He put his drink down and asked, "Would you like to join me tonight for dinner at the Captain's Table?"

I laughed a little and in so doing, a few drops of wine dribbled down my chin. Ian reached over with a napkin and I pretended I was choking to cover up my embarrassment.

"What's so funny?" Ian asked.

"The Captain's Table? I thought that was an urban legend—something made up by the Producers of *The Love Boat*." Now, it was Ian's turn to laugh, and he did it much more elegantly than I had, with my wine-sputtering.

"No, there's really a Captain's Table, and on the second night of the cruise, he invites a few high rollers to join him."

"High rollers?"

"Big gamblers."

"Ahh, are you a big gambler, Ian?"

"You could say that."

In that moment, I was almost grateful Ian had a vice. He had always seemed so perfect. Alarmingly so. Even back in the old days in Manhattan before Botswana. I liked the idea of imperfection in Ian. It allowed me to relax a bit even.

"Also, he extends the invitation to a few people willing to pay for the privilege of saying they are at the Captain's Table."

"They sell seats? Like a show?"

"Sort of. Truth is, I was just joking about being a high roller. I am not paying for my seats—not by gambling or otherwise. The Captain invited me because he owes me."

"Owes you? For what?"

"A few years back, I profiled him for an assignment. He's a third generation sea captain, a long-esteemed lineage of sea captains—but the piece was getting so boring that I told him I had done some research and traced his family tree back to a band of Bahamian pirates."

"Ian!"

"Please. Stop with your fake indignation. Tell me, which story would you rather read?" Ian's eyes sparkled. He enjoyed telling stories.

"You didn't run the pirate link, did you?"

"No. Why do you think he owes me? The seats at the Captain's Table are the least he could do. So. Do you want to come with me?"

"Yes. Definitely. Now I'm intrigued. I'll have to go dress for dinner."

I thought about my lemongrass dress hiding in the closet of my cabin. It would be the perfect occasion to bring it out.

Ian stood up and said, "Come on, I'll walk you to your cabin.

I have to dress, too."

As we walked together back to our respective cabins, the familiarity of walking side by side with Ian overtook me and I almost reached for his hand. He looked at me strangely and I wondered if he was thinking the same thing.

To distract from my nervousness, I asked Ian, "Do you really think the Captain is from pirate lineage?"

"Well, he certainly thought it was a real possibility, didn't he? The way he panicked over my threatened story. He's a bit gullible. You'll see when you meet him at dinner."

And then, as if reading my mind, as I looked out at the tranquil sea, thinking again that I had been foolish to embark on this trip thinking it would solve all my problems, and that perhaps I shouldn't have traveled so far away from home, Ian added, quietly, "He's a fine sea captain, though. A really good captain."

WHAT A PLEASURE TO DRESS FOR DINNER. I gazed into the mirror.

It had been forever since I had had the chance to lay out a dress, and put on my makeup and do my hair in peace and quiet for a night out.

Date nights with Rob had become so rare over the last few years, I had stopped bothering to dress for them.

If we could even find a Saturday night babysitter—someone I heard about at the playground that was between nanny jobs, for example—I would book her quickly, buy movie passes and throw jeans on for a quick pizza and beer dinner.

No point to putting makeup on, as the boys never let me be in the bathroom on my own anyway, and any attempt to try out my new department store counter blusher would end with Michael finger painting his brother or the bathroom walls, or something worse.

You have to be crazy to break out makeup in front of two rambunctious boys. It only took me a few thwarted efforts to realize that they saw makeup as war paint, a means to decorate themselves and their foes before running through the house at full speed and volume, programmed for mass destruction.

So no more makeup on date nights. Which really wasn't the sad part. Rob always told me—tenderly, sweetly—on date nights that I didn't really need makeup anyway. So the sad part was the fact that eventually there were no more date nights, either.

Alone in my ship cabin, I opened my new expensive makeup bought just for this trip, and smoothed the colors on my face until they blended together in a thin sheen of velvet.

I blew dry my hair and brushed it under and I could not help but preen like a peacock in my cabin terry robe as I caught my face in the mirror. I looked . . . happy . . . there was no denying it. And I felt a pang of guilt only for a moment before deciding to relinquish it. Which I decided I must do. Because I was not feeling guilty for leaving the kids. I was feeling guilty for not missing them enough right there in that moment.

❧

I glided into the Captain's Lounge. I really cannot describe my entrance any other way. I had somehow slipped into the dream of a dress, a bit heavy when it came off the hanger for its elaborate beading and sequins, but effortless, light while it was on—lined entirely in a red velvety material designed to smooth the lines and add to the comfort of its wearer. The only ugly moment I experienced while dressing was when I wriggled and twisted trying to zipper the back, the only place where the red velvet material was visible to the outside world. A small glimpse of the inner beauty of this dress.

I was about to give up hope of zipping myself up when I ducked my head outside and caught a glimpse of a cabin crew member a few doors down, getting ready to turn down the sheets and decorate our row of cabins with animal-shaped towels, while the inhabitants were out for dinner.

I motioned to him, and he looked around over his shoulder to make sure I was talking to him. "Do you have a woman . . . a female colleague on the crew who could help me with my . . ." I pointed with my one free hand to the back of my dress, while my occupied hand continued to contort to hold the back of the unzipped dress together.

He smiled and nodded as if this was the most usual, common request ever and retreated back into what looked to be a utility closet, returning promptly with a lovely woman. She took one look at me and grabbed the back of my dress. She pushed me gently back into my room, away from the smiling eyes of the crew member, giving him instructions in a gorgeous and unfamiliar dialect, that by the look of how he retreated, head bowed, back into the utility closet, seemed to be telling him his services were no longer needed.

"Here, let me," she returned to speaking English. She had a lovely, thick accent to go with her matronly shape, and I wondered briefly if she was a mother, a grandmother? She seemed unquestioningly maternal. She had thick hands but she dealt with the zipper very delicately. I felt her slide it all the way up the middle of my back and then deal with additional clasps that I confess I did not know existed, despite having admired this dress on its hanger nearly every day that I had owned it.

I didn't really know the protocol, here. *Am I supposed to tip her?* I wondered, briefly. But she had already turned on her heel and was out the door.

I had wanted to ask her how I looked, but standing in my cabin in front of the mirror admiring myself in a dress that was the color of hope, I didn't really need to hear anyone else's answer to that question. I already knew.

When I arrived in the Captain's Lounge, I surveyed the room quickly for Ian and he spotted me and excused himself from the conversation he seemed trapped in and headed over to me.

"Who were you talking to, Ian?"

"Apparently, a wealthy woman. I know this because she keeps saying so."

I laughed at Ian's candor.

"She and her husband bought seats at the table." Ian could not hide his obvious contempt.

"How crass," I responded, with exaggerated and mock

disdain. I wasn't yet sharing Ian's obvious smugness at having earned a seat at a table that was usually only up for sale, but I was having fun playing along with him.

Ian took both of my hands in his and I felt a jolt as he stepped back to look at my dress. To look at me. "You look amazing, Kate. That dress—it's just so perfect. The color. It's—"

"Lemongrass. It's supposed to be a very optimistic color." I smiled under Ian's admiring eyes. His expression was appreciative. Proud even. I pulled him to me in a hug and said, "Thank you, Ian. You look amazing, too." With Ian's arms around me and his lips in my hair, it was easy to believe that the lemongrass ballgown had found its way from Indian artisans to me for just that moment.

We headed over to the table, a long cherry wood table, decorated with a nautical theme. China and crystal bearing the seal of the ship's company lined the table and Ian escorted me to my seat. For a moment, I thought he was going to actually take the head of the table, and I was mortified, but then he passed to the other side and sat down, ushering me to his right side.

When an austere-looking gentleman sat at the head of the table to Ian's left, Ian introduced us.

"Mauricio, this is my dear friend, Kate, I was telling you about."

I stood a bit, but the Captain was already seated, so the gesture came off a bit awkward. Nevertheless, the Captain reached his hand across Ian and shook mine warmly.

"Kate. Of course. Lovely to meet you."

Then the Captain tapped his knife against his glass and announced loudly, "Ladies and gentlemen, take your seats. I would like to say a toast and get our fine dinner started here."

A few guests had already seated themselves, and the rest began choosing their seats. It was only then that I noticed there were name cards at the places. Seating had not been left to chance, and we had actually taken seats already assigned to us. It seemed the Captain had already decided who he would actually be talking to at his Captain's Table.

The "wealthy" woman that Ian was trapped by earlier was sitting at the other end of the table separated from me (and Ian) by a man I assumed was her husband. She was dressed garishly with a revealing top. Her hair looked like it was just freshly done up in the ship's salon that day, pulled back in an updo of tight ringlets. Her husband was a portly man with a reddish face, who by the way he was waving to the waiter to refill his cocktail glass again and again, was quickly on his way to becoming even redder.

Seated across from the wealthy couple was a gorgeous young woman and her date—a young man, who it would have been kind to describe as "nice-looking." In fact, his slicked-back hair was pulled off a face that was at best, homely. But he was dressed impeccably, and as he sipped his drink, his gold and jeweled cuff links caught the dim lights of the Captain's lounge and I could not help but wonder if perhaps there was something other than looks that had caught this young man the model seated to his left.

Across from Ian and myself sat a married couple, who each looked just a few years older than I. I recognized them as the couple Benton and Brie had been chatting up in line to board the ship that first morning. I introduced myself to the couple as they sat down, since we would be sitting across from each other for the duration of the meal and because I quickly decided that I would prefer to talk to them than to the wealthy red-faced man to my right.

"Hi, I'm Kate."

"I'm Anne, and this is my husband, Tom."

While the Captain turned to give some instructions to the waiter, Anne leaned into the table and confided to me, "This is our first time sitting at the Captain's Table. My husband arranged it for our anniversary."

"Oh, how lovely," I replied. Although, to be honest, it was the first pang of discomfort that had invaded an otherwise divine night.

"How long have you been married?" I asked the now obligatory question.

"Twenty-five years." Tom was the one who jumped in and answered the question.

I must have looked a little distracted, doing the math and trying to figure out how this couple could have been married so long, looking barely older than I felt.

But Anne jumped in, obviously used to this reaction. "I know, we were babies when we got married. Babies having a baby," she laughed. "Never got to go on a honeymoon, and Tom said—even way back then—don't worry honey, someday, we'll get all the kids out of the house, and we'll still be young enough to enjoy each other!

"Very smart, my Tom." Anne looked at him admiringly as he was striking up a conversation with the Captain.

"So, your kids are grown now?"

"Yes, we just sent our youngest off to college this year. And Tom is retiring. We're going to travel and enjoy ourselves. The last trip we took by ourselves was 10 years ago—a cruise just like this one. We need to start traveling a little more than once every 10 years."

Anne smiled a bit wistfully when she said that and looked down at her empty plate.

"How lucky to be retiring so young."

Something passed across Anne's eyes, as she said, "Yes, very lucky indeed," and I felt embarrassed, like I had said the wrong thing somehow without meaning to.

But it passed quickly. Anne's expression lightened somewhat

and she smiled. "So, what about you? What brings you and your husband on this trip?"

"Oh, we're not . . . not married."

Now it was Anne's turn to look embarrassed, but I absolved her quickly. "Ian and I are old friends, traveling together with some other friends on a bit of reunion trip, really."

Anne perked up with this news. "How fun!"

And then desperate to make something up to Anne that I couldn't exactly put my finger on, I took a turn leaning in to Anne while Ian, the Captain, and Tom all seemed locked in conversation and oblivious to the women's conversation at their side. The red-faced man and his wife were discussing portfolios and investments with the couple across from them and seemed altogether uninterested in me so I took advantage of the distractions and confided in Anne.

"Ian is a writer and he wrote a story about the Captain a few years back for a travel magazine. That's how we got our invite to the table."

"This is getting exciting."

"It gets better." I smiled and leaned in even further to add conspiratorially, "Seems the Captain is a descendant of pirates, but Ian agreed to keep that out of the story. Top secret." I smiled, and held my finger up to my lips and winked. Anne's face brightened with excitement. "Absolutely, I won't tell a soul. I'm so glad we got seated at this end of the table—this is so much more exciting than hearing about that awful woman's money at the other end."

I laughed and clinked my glass against Anne's glass, feeling peace and tranquility descend again as the magical night resumed.

❧

"Wait, wait, Mauricio. The women have to hear this story,

too." The Captain was telling Tom a story, while Anne and I talked about our shopping plans in port. Suddenly, I felt an electric shock and realized it was a spot where Ian had just touched my arm. "You have to hear this story—I've heard it so many times—and I want you to hear it tonight." Ian smiled down at me while I caressed the tingling spot on my arm.

The Captain continued on. "Yes, yes, I know, Ian—you think it all a bit of a tall tale—this Devil's Triangle talk—but then again, I notice you never travel through it with any other captain but Yours Truly."

"Devil's Triangle? Is that the same as the Bermuda Triangle?" I heard myself say out loud. "But we're not headed to Bermuda? What's all this talk about the Triangle?"

The Captain responded, "Actually, we are headed right through the Triangle—will be entering it sometime around midnight. Bermuda is only one apex of the Triangle—very much a misnomer if you ask me. No, I prefer its historical vernacular—the Devil's Triangle."

"Sure, that's much better." I rolled my eyes and looked over at Anne, who looked only marginally concerned by this talk.

Ian chided the Captain. "Now Mauricio, I told you to tell the forgotten lovers' tale, not scare my date half to death." It was at that point I shivered a bit, and I wasn't sure whether to attribute the chills to Ian's casual use of the word "date" or the thought that I might have left my children behind with Rob and his mistress while I was traversing recklessly, and unwittingly, through the Bermuda Triangle.

"Well, all right then." The Captain smiled at Ian, but then faced forward to address the captive audience at the table. "Every ship in these waters has its own Devil's Triangle tale. Many have more than one. Our ship's most famous tale is about the forgotten lovers."

The rest of the guests at the table were quieting now. All

eyes turned to the Captain, who was becoming more animated, clearly enjoying the prospect of holding court. And he took a dramatic pause to cut his steak and drink his tonic water as the rest of the guests waited on his next words.

"Nathaniel and Bea," Ian interjected, helping the story along.

The Captain carved and ate a bit of his steak while nodding, and then continued. "Well, I've heard them referred to by many names, really, Ian. But Nathaniel and Bea are commonly the names given by those I consider the most respected arbiters of this tale.

"So. As the story goes, Bea was the daughter of wealthy socialites and Nathaniel was the son of one of the family servants. And, of course, they fell in love."

"Of course." Ian turned and nudged me playfully, but the Captain was undistracted.

"But, they could not marry in New York in 1926. So they decided to escape both of their families and take the trip to Nathaniel's homeland, an island in the Bahamas. Nathaniel knew of a cargo ship that was leaving from New York to Los Angeles and would be making a planned stop in the Caribbean. Bea took part of her fortune, bought them passage to the Caribbean on the cargo ship, and she and Nathaniel secretly boarded the ship to their futures.

"But when the ship passed into the Bermuda Triangle, something happened."

"It sunk?" I was quite nauseous now, in spite of my best efforts to tell myself that this was all nonsense.

Anne looked positively riveted, obviously caught up in the romantic tale and not giving a second thought to the fact that we might all be drowning in a few hours.

Out of the corner of my eye, I noticed that Ian also looked riveted by this tale and remembering Ian's description of the Captain that very afternoon, I was truly beginning to wonder who was the "gullible" one at this table after all.

"No, no, it didn't sink." The Captain looked downright amused.

"But after the ship passed through the Triangle, Bea no longer remembered Nathaniel. She had completely forgotten him."

"Forgotten, like amnesia?" Anne interrupted.

The Captain continued, "She hadn't fallen, or hit her head, or suffered any other documented trauma, but yet she just suddenly stopped remembering him. Well, stopped remembering that she was in love with him. That she was there by choice."

"She remembered nothing, nothing at all?" Anne's hand moved up to her throat, and I wondered why this bothered her more than the prospect of drowning that I had raised a few moments ago.

"Well, no. She knew who she was. Knew about her life back in New York, but just didn't remember Nathaniel. She was obviously alarmed to find herself on board a cargo ship headed for the Islands with a man she did not remember, let alone was certain had brought her there against her will. She had Nathaniel ordered off the ship in the Bahamas and Nathaniel was unable to find a single crew member who would attest to having seen them come on board together, willingly, happily."

"What happened to them?" I had to know.

"Well, the story goes that Nathaniel was taken to a prison in the Islands but soon worked off his sentence and was released, penniless, and without the woman he had hoped to spend the rest of his life with.

"Bea's family sent for her and she returned to New York where her father publicized a great tale about his daughter having been abducted by a young man, named Nathaniel. Her family was obviously greatly relieved that she was all right, that

AMY IMPELLIZZERI

she was home, and that she had not, as they had feared, run off with the servant's son. His family was promptly and quietly fired and Bea had no further dealings with Nathaniel or his family. Until."

The Captain paused dramatically to make sure all the eyes of his dinner companions were on him.

"Nathaniel returned to New York several years later. Having never given up on his true love, he had managed to save and hide, even through his exile and imprisonment, one item from their trip. It was an item he was certain would release her from the odd memory loss she was suffering.

"Brazen, he put the item into an envelope, addressed it to Bea and waited outside her home while he left the envelope on her doorstep.

"He watched one of the servants summon her, watched her take the envelope inside, watched through the parlor window as she tore open the envelope.

"A few moments later, she arrived at the doorstep surveying for the messenger, and when Nathaniel stepped into view, Bea ran off the porch and into his waiting arms."

"What was it? What was in the envelope?"

Anne and I smiled at each other as we both exploded with the same questions in unison.

"A torn swatch from a dress. A simple white linen dress that Bea was going to wear on her wedding day to Nathaniel when they reached the Islands. He had somehow managed to tear off a piece of the dress and save it through his captivity and escape. When Bea saw the dress swatch—well, you could say, The Devil's Triangle curse had been broken. Bea remembered everything."

"My goodness. So what happened to them?"

"Not sure. Some say they returned to the Islands to live out their lives together. Others say they stayed in New York City and lived underground for a while. But all the varying versions

194

of the tale end with them together."

All the ladies, but me, sat back in their seats exhausted. The Captain looked thoroughly pleased with himself for his dramatic storytelling. Ian looked smugly at me as if to say, "I told you—gullible, right?"

But I was unsatisfied.

"Well, it sounds like Bea just got cold feet about a pretty daring move in a conservative time. It doesn't sound like amnesia at all."

"Well, that's an interesting theory, of course. And might be a plausible one, too. But for one thing."

"What's that?"

"While Bea later admitted fully that she and Nathaniel had come on board together openly, after paying a small fortune for passage on the ship, not one other person on that ship—not one member of the crew—could remember a white woman and a black man coming on board together. And that, my dear would have been a *very* memorable event in 1926."

"Are you saying that all of the crew had their memories erased as well?"

"I'm not suggesting anyone had their memories erased, my dear." The Captain's eyes were piercing as he turned to me. "One theory about the Devil's Triangle is that it is not cursed. That it does not devour ships. But rather that it is a very powerful energy source that under the right conditions can actually alter time."

"I'm not following you."

The Captain held my gaze alone as he replied. "There are those who believe that Nathaniel and Bea's ship—like other ships that have passed through the Triangle at the right conditions—actually traveled back in time. That once on the other side, the entire group was thrust back to some earlier time before Nathaniel and Bea had even arrived on the ship, some earlier time before they had even fallen in love."

"That's ridiculous." The red-faced man stole my line, and I was a bit disheartened to realize I was aligning now with him in my response to this tale.

"So why is that the Devil's Triangle story of *this* ship?" Finally, the wealthy woman at the other end of the table was contributing something worthwhile to the conversation.

I chimed in. "Certainly you're not saying it was this very ship that Bea and Nathaniel took across The Devil's Triangle?"

"Of course not," said Mauricio.

"But we do have a very interesting Devil's Triangle museum of artifacts on the lower level, with the 1926 cargo ship's manifesto listing a Mr. and Mrs. Nathaniel Smith as members of the crew. In a way, they are with us every time we leave port."

Ian took my hand under the table at the story's end. I felt the electric shock again. I tried to reconcile the Captain's story with reality. And I quickly abandoned it as the tall tale that it obviously was. I did not want to believe that The Devil's Triangle could take you back in time or make you forget everything you knew. Certainly, I wanted to remember every single minute that was happening to me now.

❧

After dinner, we headed out to the lounge for coffee with Anne and Tom, and Anne asked Ian about his travel mag writing. "So you travel a lot?" she asked him.

"Yes, but not as much as I used to. I used to spend a lot of time in Asia and Africa, but now I write about more local destinations. The economy is not what it used to be. People want to read about what they can discover in their own backyards." Ian smiled, and winked at us. Or at me. I really couldn't tell.

Tom was riveted. "I would love to talk more to you about Africa. Anne and I always dreamed of traveling after I retired, and now we're making every trip count." Tom looked quickly at Anne after that remark and I followed his gaze, only to see what Tom saw, quiet tears streaming down Anne's face.

"I'm sorry," she said as she quickly wiped them and made a visible effort to compose herself. Tom got up and went to sit next to Anne, patting her leg and putting his arm around her comfortably. "Now, Anne. Let's talk with Ian about Africa. A safari adventure sounds nice, doesn't it?"

Anne nodded and forced a smile. "I think I'll just run to the restroom. I'll be right back."

"I'll wait," Tom said. "You go. I'll be right here." Anne looked uncomposed for a moment again and headed quickly down the hall.

I looked at Tom, questioningly, as Anne hurried down the corridor to the restroom.

"No, don't worry about my wife. She's just fine. She's a worrier, is all. I've been having a few medical issues that forced me into an early retirement. Early onset of dementia, they say. Not sure how long I'll remain status quo. Doctors keep trying to put numbers on me . . . six months . . . two years . . . I wish they'd never said any of it in front of Anne."

Tom smiled and I patted his arm warmly, while wiping away a tear of my own. The emotion overcame me and I was embarrassed for a moment, but Tom kept on. "So you'll have to excuse my wife. Like I said, she's a worrier.

"Listen, you kids go enjoy yourselves. I'm going to take Anne back to the cabin and turn in early. Maybe we'll see you at breakfast tomorrow. Would love to talk more with you, Ian. And you of course, Kate." Tom shook our hands warmly and left Ian and me sitting on the lounge sofas with our drinks.

"What now?" I looked at Ian.

"You up for a gamble?"

I had no idea what Ian was suggesting and I nearly choked

on my coffee as he stared at me.

"Seriously." Ian grabbed my hand and pulled me off the sofa. "Let's head to the ship casino."

"YOU HAVE TO ASSUME the dealer is going to break every time."

Ian began coaching me at the bar after a pretty serious game of blackjack.

So serious in fact that there had been audible groans from the table when I failed to play my hand "correctly." Apparently, when you do not "stay" or "hit" when you are "supposed to," you mess up the entire table. At least, this was Ian's polite translation of some of the drunk cursing that had erupted from the table when I asked the blackjack dealer for "one more card, please" while I had a "16" showing and so did the dealer. I got a jack and the dealer got a five and everyone who was not cursing at me was simply glaring at me while the chips were being shuffled toward the dealer as he announced for the mathematically challenged at the table:

"21."

Ian put his arm around me. "Let's go get a drink before you make any more friends at this table. I'll teach you how to play and then we'll come back for a bit of redemption."

At the bar, Ian ordered a Manhattan and I ordered a glass of wine, and he repeated his instructions—obviously feeling that repetition was necessary given my perplexed look.

"You have to assume that a dealer, sitting with any hand showing from a 12 through a 16, is going to get a 10 and break."

"Well, that sounds pretty unrealistic," I challenged. "Look what happened there. 21. The best hand you can get."

"Yes, but you took his break card."

"I what?"

"If you had stayed on your hand, the dealer would have gotten the jack, would have broken, that is—gone over 21—and you and everyone else at the table would have won. You have to assume the dealer will get a 10 for the game to work correctly. You have to assume the dealer will lose."

"Sounds pretty optimistic to me."

"That's how gambling works, Kate. To succeed, you can't be too practical. Or too conservative."

"Ah, it's the great inverse of life." I clinked my glass on his.

Ian actually looked startled. "Inverse? Kate, it's the precise *analogy* of life. By the way, let me see the inside of your purse."

"What?"

I instinctively clutched my handbag more tightly.

"Come on, there can't be anything too incriminating in that little bag there. And I want to prove my point."

Ian leaned over and stacked the chips on the bar counter that were sitting next to my glass of wine. I had brought them over from the blackjack table and lined them up in neat color-coded piles. Before Ian had accused me of wrecking everyone's blackjack mojo, I had in fact, doubled my initial one hundred dollars, playing my way, ignoring the groans and curses from my table mates.

I held tightly to my bag and Ian stared at me over his Manhattan. I couldn't read his smile. Was he amused? Or was he mocking me? I was a little uncomfortable so I sat up in my chair a bit straighter and glanced around for a diversion.

I found my diversion in a cruise employee, who came by just then to sell raffle tickets and I gave her $20 in chips for two raffle tickets without even asking what I would be trying to win. "One hour til the drawing, dear."

"How's that for conservative and pragmatic?" I was pleased with myself, until I saw Ian grabbing the purse I had neglected on the bar as I had counted out chips for the raffle tickets.

"Ian!"

Ian held up the bag out of arm's reach and then when I sat back in my seat defeated, he moved the compact, NARS lip gloss and ATM card to the side of my clutch before pulling out exactly what he had been searching for in one handful—$100 in gambling chips.

"I knew it. You sacked these away when you started winning, didn't you? Your initial investment? This way you can't lose?"

I suddenly felt a little sheepish with a decision that only a half hour earlier had seemed so wise and prudent.

Ian leaned in and whispered quietly into my ear. "What do you think will happen if you gamble away $100 Kate? Wouldn't you like to just try it for once and see?"

I didn't answer.

Well, I couldn't answer.

Actually I could hardly breathe.

Ian was so close, I could smell the citrus undertones of his aftershave and the boozy scent of his last gulp of his Manhattan. And in that moment, I wasn't thinking about the $100 or my life at home or Rob or Celeste. I was thinking about what it must be like to live with a man who had so much exuberance and optimism that he could assume the dealer was going to lose. Every time.

I was still a bit woozy but I let Ian pull me out of my chair. A band was playing nearby and we headed to the dance floor. Ian held me close as we danced.

Ian and me and the lemongrass ballgown.

"I love this dress, Kate. Is this the first time you've worn it?"

"Yes. I bought it a few months ago, even though I didn't have a clue where I would wear such a thing." I looked down and smoothed my hands over the beading, admiringly. I looked up to see admiration on Ian's face as well.

"I'm so glad that you found an occasion."

"Me, too."

Ian held me and I was vaguely aware that the song was ending.

"Come on." Ian began reaching into his moneyclip for some well-worn $100 bills that didn't seem to have just come from the nearest ATM machine. These looked like they could be part of a small treasure trove that had just come back from the African continent or some such adventure.

I followed Ian as he took my hand, and we walked over to the nearest blackjack table.

I lined up my gambling chips (even the ones I had stashed in my purse) in front of me as Ian and I took our spots at the end of the table. The dealer nodded and smiled at Ian as she converted his worn $100 dollar bills into plastic gaudy chips. This time, I followed Ian's lead and nodded at the dealer when he told me to. Waved my hands over my cards to stay. Pointed firmly at my hand to hit when Ian indicated. I felt like I was under some spell. Ian's spell. I watched as cards flew over and back again, and chips piled up in front of Ian. And in front of me. After an hour, a new girl arrived on the arm of an older, gray-haired man. The girl took a few chips that her companion gave her and when she hit on her "13," in front of the dealer's 16, I groaned a little, and then caught myself as I put my hand over my mouth and without thinking, leaned into Ian's shoulder to stifle a small laugh. Ian reached his hand up to my hair.

It was just a small touch. In my hair. But I felt it right down to my toes. It was palpable. I looked at Ian and he had the strangest look in his eyes. It was as if he was . . .. sad? I didn't have long to analyze it, because the look was gone in a flash. Replaced by the trademark smirk. And then he said to me, "I love how easily you laugh. It's one of your most endearing traits."

His hand was still in my hair and he caressed my head for a

minute before dropping his hand and reaching for a pile of chips to play the next hand.

I waved off the dealer as he asked for my bet and stood up. "I think I better call it a night." Ian nodded but kept his eyes on the dealer. Since my spot remained empty, Ian got dealt my hand.

Blackjack.

The dealer paid him and Ian tossed a few coins back as a tip before standing up. "I'll walk you back to your room."

"Such the gentleman," I smiled.

Ian reached for my hand but I jerked it away a bit too quickly, just before Ian looked at me puzzled.

"No, no, it's not—" I smiled as I tapped my clutch. "I have to check my raffle ticket."

I pulled out the ticket and checked the digital display board over the bar which was just now showing the winning ticket number. And—

"Oh my gosh. I won. I can't believe it."

"See," Ian leaned over and kissed my cheek. "You have to be optimistic or you will never win anything in life."

❧

If Ian was expecting more than a kiss on the cheek at my cabin door, he didn't betray any surprise as I simply said goodbye at the door. He took my hand and said, "Listen, let's have breakfast together in the morning. I'll meet you upstairs at 9 am." I nodded and squeezed his hand. I was thinking about hurrying inside, more afraid of my own lack of resolve than any ungentlemanly behavior on his part. I had already decided that a kiss goodnight would be much too intimate. Too confusing.

Please don't let him ask to kiss me. Please.

"Thanks for teaching me to be a degenerate gambler," I laughed and reached my arms around his neck for a warm hug.

I felt his heartbeat next to mine under my dress as we hugged and his hand reached up into my hair again the way it did at the blackjack table. As I leaned into his hug, I thought how close this was to a goodnight kiss and yet, how much more intoxicating.

Ian stepped away and looked at me again, and the dress, the way he had in the Captain's lounge. "Thanks for a wonderful evening, Kate. I'll never forget it. And that dress. That dress. Everything was perfect." He shook his head and turned to walk away down the hall.

It was shortly after midnight when I swooped into my small cabin and admired myself in the bathroom mirror. My raffle prize turned out to be costume jewelry from the ship store. A gorgeous gemstone pendant. After leaving Ian, I stood in my cabin, drunk and happy, trying it on in front of the mirror, turning this way and that to catch the pendant in the light.

And I remember thinking that it was gorgeous. That I was gorgeous. The sea air or the cabin lighting or the booze or some combination of all three had given me a glow of a woman several years younger. Several worries younger. I did not look like a woman who worried about sick kids or carpools or healthy snacks in the school cafeteria. I didn't look practical or conservative. I looked like a woman who was about to embark on a brand new life.

I tucked the pendant back into the felt drawstring bag in which it was given to me. And as I swirled around my small cabin in my lemongrass gown one last time before undressing and hanging the gown back in my cabin closet, I wasn't feeling like a gambler at all.

"Lemongrass," I said aloud only to my reflection. "It's the color of hope."

38

AT 9 AM, I CHECKED MYSELF one last time in my bathroom mirror, and headed out to meet Ian for breakfast. Walking along the deck to the inner stairwell of the ship, I caught a glimpse of myself in a mirrored column, and I gave a slight start at my reflection. I was dressed in a long chiffon sundress and gold sandals and I looked. . .pretty. Almost gazelle-like, I found myself thinking. Out here on the open sea, it was easy to shed your cares and responsibilities for a short time. I felt momentarily guilty. But it passed quickly.

I had emailed the kids some pictures earlier that morning via Rob's work email as my cell phone connection was non-existent now. The internet connection was slow but the email seemed to go through.

There would be very little ability to communicate for the next few days. Emergencies only. I had told Rob via email to make sure the kids knew how much Mommy loved them, as I wouldn't be able to tell them myself for a bit. I signed off to Rob with only a "See you soon." Because with all of the swirl of emotion I was feeling about Ian, this was the only thing I could think of saying that would be, in fact, true.

❧

When I arrived outside the dining room, I found Ian sitting on a lounge sofa flanked by Anne and Tom who were grilling him about his African travels. They seemed to have hit upon the trip to the Okavango Delta just as I arrived.

"To live among the elephants—can you imagine just giving

205

it all up to do such a thing?" Tom looked mesmerized, and Anne was studying the men as they remained deep in conversation even as I walked up and took my seat across from the group. It was evident that no one was willing to interrupt and head into breakfast just yet.

"Well, if you're serious—truly serious about an African safari," Ian said, "I would have many recommendations for you. It is an amazing, life-changing experience, really."

Ian looked over at me and winked to acknowledge me without interrupting his conversation.

It's funny. He can make me feel like I'm the only one in the room.

He was doing that to everyone, I suppose. Making each of us feel like we were the only ones there. Which is why Anne and Tom barely looked away to acknowledge me. For a moment I even thought they did not recognize me from the night before. They seemed to be under Ian's spell. Like I was.

Tom continued his conversation about African elephants with Ian. And I struggled with shock and disbelief thinking about the admissions from the night before about Tom's health. Tom certainly looked the picture of good health as he slapped Ian on the back. Was his disease terminal? I had so many questions.

I found myself thinking about Rob. What would it mean if Rob were diagnosed with a terminal illness? With Alzheimer's? Would we travel? Would we get a divorce or try to work on a reconciliation?

Strange thoughts swirled through my mind but they were interrupted suddenly as I heard Ian saying something that took me by surprise and woke me from my daydreams.

Ian was telling Tom a story about being in Brazil with "my wife."

༄

"So you are married."

"I am. So are you."

"Yes, yes I am."

"We are both married."

I sipped my coffee and leaned back in my poolside chair waiting to see how this would all play out. I thought about Max and her admission to me. Her belief that I would soon start to see adultery and love affairs outside of marriage as much more complicated that I once had.

Max was right.

What more would Ian reveal to me? I wondered.

Ian didn't make me wait long.

"I've known Stella since we were kids. Our parents were best friends in college and then stayed close after they graduated. I think our parents actually had us engaged in the wombs."

"Sounds nice," I said, without meaning it. "You never mentioned Stella. You know, back then."

"No, we weren't seeing each other then. We were just friends at that time. We started dating years later actually. See. There are many, many things you need to know about Stella." Ian sounded like he was about to start making a list. "And I want to say them in the right order. But this is very hard."

"Take your time, Ian."

"I didn't love Stella when we got married. But I never felt badly about that fact. I felt badly that it was my fault we needed to marry in the first place—that's what I have always struggled with—not the fact that I didn't love her when we married."

"Why did you *have* to marry?" My mind raced back to Rob's emergency room proposal. To my miscarriage and the unconfessed reason that brought Rob and I together. Did Ian have children after all? After denying that he had any children? What else was I about to find out about my Ian?

"Stella and I dated on and off again through our late 20s—

but we were—I thought—so half-hearted about it. We would break up when I would leave on a trip and then pick up like nothing had happened when I'd return. We were comfortable together. I don't know why we mistook that for love, but we did.

"We were out taking a drive after a family party one Christmas Eve ten years ago. Stella had asked me to take her for a ride. She needed to talk. I thought—no I hoped, that she was about to break up with me. For good, this time. I wanted her to do it so I wouldn't have to. I had already decided this would be our last Christmas together. We needed to pursue real happiness. Not our parents' idea of happiness. And I had this crazy idea that I should come whisk you away from Rob, once and for all."

"Ian."

Ian looked right at me for the first time since he had started this story.

Ian looked away again. "But in the car that night, Stella told me she loved me. Had always loved me. And she asked me, did I think I would ever love her, really love her? Did we have a future together? She needed to know. It wasn't an ultimatum. Stella isn't like that—she's not an ultimatum girl.

"I was trying to think of an answer. I was trying to think of a kind, gentle way to say 'I have never, and will likely never, love you.' Do you know that it is a hell of a lot harder to tell someone 'I do not love you' and mean it, than to say the words 'I love you' even if you do not mean them?"

When I looked over at Ian at that point—tears were streaming down his face and I felt suddenly like a voyeur.

"Ian, we don't have to talk about this."

Ian ignored me and kept going. "I never told her I didn't love her."

"You told her you loved her and then you married her?"

"I told you, Kate. Order is very important, here." Ian's words were curt and jostled me a bit. But I kept my gaze on him as he turned, looked me in the eyes and said, "Because before I told Stella I loved her and then married her, I accidentally crashed the car that night and caused her to go blind."

∽

I sat still and quietly with Ian for a few moments, waiting. I felt that he needed me to be patient and so I was.

"A month ago, Stella asked me for a divorce. She said she is tired of me." Ian gave a wry laugh. "Tired of my optimism. It's draining, she says." Ian stared ahead and I wondered what he was thinking about.

And then something he said stuck in my mind. "Ten years ago?"

Ian didn't look surprised or confused by the detail I seized upon. He smiled. He looked almost relieved.

"Right. Ten years ago."

"That's right when Rob and I were deciding to get married, too."

"I know."

Before I could make sense of his simple statement, Ian checked his watch and then stood up and grabbed my hand.

"Come here. Stand up. It's almost time."

We were on the uppermost deck of the ship. Ian pulled out a small compass from his pocket, and showed it to me. The needle pointed north behind us. And Ian pulled me over to the rail on the side of the ship.

"We're almost in the middle of it now."

"What are you talking about, Ian?"

"The Devil's Triangle."

I felt the same nervousness I had felt yesterday at the Captain's Table when he had first revealed that unsettling news to me.

"What is it, Kate?"

"I just never thought we were going through dangerous waters when I decided to come on board." I gazed out at sea and smoothed my chiffon sundress nervously. I tried to quiet my nervous heartbeat clucking with the steady throb of guilt.

My boys. What was I doing out here at sea? Away from them? What was I thinking?

I pictured them as they would look in the morning—waking up sleepily. Would they have slept through the night? Would Rob remember to help them brush their teeth? What sort of clothes would they all be picking out together without my help?

But Ian brought me back from my guilt-laden daydream by holding out his compass to me. "There. Look at this, Kate. It's not dangerous out here, it's mystical."

The compass arm was dancing frenetically.

I took the compass with the dancing arm from Ian and turned it over and over in my hand.

Ian wrapped his arms around me and buried his lips in my hair.

I exhaled and leaned into his hug the way I had the night before in front of my cabin door.

"You were keeping tabs on me and Rob back then?"

"Yes. I used to ask Benton about you all the time. She hated it. She said you were happy and I should leave you alone. I couldn't let go of you, though. So I'd keep asking and keep wishing the best for you. Mourning the fact that you were not mine. Loving you from afar."

I inhaled sharply at his confession. "Loving me?"

"Yes, loving you. Since that first night I saw you. That first night at Rocco's. Kate, I always told you that. I meant it. I never stopped loving you, Kate."

"But how—Ian, you don't even know me anymore."

"I don't know you?"

Ian's hands were in my hair and his lips were in my ear. "Here's what I know, Kate. I know that you are so strong but also so, so vulnerable. I know the claws that you use mercilessly to take care of yourself, and the soft touch you use to take care of those you love. I know that you fall in love completely, deeply. Even if you don't say the words. The ones you fall in love with can feel it."

Those fuzzy Manhattan days, in which I avoided telling Ian how much I loved him, gradually came into sharp focus with Ian's words.

"I know that you like to think you are practical. Maybe you are practical. In some ways. Like when it comes to money and blackjack. But not when it comes to love. You are just so damn reckless when it comes to love. You will throw away perfectly good love just because it doesn't make sense. To you.

"But I know, too, that you are a devoted friend. You will never let go of your true friends. And you are open to so many ideas. So many philosophies. Time travel and mystical serums. You entertain them. You listen. You have the most open heart of anyone I know. You give me hope like no one I have ever met in all of my travels.

"I know that you are a born teacher, but not as an occupa-tion. As a vocation.

"And I know now that you are an amazing mother—the mother I always imagined you'd be. The kind of mother who would rather pretend to like chairs instead of tables than have her son be disappointed in her.

"I know that you think New Zealand sauvignon blanc is the world's finest white wine. You know nothing else about wine but because of an article you read in the 1990s about the govern-ment and wine growers, New Zealand sauvignon blanc is *always* your first drink of choice.

"I know that you laugh readily and beautifully. And when

you wake in the morning, unretouched, I know that you are, in fact, the most beautiful woman I have ever known.

"I know you, Kate, and I *do* love you."

I could *hear* Ian's heart beating, after he stopped talking. I was as dizzy as I'd been that day on the Bryant Park carousel all those years earlier. My arms and fingers were tingling and I grabbed more tightly to the compass to keep from dropping it.

I love Ian. I have always loved Ian. I never stopped loving Ian.

The realization was as shocking as it was exhilarating.

"Please, Kate. Please. Can I kiss you?"

❧

Two hours later, we were still lying in Ian's cabin bed. I had wrapped myself up in his bedsheet as if I was suddenly modest.

It was as if no time had passed at all since those summer afternoons in Ian's Manhattan sublet. He was just as I remembered. The most attentive and generous man I have ever known. I was only mildly surprised by how natural being with him felt in the moment. After all, I had not been with any other man since Rob.

But Ian was the last man I had been with just before Rob. In many ways, it was like we were picking up right where we left off.

"How do you feel?" I asked him.

"How do *you* feel, beautiful?"

I thought for a moment. Trying to reign in my emotions. I must have been silent too long, because Ian jumped in to respond, "Kate, I feel so many things. It's hard to put it into words."

I traced his chest with my finger. "I feel warm. And full. And . . . ."

"Loved." The word came from both of us. At the same time.

My tears fell onto Ian's chest, as I let go. Me, who never let my guard down with anyone. Finally. After all this time.

Ian felt my tears on his chest, of course, and wiped my closed eyes gently with his fingers before lacing his wet, tear-stained fingers into mine and kissing the top of my head.

"My Kate. So many years of loving you from afar. And now you're here."

I pushed up on one elbow as I leaned in to kiss him. As we kissed, Ian traced my hip with his hand over the bedsheet.

"Promise me that you're really here," he tugged on the sheet and pulled me to him.

"Again?" I smiled at him as he continued tugging on the sheet.

"Always," Ian said as he kissed me, this time without asking.

～

We separated briefly after we re-dressed in the morning's clothes. By then, it was dinner time and I told Ian I wanted to go back to my cabin to shower and dress for dinner.

"I need to put on a little lip gloss and brush my hair." Ian seemed disappointed that I wanted to leave, however briefly.

"Do you really have to brush your hair? I like your 'love knots.'" Ian smiled as he caressed my tangled head and then took my face in his hands lovingly. "I like you best like this—unretouched."

"You melt me, Ian."

"I know the feeling." He was looking at me. Really looking at me, as I headed out of his cabin door. And then, as I walked down the ship corridor to the elevator, I looked back over my shoulder. Ian was still leaning in the doorway and he said quietly, "So, listen. Hurry back. I've already waited too long for you."

～

When I returned to my room, the housekeeper was finishing

up straightening up and turning down the bed for the evening. The same woman who had zipped my dress the night before. I thanked her again for zipping me, but she didn't seem to remember me as she quickly left me to shower and change from my day.

I climbed into the shower and tried to sort through my feelings. Not much to sort. I was feeling euphoria.

I wanted to get back to Ian as quickly as I could and I didn't want to leave him again for a long time. So after my shower, I packed up quickly, not delaying for long when I couldn't find my new expensive cosmetics or even some of the new dresses I had packed for the trip, wondering only briefly, how much "straightening" the housekeeper had actually done.

I grabbed a few dresses I didn't even remember packing, an old makeup bag from the bathroom counter, and a few books, and headed back to Ian's cabin.

When I arrived in Ian's room less than an hour later, dressed and primped for the night, I had an overnight bag. A nightgown. A toothbrush. Clothes and toiletries for the next few days. Ian hadn't mentioned it. I hadn't asked. But I was moving in.

Without a word, Ian took my bag and put it on a chair in his cabin as if it was the most natural thing he and I had ever done.

And then we headed up to a late dinner hand in hand.

WE DIDN'T SEE ANYONE we knew at dinner. Benton and Max had mentioned the day before that they would be doing early dinner seatings during the duration of the cruise, so we assumed we had missed them. We asked our waiter for a table in the back and he accommodated us with a smile.

"Not exactly the Captain's Table," Ian said as we sat down in the back corner of the crowded dining room. He reached over and took my hand across the table.

That simple act of holding his hand, of his fingers intertwined with mine, was so intimate. For a silly moment, I daydreamed that it was only he and I in the dining room. Only he and I on the ship. In the world.

So it was a little jarring when Ian smiled warmly at me over our interlocked hands, and said, "Tell me about your husband." I could not meet his eyes. I looked over him for our waiter, hoping wine was on its way, and all I could think to respond was, "Well, it's hard to convey the details of ten years of deterioration over dinner. Suffice to say, our marriage has been pretty rocky for some time now. A few months ago, I found out he has been having an affair. I shouldn't have been surprised. But for some reason, I was."

Ian's eyes looked sad, and that made me desperate. So I blurted out, "It's fine. It'll all be fine. I just need to sort out what to do." The words I didn't want to say to Lex when I first confided in her the news over egg white omelets and talk of motherhood's evolution, or lack thereof, came pouring out of me without warning.

Ian shook his head and I knew, of course, that he would not be letting me off the hook that easily, and I wasn't sure if I was relieved or annoyed by that fact.

"Kate, it's obviously not fine. It's terrible. It's a terrible position to be in. Talk to me."

I stared off to the side of the dining room. Nearby, a young couple caught my eye. There was an infant carrier sitting at their feet with a small sleeping baby bundled and swaddled while they poked at plates set out on the table before them. The husband was trying to talk to the woman, but she seemed hopelessly distracted by the sleeping baby. He looked frustrated, sad even. Despite her pretty dress and makeup, the woman looked tired and absent.

I created a narrative for them as I sat there trying to think of something to say in response to Ian's questions.

They booked this trip over a year ago, before they found out they were pregnant. The husband wanted to take the trip anyway. A babymoon of sorts. A celebration of their new family, and an opportunity to be together somewhere outside of their little home, now cluttered with diaper genies, and baby clothes, and exersaucers. The woman went along with the idea at first, determined to be a fiercely independent mother, raising a baby that would be easy to travel with. But after the baby was born, this tired mother quickly began having second thoughts—sleep deprivation and lactation problems becoming the new norm. Packing for a baby suddenly became daunting. She fought with her husband. He won the argument. She lost the argument. They came on the cruise.

Now it is no longer clear who won or lost.

The waiter finally arrived to fill our wine glasses. I turned back to Ian. "Remember I told you about my friend, Lex? The one who is working on a book about the evolution of mothers? Her premise is that our generation of mothers is actually defying the laws of Darwinism. That we are in fact becoming weakened and crippled as mothers, and that our weakened generation is raising women who are in turn, even more weak." Without letting go of my hand, Ian raised his wine glass to his lips. He began looking at me with a familiar look of bewildered amusement. And he said, "I am remembering something again. You are an interesting bird, Kate."

"How so?"

"When you don't like the topic at hand, you will change it—rather dramatically, I might add, to one that I know absolutely nothing about. It's your secret weapon. Deftly played, my dear."

I glanced at the couple again. I nodded their way to Ian. "That is what happened to Rob and me."

"We thought we loved each other until our kids arrived. And then, we realized we had had absolutely no idea what love was. It was disconcerting. We flailed around trying to reclaim it for a while. Then we gave up. To be honest, I think I gave up first.

"He was the one who eventually had an affair, of course. But I had given him permission to have an affair long before that. When I had given up any hope that love would appear in our marriage again. Ever.

"Because here's the thing. I never really got over the feeling that our marriage was doomed. Rob actually proposed to me ten years ago in the emergency room after a miscarriage that I had before my boys. I never told anyone that. But it's the truth. I was devastated by the miscarriage, and yet, I thought in that moment as Rob proposed in the most horrific of circumstances, that Rob and I still had a life that was meant to be. But I never really figured out whether the marriage was a conscious choice or something we fell into after the miscarriage. I never gave the marriage a real chance, but I'm not sure it ever had one to be honest. Hindsight is *not* 20/20 as they say. It's contorted and confusing."

I no longer felt like I needed to look away. I looked Ian in the eye, and he looked satisfied with my response. His eyes were so warm and empathetic. He was eliciting these words, this confession, from me with those eyes. And I was confessing my part, my responsibility, in the breakdown in our marriage. Something I had not previously admitted to anyone. Not even to myself. He was making me feel bare and naked, but just like in his cabin room hours before, I was not uncomfortable. I was strangely at ease with my vulnerability.

"Ian."

"Yes?"

"Before I found you again this week, I was thinking of reconciling with Rob. I was willing to forgive him."

Ian nodded, not visibly shocked by this admission.

"And I think the reason I have been willing to forgive him is that I have been absent in our marriage myself."

"I know, Sweetheart."

"As it turns out, I still love you, Ian."

"I have *always* loved *you*, Kate Monroe."

Kate Monroe. My maiden name. He used the name I had had when we first met. I didn't realize that I was holding my breath until I audibly exhaled. Ian patted my hand and let go as the waiter set down our dinner plates before us and we ate in comfortable silence.

❧

The next day, we spent the entire day in Ian's cabin. There was still no reliable internet service. It was a day at sea, and the rest of the ship's passengers were busy playing bingo, casino games, and a nighttime trivia contest.

But Ian and I rented movies and snuggled in his cabin all morning. We left the bed only to shower together midday, and then we collapsed back into bed, pulling out books from our respective piles to read next to each other. I felt a little sorry for having deserted Benton. I wondered if she and her travel companions had figured out yet what was going on between Ian and me. It didn't bother me that they might have guessed. I only wondered. The fact that there was still no reliable internet service absolved me of any responsibility to communicate with Rob and the boys. Truth be told, guilt simply had no room next to the happiness I was feeling just being near Ian.

Ian was reading a travel guide to Madagascar, and I was re-reading *Life of Pi*. I lay my head on his chest and settled into the book.

After a few hours, I glanced up at Ian. He closed his book and put it on the nightstand next to his side of the bed and asked me, "How is that book? I've started it a few times, but never finished it."

"I love this book. I've read it countless times. The story blends realism and mysticism beautifully. The language is amazing. I am positively transported every time I pick it up."

"Read something to me."

I flipped to a dog-eared section of the book. A part I had read and re-read so many times I had practically memorized it.

"This is the part that breaks my heart every time. The tiger, whose name is Richard Parker, is leaving Pi, after their ordeal at sea. Richard Parker leaves to head into the jungle and he never looks back." I explained to Ian. Then I read aloud to him from the book.

"I wept like a child. It was not because I was overcome at having survived my ordeal, though I was. Nor was it the presence of my brothers and sisters, though that, too, was very moving. I was weeping because Richard Parker had left me so unceremoniously. What a terrible thing it is to botch a farewell." When I finished reading, I was crying as I always did at this part, and Ian reached over to wipe my tears.

I thought, strangely enough, about Max. About her botched farewell to Allen at the age of 15.

See you around.

Perhaps if they hadn't botched that farewell all those years ago, they would not have needed to resurrect the love affair all those years later. Who knows? Perhaps if Ian and I had not botched our own farewell on that New York City night we would not be here now. Trying to fix things.

Lying there with Ian, wiping away my tears and thinking about Pi and Richard Parker and Max and Allen, I could not imagine ever saying farewell to Ian again.

"Ian. My heart has not stopped beating at this pace since you kissed me on the deck yesterday morning." I took Ian's hand and placed it on my chest to prove it to him—but he moved my hand and instead pulled me on top of him so that I could feel his beating heart under mine, matching mine, beat for beat.

"I'm afraid."

"Of what, Sweetheart?" Ian pulled away and looked me in the eye with genuine alarm and I leaned down and kissed him softly to reassure him before I answered.

"I am afraid that my heart will actually stop beating if I have to say goodbye to you at the end of this cruise. No pressure." I smiled to add levity to the statement, but even so, Ian could tell that I was somewhat serious.

"Sweetheart, you know that's not true, right? I mean I don't want to say goodbye to you, either. But you understand that you would not *die* without me—right?"

I was tempted to be insulted by Ian's matter-of-fact response to my emotional appeal, but Ian was so sweet as he said it. He looked genuinely concerned, for my mental well-being. And I wanted to pretend to him that I was just like any other lovestruck woman, even though what I was feeling was extraordinary— other-worldly even—so I laid my head on his chest and said softly as I fell asleep in his arms, "Of course, I know that, Sweetheart. Of course."

But as I was drifting off to sleep, what I was actually thinking was, "What a terrible thing it is to botch a farewell."

WHEN I WOKE THE NEXT MORNING, Ian was not in the bed. My eyes adjusted slowly to the darkness in the room, cut only by a sliver of light coming from the curtains pulled apart slightly at the cabin window. I turned my attention to the sliver of light and eventually saw Ian standing in it.

"We're pulling into port. Do you want to see the Bahamas?"

"Of course," I murmured as I wrapped the sheet around myself and walked over to join Ian by the window. He opened the curtains and I could see the dock and a flurry of activity below. The window was fogged up with some combination of the warm air in our cabin and the cool morning air outside the ship, and I had to wipe a section clean with my hand just to see out. Ian reached over and traced a shape on a corner of the fogged window. It was a heart with our initials: I.C. + K.M. He smiled impishly at me and was just about to erase it with his hand, when I grabbed his hand to stop him.

"No, Ian, leave it. You are wrong."

"Wrong?"

"My heart *will* stop beating if I have to say goodbye to you."

Ian pulled me close and rested his chin on the top of my head as together we watched the ship dock.

"Did you sign up for any of the excursions for today?" Ian finally interrupted the silence.

"No. I was going to research those during our day at sea. But I seem to have gotten distracted." I pulled away and smiled up at him. Ian leaned in to kiss me, but I made a face and waved him away from my morning breath, clamping my lips shut.

"What do you have in mind?" I said, as I headed to the bathroom to brush my teeth and splash soapy water on my face. Ian called in to me from the cabin window. "I know a fabulous place on the beach that none of the excursions will hit. It's a place for locals, with the best conch fritters you will ever taste. Let's grab a cab and spend the day there." I leaned my head out of the bathroom while I brushed to say "of course." But something stopped me. Ian was still standing at the window and I could see his profile from this angle. He was retracing the letters of our initials in the window, and he looked pensive.

Is he sad? I wondered. I wanted to ask him aloud but I was petrified of the answer. I was scared of what he might be thinking.

About us.

About Stella.

We had talked about Rob and me. But we had talked little more about Ian and Stella. I didn't know what to ask. What more I should know other than what he had revealed to me about their loveless marriage and her aversion to the thing I found most compelling in him—his ceaseless optimism. But I wanted to know more about what Ian was feeling about his future. About our future.

I wondered what sort of plans Ian and I would make over conch fritters and out of earshot of anyone but Bahamian locals. I felt something akin to panic, but I buried it, finished brushing, and spat out the remaining toothpaste, before yelling out to him, "That sounds like a great way to spend the day, Sweetheart."

I paused a moment to hear his response. Desperate for some loving words, and some reassurance about how he was feeling today about me—about us.

But there was nothing but silence in response.

❧

There was neither air conditioning nor one working seatbelt in the cab we jumped into at the dock. So I rolled the window way down, held fast to a handle on the door, and my hair blew about furiously as we sped off to the beach. Ian gave some directions to the cab driver, who quickly figured out where we wanted to go. After about 15 minutes, we stopped on the side of the road, and Ian slid a small wad of American money into the cab driver's hand, and asked him to come back for us at 6 pm, as we hopped out.

We dodged traffic across a busy but pothole-ruined road. American hotel chains littered the beach areas in the distance to the left and right, but we had arrived on a stretch of beach that was pristine and untouched, decorated only by a shack with a hanging weathered sign that read "Jack's Bar" in faded black letters. The shack itself was far from faded, painted in varying pastel colors ranging from light green to pink.

As we headed closer to the shack, I kicked off my sandals and carried them, digging my bare feet into the cool, powdery sand. I heard music playing and as we stepped onto the shack's creaky wooden deck that seemed to double as the dining room, I realized it was live music. A beautiful Bahamian woman was singing as she washed down and set the handful of tables that were scattered across the deck of "Jack's Bar." When the singing woman saw Ian, she lit up in a way that made me (embarrassingly) jealous and I could do nothing but watch somewhat uncomfortably as they hugged each other fondly.

Ian and the woman exchanged a few unheard words and I stepped back to allow them to talk, but then Ian seemed to be introducing me, because the Bahamian beauty quickly glided past Ian and came toward me, arms outstretched. I leaned in to hug her, not quite sure what else to do, since she seemed to have already decided how friendly this greeting was going to be.

"Kate," she said as we hugged. "I am so happy to see you."

I wondered briefly about the cultural/language nuances that had caused her to say this instead of "Happy to meet you," but I simply responded, "Me, too."

She waved her hand at the table closest to the edge of the deck—with the best view of the nearby ocean, and we sat down next to each other facing the water. Ian rubbed my leg tenderly as he sat next to me and I leaned my head comfortably onto his shoulder.

Ian ordered for us—some Bahamian beers ("No, it's not too early—you're on vacation," he laughed at my protests) and a buffet of seafood that seemed to include conch fritters and fresh fish that some men were busily cleaning in the back of the shack. So fresh that it apparently had just been caught that very morning.

Until that morning, I had never had beer and fresh local seafood at 10:30 am, but I was quickly realizing that I was much more adventurous than I once thought, and so, after Ian ordered for us, I settled in and decided to just enjoy myself.

The Bahamian waitress continued singing as she headed back and forth from the kitchen. In no time at all, the tables filled up with more locals who greeted the fishermen in the back and then took their seats with beers of their own.

After the coziness of my first Bahamian beer had washed over me, I felt comfortable finally exploring the topic Ian and I had been conspicuously avoiding the last few days.

"Ian, what do you think will happen to us at the end of the cruise?"

Ian smiled at me. The smirk was back. But also that look.

"Kate. Certainly we have moved past the are-you-ever-going-to-call-me-again stage of our relationship?"

I laughed as I sipped my beer, and I dribbled a bit out—grabbing for a napkin from the center of the table.

Ian broke into a laugh as he tried to help me reach the napkin. "Was that a snort?"

I punched him playfully in the arm. "No! Just don't make me laugh while I'm eating or drinking."

Then I took his face in my hands, to try to make him understand my mood in the midst of the snorting and dribbling. "I'm serious, Ian. What would you like to happen next?"

Ian looked away from me and out at the ocean quietly.

And I don't know why I felt compelled to say it out loud but I did. As if perhaps Ian had let himself get lulled too far from reality. Something I was trying very hard not to do. "We haven't been together in the real world in a very long time. And this was already going to be a very complicated time for both of us, even if we had never found each other again. Do you really think this—us—has a future out there?"

Ian took my hands in his and answered in his wise and calm tone. "I feel like things will work out exactly as they are supposed to and we don't need to solve all this right now. I love you, Kate. I have been waiting for you and hoping for you for so long. Complicated or not, we have found our way back to each other. That must *mean* something. It must."

I welled up at his earnestness. I was so desperate in my desire that he be right.

"Come on, Kate."

Ian pulled my hands and stood up. Then he walked me down to the water's edge.

We stood barefoot in the warm blue ocean and I put my hand up to shield my eyes. I wished I was wearing a beautiful sarong and an elegant wide-brimmed straw beach hat—I could almost picture how we would look, standing there, dressed for the moment. But instead I was wearing a black bathing suit covered by a black sundress and a baseball cap and Ian was wearing black swim trunks and a faded NYU tee shirt that looked to be about a decade old. My daydreams and realities felt like they were competing grandly with each other.

"I love it here," Ian said seemingly only to the ocean.

"I can certainly see why." And then I suddenly wanted to know something. "How many times have you been here, Ian?" I asked, remembering how comfortable Ian was with the cabdriver and the Bahamian waitress.

"Many times, Kate." Ian smiled and looked out over the water, vaguely. "I would love to have a place here someday."

And just like that, I was struck with another pang of irrational jealousy. "Ian, have you ever brought another woman here?"

Ian looked startled for a moment, and then shook his head vigorously, as if shaking off the startle. "Of course not, Kate. Only you."

❧

"I wonder if our lunch is ready," Ian said, as we walked back from the ocean to the deck, hand in hand. "Or maybe—"

"Maybe what?"

"Wait here." I stood near our table as I watched Ian head back to the kitchen where the men were still cleaning the fish and our pretty waitress continued walking in and out of the kitchen retrieving meals for the locals who came in after us.

"Kate, come here." Ian leaned his head out of the kitchen and summoned me. I followed him into the kitchen and he pulled a cook's apron off the wall and handed it to me. He had already tied one around his NYU tee and swim trunks.

"Let's make our own lunch." Ian smiled at my obviously puzzled expression.

The men cleaning the fish in the back handed Ian a tray of fresh fillets, and he started rummaging around the kitchen, laughing along with the men who were breading conch and fillets as if he belonged with them, side by side.

I, on the other hand, felt very out of place.

My apron looks clean enough, I thought as I tied it around me. I washed my hands in the big sink next to the tray of fillets. The kitchen area was largely clean, but just beyond the doorway, the outdoor deck was splattered with blood and fish guts. I tried not to focus on this as I turned my back on the fillet station and looked at Ian, who was grinning ear to ear as he poured what appeared to be flour from a sack he reached on a high shelf into a wooden mixing bowl and summoned me to him.

"Come here. Help me make our lunch," he smiled. He reached into the large industrial-sized refrigerator behind him and pulled out what looked to be a basket of fresh eggs. He cracked some eggs into a second wooden mixing bowl, and then leaned past me to wash his hands in the oversized sink. "Come on—when in the islands, do as the islanders do."

One of our fellow cooks handed him a shaker bottle with a mixture of herbs. Ian sprinkled the mixture into the flour and rooted around the drawers in the kitchen until he found a fork which he handed to me. "Mix it up, Sweetheart."

While I was mixing, Ian pressed some fillets into the egg and then into the flour mixture. He was using his bare hands, and our hands touched as he coated the fillets. Just that light touch was jarring. I almost dropped the fork into the mixture before I caught it quickly. We made our lunch in silence, bathed only in the foreign chatter of the men through the doorway cleaning fish, and the humming of the waitress, who came in and out of the kitchen, and who never seemed to be looking directly at me, but always at Ian, and always smiling.

I started to feel less out of place, as Ian and I fried the fillets, dodging hot oil splattering up at us from the large stove. The smells of the cooking fish enveloped us and I smiled broadly and wordlessly at Ian as we cooked and flipped and together watched the fish fry.

And I couldn't help it. I let my mind wonder what it would be like to be here with Ian.

Making our lunch each day with these Bahamian fishermen. Learning their slang and chatting with them over the morning's catch. Learning the melodies of the waitress and humming with her.

I will help her. Work here with her feeding the locals. I will be a local, too. I will bathe in this blue ocean with Ian.

I created an imaginary daydream where Ian and I had a place there in the Bahamas, and Rob would let me bring the boys, and we would all spend our days, brown and carefree in this world.

Standing in the kitchen with Ian, side by side with the locals, I let the daydream overtake me.

I could not imagine leaving Ian at the end of the trip. I could not wrap my mind around a world that did not include him.

❧

When we returned to the deck with our plates of fried fresh catch and conch fritters, Ian and I were coated in flour and grease. There was more Bahamian beer as we ate. The food was delicious, and I wondered only fleetingly what was in that shaker bottle. The food was like nothing I had ever tasted at home.

Over lunch, Ian told me about research he did for a free-lance article he wrote on his first trip here about the pirating history of the Bahamas in the late 1600s to the early 1700s.

More pirate stories.

"Most people are fascinated by the stories of the more famous pirates like Blackbeard and Benjamin Hornigold. But I was always interested in the stories of the lesser known pirates, the ones who hid their treasure around the Islands. The ones who stayed on the Islands after the age of British privateering all but destroyed the pirating culture. The ones whose descendants are still here on this island, still with pirate blood in their veins."

Ian smiled as he talked about "pirate blood," and I put my fork down to chide him.

"You sound like a young boy, romanticizing the pirate life. Honestly. You've seen too many Disney movies. Real pirates were not adventurers. They were bad men. They were murderers and rapists and thieves. Why do you think Captain Mauricio doesn't want to be associated with them? Honestly. Rob and I won't even let the boys watch those ridiculous pirate movies. We don't want them to grow up emulating that kind of so-called hero."

Ian looked taken aback. And for a moment, I wasn't sure whether it was my firm stance on pirates or my too-casual mention of Rob in this conversation. Ian resolved my internal questions pretty quickly, after he swigged the rest of his Bahamian beer.

"So Rob agrees with you on the no-pirate-rule? Or is it his rule and you go along with it?" He was smirking again.

"No, it's my rule, and he goes along with it, actually. I'm the historian in the family, remember? I don't want my boys to emulate false heroes. I want them to know about the real heroes of history. Martin Luther King, Jr., Charles Lindhearst, Amelia Earhart, Abraham Lincoln. Not pirates."

Ian seemed satisfied. "Fair enough, Kate Monroe. We will agree to disagree on this point. But, I promise, for now, no more pirate talk."

I wasn't sure whether to feel vindicated or not.

Ian interrupted my thoughts. "Hey. You just gave me a great idea. We're still docked in the Bahamas tomorrow. Why don't we go on a historical tour. But not through the ship. Those excursions are trite and pandering. I have a guide friend here who can take us on a private tour of a wonderful spot. Strictly historical."

I decided to forgive his romantic feelings about pirates.

"That sounds fun. I would love that."

"One condition, though."

"Oh no. Please don't tell me we have to go to Blackbeard's former residence on the tour?"

"No, no," Ian laughed. "That will be on the ship's excursion menu, I guarantee it. No, but the condition is that you let me make all the plans. The condition is that you trust me."

"I would love that."

"Good. It's all settled then. So, tell me, Professor. Where does all this adherence to historical accuracy come from? All this anti-pirate sentiment and lack of romance? Do I have Rob to blame?"

Ian winked, but I flinched a bit hearing Ian refer to Rob in an otherwise idyllic setting.

"No. I think I inherited my father's devotion to historical accuracy and my mother's complete lack of romance." I shrugged as I ate our beautifully breaded fillets and welled up at the thought of my father.

"Although, my mother surprised me recently with her hidden romantic side. Really surprised me."

A tear streamed down my face.

"Kate, what is it?"

"I lost my father a few months ago. A sudden heart attack."

"Kate. I'm so sorry—I didn't—"

"Of course not, how could you know? He was my mentor in so many things. History. Teaching. Life. I always knew I took after him more than my mother. Although my mother is so terribly practical, a trait you know I tend to favor."

I winked as I said this, to try to lighten the mood.

"I remember, Kate, how much you looked up to him."

"I did. But at my father's funeral, I saw something in my mother. Something I had not appreciated until then."

"What was it?"

"Tenderness. Love. Devotion. I saw how much she loved my father. Depended upon him for her own happiness. It was shattering to say the least. She only let me glimpse it for a moment, but it was enough.

"My selfish need to escape her grief—really her stoic dealing with her grief—is part of the reason I ended up running away. Here."

Ian nodded.

I looked at him, wondering if I could confess the awful thing I had felt at my father's funeral.

"I felt something at my father's funeral that threw me. Something when I saw my mother's raw grief, that I haven't been able to get past."

Ian sat patiently.

"Jealousy. I felt jealous that someone could feel that way about another human. I hate to admit it. But I felt jealousy."

Ian didn't look shocked. He nodded. And he reached his arm around me and pulled me to him. I don't know if he did it so that I could feel his heart beat, but that was the result.

❧

Our Bahamian cab driver was punctual, and we were a little tipsy when we greeted him at the pre-ordained spot on the roadside at 6 pm. We had had a leisurely afternoon by the ocean, on some wobbly beach chairs we borrowed from Jack's Bar. We spent the afternoon alternately reading in our chairs and cooling off in the ocean, and then headed back up to the deck for some rum drinks and more conch fritters before meeting the cab.

As we left the bar, Ian had hugged the Bahamian waitress. I was no longer jealous of her. I felt a kinship with her. Perhaps it was the Bahamian beer and rum, or the fact that I had fried fish in her kitchen with Ian, or just the luxurious day we had spent listening to her sing and hum as she cleaned, and served, and cooked. I no longer felt like an outsider. I had heard one of the locals address her by name, so I hugged her easily as we left, "Goodbye, Dee." She pulled away, smiling, as if I had pleased her enormously, just by saying her name.

"Goodbye, Kate. He loves you so much, you know," Dee said into my ear in one last warm embrace just before we left the shack. Ian saw us hug again and looked at me questioningly but I just shook my head and grabbed his hand. I led him off the deck, looking back at Dee who was grinning at us with her hands folded up under her chin as if in a silent prayer of thanks or good wishes or maybe just goodbye.

Ian and I were both giggling a bit too loudly when we found our driver waiting across the road from us at the same spot he had dropped us off earlier that morning.

As we were driving back to the ship, the cooler temperatures allowed me to keep the windows rolled up. I watched the trees and the scenery pass by in a blur as I leaned into Ian's arms wrapped around me where a seatbelt should be. I had thought from my tour books that the effects of the hurricanes from 2004 would still be evident. But the Island looked so lush and good through my rum haze. "I'm surprised the Island doesn't look worse from Frances—," I murmured. The cab driver looked at me in the rearview mirror and laughed a hearty laugh. "Frances?" Ian shook his head at the driver, gestured at me, and laughed. "Don't mind her, she's had plenty of rum drinks." The driver nodded and turned up his static-buzzed radio. I leaned deeply into Ian, not sure why the driver knew nothing about the hurricanes that had hit his island seven years ago, but I was suddenly warm and tired in Ian's arms. I closed my eyes for a few minutes and dreamt of pirates while we rode back to the ship.

Pirates who cook conch fritters after they search for buried treasure.

THE NEXT DAY, we woke early and headed to the dock. The ship had moved to another island in the Bahamas, and I could not be sure how Ian had arranged this tour sometime between the booze-fueled haze at Jack's Bar and the following morning; when I asked Ian, he just kept telling me to relax and let him take care of things for a little while.

"Remember my one condition?"

A man leaning against a cab waved us over when he saw Ian scanning the cab line, and Ian yelled out to him, "Pedro!"

The two men clapped each other in a warm hug and Ian pressed what appeared to be money into his hand before Pedro hugged me, too. "Hello, Kate."

Ah, he's already heard of me, too. Wonder what he's heard? I was momentarily distracted by my thoughts as I reached for the cab door handle.

I started to climb into the back of the cab, but the men laughed. "No, no," Ian said. "Cabs are for tourists. We're walking."

"Walking? Where?"

"To Fort Charlotte," Pedro answered.

"It's my favorite fort," Ian nodded.

"You have a favorite fort?" I teased dubiously.

"Fort Charlotte was erected as a show of strength by the British in the 18th century. And yet not a single cannon was ever fired from it on an invader. It was never used in battle. Never had to be. Once it was built, it was enough."

"Ah, yes." I linked my arm in Ian's as we followed behind

Pedro. "Well, that makes it a very good candidate to be *my* favorite fort as well."

"Pedro can get us in past the tour lines and into the underground passages. I've tipped him heartily so that we can get lost down there." Ian smiled mysteriously at me. I wasn't sure whether to believe him or not. But I kept walking up the steep hill in front of us. Pedro was leading us toward a sturdy looking fortress in the distance.

With Pedro, we walked past the already accumulating tour lines at Fort Charlotte's ticket entrance, and headed to a stone stairwell which spiraled downward. Ian thanked Pedro and shook his hand just before Pedro said goodbye and left us there. Pedro turned and headed back toward the crowds—for more tours—and more tips, apparently.

"We're going alone?" The nervousness in my voice betrayed me somewhat.

"Too late for second thoughts, my dear. You agreed to do this tour on my terms—and to trust me." Ian took my hand firmly in his own.

I asked myself again—not for the first time—whether I should trust this man I had not seen in nearly 15 years. I answered myself the way I had every time I had asked this question over the last few days. With a resounding—albeit silent—*yes*.

As we descended, I put my hands up against limestone walls that felt cool to the touch. The air was getting crisper as we moved further and further below—a welcome respite from the temperatures above—already climbing rapidly despite the early morning hour. Ian held my hand and I listened to his admonition to watch my step as we climbed downward into the darkness, the stone steps irregular and hazardous in spots.

We arrived in what appeared to be an underground tunnel. Ian took a flashlight out of his pocket and shined its light on the walls, where I saw a few remnants of carved inscriptions on the stone. It was hard to make out anything with accuracy, but I didn't have much time to examine, as Ian grabbed my hand and said, "Come on." He continued shining the flashlight with one free hand ahead of us.

We navigated the darkness together and it was exhilarating. I trusted Ian completely. The feeling overwhelmed me with its simplicity. We stopped to examine inscriptions on the corridor walls. We touched them together, words carved into the soft stone by soldiers. We tried to interpret their meanings together. Ian knew the tunnel and I deferred to his choices and we moved left, right, and continued straight ahead in some spots.

"How do you know this tunnel, Ian? How many times have you been here?" I asked again as I had at the beach the day before. Only I was not jealous this time. Just curious.

"Many times," he answered again, just like he had the day before at Jack's Bar. But this time, I didn't ask him who else he had brought here. I knew he would tell me no one else. I already knew that. And I would believe him.

Ian leaned down to kiss the top of my head a few times, while I was tracing words in the stone. Each time he touched me, took my hand or kissed my hair gently, I was surprised by how easy it was for us to be together, but grateful, too.

When we turned a corner after what must have been close to two hours of navigating the dark tunnel, I jumped as Ian grabbed my arm and pulled it back.

I looked up at him in alarm. He put his finger up to his lips in a quiet sign and grabbed my arm tighter.

And I heard it then.

Voices. Men's voices. Perhaps two of them. Quietly arguing.

They were speaking a language that was not familiar to me, but they were clearly arguing. Their tone and rushed inter-rupting of each other left little room for another interpretation.

My heart caught in my throat as I realized we were not alone in the tunnels, and that our tunnel companions did not appear to be very friendly, either.

Ian pulled my arm and navigated back in the direction from which we had just come.

I followed him, trying to keep my steps careful and deliberate but still quiet. He kept the flashlight off. I saw him put it back into his pocket and use his hand instead to feel the walls and guide us back the way we had come.

In the silence, we could hear the arguing voices, faintly, and then we heard a loud "shush."

I looked at Ian wide-eyed. They had heard us.

Ian's expression remained calm, but he tugged harder at my arm as he pulled me along the corridors, feeling his way as he turned us left, left, right, straight. I strained my ears to hear the men. To hear voices or footsteps or something. Something that would tell me if they were close by or not.

Then I saw a light, and I turned in horror to look at Ian. Had he put his flashlight on? Was he giving us away?

But no, the light was coming from a stairwell—a narrow stairwell—much smaller than the one we had descended. Ian nodded and pointed up—directing me to go first. We ascended the small stairwell, just as we had descended—hand in hand. All of my trust in this one man. At the top of the steps, the full sunlight hit my eyes. I reached into my bag for my sunglasses and put them on quickly as I struggled to adjust to the light. Ian shielded his eyes for a moment before grabbing his sunglasses off his head and putting them on as well.

Ian peered down the stairwell, and then grabbed my hand, directing me to a spot on the other side of the old cannon that had never been fired. Some tourists were standing there, listening to a guide, and Ian pulled me over to the group so that we would blend in among the other tourists.

After a few moments, I watched as two men emerged from

the stairwell we had just ascended. One had a black eye and a fresh bruise on his face, and the other had a scowl on his bruise-less face. It was easy to make out the winner of the arguing pair. The bruised man reached into his pocket for some money and handed it over to the victor who looked around and glanced at the group of tourists we were standing with just before he headed off in the opposite direction.

"It's ok. Just two locals arguing over tips, likely," Ian suggested. I put my face in my hands and started crying, relief and fear mixed with my sobs.

"Hey. It's ok." Ian grabbed my face in his hands. He held me out arm's length and said, "Is this real world enough for you? We can survive a lot together. Don't you think?"

Then he pulled me into him, and I let him hold me and I sobbed big tears, my body shaking. I couldn't stop thinking about my boys. I had left them and was here putting myself in real danger with a man I loved.

A man who was not their father.

❧

When we got back to the ship after our trip to Fort Charlotte, it was empty, most of the ship's passengers having gone ashore for various excursions. Ian and I agreed that a quiet day on the ship would be good for us. The following day we would be at sea, headed back to New York City, and the crowds on the ship would be excruciating.

We agreed to meet at the pool but first, I excused myself to go back to my room and freshen up.

"Are you sure you're ok?" Ian looked a bit concerned. "Why don't you get showered in my room instead?"

In truth, I *was* feeling a little shaken up by the Fort Charlotte tour and our near encounter with the arguing locals. But I hadn't been in my room in days and I thought it would be good to go get the room a little organized—perhaps even begin packing for disembarkation—a sad thought if ever there was one.

"I'm fine, Sweetheart. Let me get changed and then we'll have a quiet day at the pool."

Ian kissed the top of my head and held my hand for a moment longer before he let go, turned, and walked toward his cabin room.

As I walked by the ship's boutique on the way to my room, I saw Anne and Tom inside shopping. Perhaps I was dreading being alone more than I had let on to Ian, since I detoured into the shop to say hello to the couple.

Anne was just headed into the dressing room with an armful of dresses, and gave me a polite smile as she saw me, and so I greeted Tom with a smile. "No excursions today?"

Tom looked startled by my question and I immediately regretted my decision to come inside the boutique. "Tom, it's me, Kate. From the Captain's Table."

I put my hand on his arm gently. He looked at me a little strangely, and then he said, "Oh, you are with that nice man, Ian, right? The world traveler? He has really piqued my interest to do some exotic traveling—maybe someday after I retire."

I felt a pit in my stomach, and I looked over his shoulder waiting for Anne to come out and rescue me. I was so uncomfortable about Tom's memory loss and unsure how to handle it other than with a gentle smile and nod. I didn't want to race out of the boutique, so I simply said, "That's a wonderful idea, Tom."

I pretended I had come in to shop, grabbed a few dresses, and excused myself into the dressing room to try them on.

I took my time in the dressing room, not really wanting to rush back to my empty cabin room, and not really wanting to run into Anne and Tom again, either. I tried on a few sundresses, and after swirling in front of the mirror a few times, I decided to actually buy one or two of them, thinking that maybe I *would* just go to Ian's room to freshen up and avoid my cabin and packing for another day. All my toiletries had been there in Ian's room for the last few days anyway.

After the boutique shop detour, I stopped in the ship's computer room to try to send an email to my boys.

I kept attempting to send an email to Rob's work email address, the only one he ever used, but my emails kept getting bounced, and I grew increasingly frustrated until I gave up and headed to Ian's cabin.

Ian greeted me at the door with a wet head, in fresh clothes. I held my bag of new sundresses up to him and said, "I never made it to my room. I did a little shopping instead. Why don't you pick something you like? Mind if I get changed here?"

"Of course not," Ian smiled.

"I needed to see a friendly face rather than my quiet cabin room. I had the most disconcerting encounter with Tom," I said as I headed into Ian's open arms.

After I showered, we decided not to leave the cabin for dinner. We ordered room service and we wrapped around each other.

After a long silence, I asked the question I hadn't been ready to hear answered until then.

"Ian, what is Stella like?"

Ian sighed as if he had been waiting for this question for days now. Perhaps his answer was always prepared as he responded easily.

"Stella is not like you. She has wonderful amazing traits. But she is not like you."

I was unsatisfied.

"What does that mean?"

"She is fierce. Uncompromisingly fierce. I've seen a strength in her that has truly inspired me. But she has no soft edges, and she has little hope that things can ever be anything but what they are.

"I would be lying if I said I don't love her now. I *have* grown to love her. I love her determination and grit, which is ironic, really, since I started out the marriage in a state of hopelessness. I viewed it as a situation that had been thrust on me by fate and bad luck. But not too long into the marriage, I realized I had a choice. And, when I did so, when I chose to love her and love our life, she grew to find me exhausting. She does not want to live in hope. She fights hope like it is a toxic disease with a ferociousness that is difficult to describe.

"Still. If she hadn't ended our marriage, I don't think I would have ended it voluntarily, unless—"

"Unless what?"

"Unless you had come back to me."

We fell asleep like that while there was still daylight streaming in through the ship window, but just before we did, Ian asked, "Kate, are you awake?"

"Hmm," I answered just barely audibly. I was almost asleep, but not quite.

"I love you, Kate. I've loved you since that first day. That first day at Rocco's. Just like I always told you. And I love you even more today."

"I love you too, Ian. I do."

Ian's fingers twirled in my hair and I felt him exhale under my words.

In the middle of the night, I woke and looked over at Ian who was awake, pensive as ever. He had the same expression I remembered seeing as he traced our initials in the foggy window that morning we arrived in the Bahamas. I lay my head on his chest.

"Hey."

"Hey." Ian's fingers weaved in and out of my hair familiarly.

"Thank you, Ian."

"For what?"

"For showing up when you did and turning my whole life around. In an instant."

"That's silly."

I felt foolish and childishly romantic about my words for a split second before Ian continued on.

"That's like thanking the river for reaching the ocean. It's just what was always meant to be."

Sigh.

"Ian, I asked Benton one time why you and she never got together."

"Benton? And me?" Ian laughed. "Did she tell you that I never asked?"

"Actually yes, that's exactly what she said. But she also said that you were too much of a gypsy. That you never wanted kids and—"

"I never wanted kids until I heard you talk about yours, Kate. And that's the truth."

Sigh. Again.

"And that you are always stuck in the past."

Silence.

"Do you think you are always stuck in the past, Ian? Do you think we are always stuck in the past?"

"Kate, we're right here. Right now. Doesn't that answer your question?"

Yes, it does.

IT HAPPENED ON THE LAST FULL DAY of the cruise.

I was brushing my teeth in Ian's cabin, planning for some breakfast poolside and a relaxing day at sea with Ian before early disembarkation the next morning. I was feeling buoyed and not at all restless about the cruise ending. I was eager for Ian and me to start figuring ourselves out again in the real world.

And I was so very anxious to see my boys.

I had not been able to communicate with them for days.

"My emails keep getting bounced." I leaned my head out of the bathroom in the middle of brushing my teeth to ask Ian, "Have you been able to send any emails since we've been on the ship?"

Ian shook his head, but he appeared distracted. Like he was thinking of something entirely other than emails and inadequate wifi technology. He was rifling through a worn leather bag and looking curiously at some papers.

He quickly stashed them back into his bag and turned to me.

"Come with me to the pool. Let's have a drink. I want to talk with you."

The tranquility I had been feeling a moment earlier evaporated dramatically.

Here we go. I thought.

This is where it all ends.

This is where he tells me this is all a bit much for him. Me and a cheating husband and two small boys. Here is where we welcome reality back into our lives and stop living on a cruise ship.

Ian looked a little rattled, something I really wasn't used to seeing, and it shook me a bit as well.

"Ok," I conceded. "Let me just get a shower and freshen up first."

Under a cloak of steam and soap, I tried to shake the feeling that something bad was happening—had already happened. I thought about how far I had traveled away from Rob in just a few short days. And I thought about how much I missed my boys.

After I showered and dressed, Ian and I headed to the adult pool area—a quiet oasis at the stern of the ship. On our way, we ran into Benton and Brie who were just headed to a last Broadway-style show in the ship's lounge. It was the first time I had seen anyone familiar other than Ian in days. And I was jarred a bit seeing them. They looked different. They'd gotten sun and they each looked lighter and happier—younger even. I wondered if I looked the same to them.

"Well hello, you two lovely strangers. Do you want to join us?" Brie asked.

"No, we're headed to the pool for a quiet afternoon. What did you do yesterday? We had a very interesting tour of Fort Charlotte." I looked at Ian and we shared a conspiratorial wink. Benton looked at me strangely. She pointed over to a dining crew member across the hall, and said, "Ian, that reminds me. Charlotte over there was asking for you. She has a problem with your dining table assignment for this evening, and asked me to let you know if I saw you that she would appreciate you coming over to her to work it out."

Ian looked from me to Benton and back again. He looked almost reluctant to leave us alone together. "Ian, go. I want to catch up with the girls for a minute. Then we can go hang out by the pool."

He nodded and headed over to Charlotte, the crew

member who had now spotted him and was calling out his name heading over to meet him. Benton took advantage of Ian's distraction to stage whisper to me.

"Everything ok, Kate?"

"Of course. I'm having a wonderful time. So sorry, I haven't seen much of you guys. Ian and I have been catching up and spending a lot of time together. It's been really amazing, to be honest."

"But Kate, what about Rob?"

"Well, Benton, this is confusing, but you know Rob and I had some tough decisions to make when I got home no matter what. Ian complicates things, but I don't think I really want to discuss this now."

"Well, ok. It's your business obviously. I just had this pang of regret that you might actually call things off with Rob. You and Rob always seemed so meant for each other. It's none of my business, of course. Just because I fixed you guys up. I get that. It's just that I always pictured you guys married with a passel of kids, one of them named after me. Silly and romantic, I suppose."

"Benton, I—" I was interrupted by Max who headed over at that moment.

"Hi girls, you haven't left yet. Good. I decided I would like to join you after all."

Brie hugged her mother. "I am so glad, Mom. I know you're having a rough time. You are such a trooper. You need a good last day on the ship, relaxing and letting your hair down a little."

I looked at Max. Her eyes looked so sad. She looked very different from the last time we had spoken. Benton leaned down and did her stage whisper again. "It's been hard for Max, traveling so soon after her husband's death. I'm so glad she's here though."

I looked again at Max. So soon? Her husband had been dead

a decade, and when we last spoke she had seemed so healed, so different. What had happened in a few short days? I took her hand, and said, "I'm sorry, Max. I'm sorry to hear you've been having a rough few days." Max's eyes met mine, and that familiar kindness crept into her expression as she looked at me. Searchingly—in a way, not unlike the look I was used to getting from Ian.

"Someday, I think it would be very nice to sit and chat with you at length, darling," Max said. "You have such a warmth in your eyes. Something about you reminds me very much of myself at your age. Yes, I think we could have a lovely chat, someday."

And with that, Max, Benton, and Brie turned together and headed off to the ship's lounge and I was left puzzling all of the strange words just uttered by Max, and by Benton before her, as Ian returned.

"I just had the strangest conversation with Benton—and with Max, for that matter."

"I was afraid of that. I didn't want to leave you alone with them until I could talk to you about all this myself."

"Talk to me about what?" I felt a wave of nausea come over me.

Was I going a little crazy? Why was Benton talking about me marrying Rob? What had happened to Max?

We continued on to the stern of the ship. We chose comfortable oversized chairs on the side of the pool and I settled in to hear what Ian was about to say.

"Kate, I don't think you understand what has happened to us."

"But I do. And I'm terrified of it, too. Oh dear, there are Anne and Tom. I really wish we could sit somewhere else. I don't think I handle his erratic memory in the best way."

Anne and Tom walked by us and Tom clapped Ian on the back warmly as he passed. Anne was wearing a new sundress that I recognized from the boutique.

"So nice meeting you, Ian. And you, Kate. Don't mind if I look you up in about 20 years when I retire and head off on an African safari?"

"I would be delighted if you would. Even earlier, if you'd like. Try to make time for traveling more often. You deserve it." Ian shook Tom's hand warmly, and Anne had such a calm, peaceful smile as they walked off.

"Well, even though his memory is playing tricks on him, they seem well now. When I saw him earlier, he didn't even seem to remember our discussions at the Captain's Table." I shook off the memory uncomfortably.

"Tom isn't having any memory problems yet, Kate."

"What are you talking about? Didn't you hear him? *When* he retires? Didn't you hear his own admissions that night after the Captain's Table dinner?"

"No, Kate, don't you see? What's happened? What's really happened?"

Suddenly, I was not sure Ian and I were on the same page at all.

"What are you talking about, Ian?"

"Do you want to know what I think happened to Bea and Nathaniel?"

"The Captain's legend? That's what we're talking about now?" I tried to hide the annoyance in my voice, but it was tough to do. I was trying to think about our futures, about how we were going to navigate our complicated lives, our possible divorces, and our rekindled love affair, and Ian was talking about star-crossed lovers from a gullible ship captain's tall tale.

But Ian was undaunted by my tone. "I think time shifted when they went through the Devil's Triangle. Time shifted backward and they were given the chance to start again. If they wanted to. Nathaniel didn't want to start over, but Bea did.

"Bea used the opportunity to pretend she did not remember, but she did, probably all along. She took the opportunity to undo what had been a difficult, complicated decision. She took the re-do. Of course, eventually, she learned that, no matter how hard you resist, you find yourself right where you should be, where you are meant to be, no matter what. That's the real message for us, I think."

"What—what are you saying?"

"*We're* back, Kate. We're right where we should be. All those years of missteps, of walking away from each other. Where has it all led? To unhappiness? Sure. But ultimately, to right now. To where we should be. Where we were meant to be all along.

"Back before we got ourselves trapped in those all-wrong marriages. Back before we lost each other and ourselves. We can have a real chance. At love. Don't you deserve that? Don't *we* deserve that?"

Ian had been holding my hands. But I pulled away, panicked, suddenly trying to decide if all of my trust in this man had been misplaced. Trying to sort through my brain to understand what he was telling me. What he thought had happened.

"Where are we, Ian? How did this happen?"

"You asked me about that summer in Botswana, Kate? About the marula fruit and the agate? I learned things that summer in Botswana after I left you, Kate. Things that I believe are true. The mystic taught me about the universe's energy, about harnessing it. There are places where the energy is unique. Places like the Botswanan marula forests and other places, too. Places like The Devil's Triangle.

"I think that being here on this ship with people who had been on this very ship 10 years ago without us—Benton, Brie, Max, Anne and Tom—somehow allowed time to shift for us.

I pulled farther away from Ian but he continued on, undaunted.

"Another thing I learned that summer in Botswana is that there are people who have a special energy—people who together have a special symbiotic energy. I *believe* that, Kate. I really do. And I know you do, too. I know you felt it from the moment we first touched in that Tribeca bar. I have felt it every day we have been here, too. From that first night, yes, but ever since we passed completely through the Triangle—well, it's been indisputable—the energy between us—around us."

I thought about that peaceful, unfamiliar electricity I had felt the first time I put my hand on Ian's at the Tribeca Bar on that Cinco de Mayo all those years ago. That night he told me he was going to Africa. That he was leaving.

I had been chasing that electricity ever since Ian left. Like a drug addict, I had been chasing that dragon through city living, through window treatments and suburban utopia, through motherhood.

Perhaps it was all an illusion. Or perhaps it was very real after all.

"Ian. Where do *you* think we are?" I spoke slowly. I was trying to be rational. I was trying not to believe anything he was saying. I was trying to calm Ian and calm myself. Because if what he was saying was true—if there was any way *any* of this could be true . . . .. my mind raced uncontrollably.

"There have been clues all along of course. But I think I ignored them. Deliberately. And then this morning, I found notes in my bag. The notes I made in preparation for a trip to India to live among local artisans in 2001. I hadn't seen or thought about those notes since that trip. I—"

I looked at him, paralyzed. I could do nothing. Say nothing.

"I shredded those notes in India in 2001 after I wrote the article."

"Ian, what are you saying? This is a mistake? An elaborate hoax? What?"

Ian took my hands firmly in his. "I think it is 2001 again, Kate. And I think we have a chance to fix that goodbye we botched the first time around."

"But, Ian, my kids? My boys?"

I felt my hand reach up to my throat as the full ramifications of what Ian was saying hit me. If Ian was right—and suddenly, inexplicably I felt as though he might be—I was now living in a world where my boys *actually did not exist.*

I felt grief-stricken and weak.

I stood up. "I need some water. Something. This can't be. This can't be real." I backed away from Ian, recoiling really. There was static in my ears and I was trying to see through the blackness that was closing in on my vision.

Ian pulled me back down into the seat; my legs were barely strong enough to hold me upright anyway. "Kate, who is to say which reality is the reliable one? But right now, we are living in a reality where you don't have to marry Rob. I don't have to marry Stella. There's no lost baby. Stella is not blind."

At these final words, I looked at him lucidly for a moment. Through my haze of grief—I actually felt unbridled joy for him. This wonderful man who would now get his life back in a way he deserved. I was so happy for him. So unconditionally happy for him that I knew in that moment, *I must love him so very much.*

But love quickly gave way to despair again, as waves of grief poured back over me. My boys. They were gone.

❧

I feel shards of glass all around my body, piercing my arms and legs and torso, and I realize that I am going under water. I try to push myself up, but I am still being pulled down by gravity. I push up against the crushing water with all my strength and soon I am going back up, up, up, but not quickly enough.

I am losing air and my lungs are starting to pain me. My

thoughts turn quickly toward a funeral. I know it is a funeral because there is a coffin and everyone is wearing black. Rob is there. Well, I think it is Rob because he is standing next to the boys. My boys. But he is faceless. A dark-haired faceless man.

But my boys are not faceless. They are standing next to the dark faceless man. They are standing next to a coffin in small dark, misshapen suits that some well-intentioned soul has picked out for this funeral.

They look distraught.

Through the broken, piercing shards of glass, I see the contorted faces of my boys so clearly. I want to talk to them. To reach out to them. I want to comfort them. But I cannot talk. My lungs are collapsing with pain and I try to scream.

I push harder against the broken glass and the heavy crushing weight all around me, and I soar free into the light above me.

I gasp just as I see the boys—*my boys*—choking with sobs next to the coffin.

Next to the coffin of their dead mother.

∾

The next thing was blackness. I heard Ian talking and I struggled to open my eyes. "Kate. Come back to me. Come back to me."

Ian sounded like he was crying, but I could not see him. I realized that my eyes were closed and I could not open them. I reached within myself trying to find the will to open my eyes. I pushed hard. Finally, I saw Ian. And he *was* crying. I squeezed his hand that was holding onto mine.

"She's awake." He smiled. His hair was wet. *I was in the water,* I recalled. *Was he in the water, too?*

Ian looked relieved but not shocked to see my eyes flutter open.

Because Ian is ever the optimist, I thought to myself.

Someone wearing a ship badge shined a bright light in my eyes and I winced hard.

"What happened?" I tried to remember what was happening before the shards of glass took over. The grief began to overtake me again. The grief that led me to stand up and to back away from Ian—apparently straight into the pool, nearly drowning myself.

"I'm ok," I assured the ship doctor. Although I had no basis for such a confident assertion. I looked down to see that I was resting on a cot in a strange cabin that was neither mine nor Ian's, and that I was wrapped in a plush robe under warming blankets.

It turned out that I was in the medical cabin and the ship doctor asked me to spend the afternoon there resting. We were scheduled to disembark first thing the next morning. She assured me she would arrange for assistance leaving the ship. But Ian interrupted her to tell her that he would take care of me. That I was with him.

With him.

I was shivering from grief, but Ian mistook it for cold, and wrapped another towel around me.

"I need to go pack up my room." I hadn't actually been in my room for days, I realized with a start. I was fearful and curious about what it might actually look like given what I was starting to believe had happened to us on this trip. I began to sit upright, but Ian stopped me gently.

"No. No. Let me go. Let me do that for you. I can pack up your things and you can rest."

Ian was not looking at me with his familiar searching expression. He seemed to know what he would find. He just kept looking at me, with a sad, defeated smile, as if he knew all along this was how it would be.

And so I agreed to let him pack up my room, because he seemed so helpless, a state I was sure he was quite unused to feeling. And I hoped that a small thing, like helping me pack up, would actually help him, too.

Ian patted my hand and left me alone in the medical cabin and I thought about what an intimate thing it was to let someone pack up your belongings. The last in a series of intimacies between Ian and me. It was all ending now.

I closed my eyes and tried to decide if the last seven days were real, or just a figment of my imagination, the conjurings of a drowning woman, a near-death experience.

One thing was sure. I had received a gift. A glimpse at what my life could have been if I had gone the other direction at the fork all those years ago. Had not botched my farewell with Ian on that Manhattan street corner more than a decade ago.

And it was beautiful, and spectacular, and would have been all I could ever want.

If I had not—in the meantime—chosen Rob, and had my children.

And now it seemed, I could not choose any other road besides one that included Rob.

So who was to say what was *really* meant to be?

IAN RETURNED SEVERAL HOURS LATER with a small bag of toiletries and a change of clothes. He took my hand, guided me off the medical cot and helped me dress.

I was dizzy as I stood up and leaned comfortably on Ian until I started to feel a bit stronger. I turned away from him to comb my hair in the cabin mirror. As I did so, I looked hard at my reflection. Was I really a decade younger? Did I look a decade younger? So hard to say, as nothing was vivid in my memory from the last 10 years.

"How long was I under water, Ian?"

I turned to look at Ian who was watching me sadly. "Not long," he said. "I jumped in right after you fell in."

"Of course you did. You saved my life."

He smiled wanly. "Listen. I told the ship doctor that I would be taking care of you for the rest of the trip." Ian took my hand as we walked out of the cabin. "I only have a few more hours with you. I need to savor them. Let's go to an upper deck and watch the sunset."

We headed upstairs and located two chaise lounges near the ship's railing overlooking the setting sun. I took a seat, and Ian collapsed into the chair next to me.

He ran his fingers through his hair before looking up at me again wild-eyed. "Do you really have to leave me, Kate? Are you sure?"

"Ian. I am sure of two things. One: that I love you. That I have always loved you. And two: that I have to go back, or the grief I will be forced to live with will doom our love like a poison.

We could never survive that kind of choice."

Ian nodded, and for a moment, I thought he understood what I was saying, until he said, "Then I will wait for you. I will wait right here for you. Marry Rob, have his children, and then come back to me. Come back to me again. We'll make it work then."

I shook my head violently. "No, Ian. What would that even look like? How can I go back to Rob and wait for everything to fail? I can't doom all of our lives with my pessimism. How can I do that to my boys? I have to *choose* to make my marriage work—otherwise there is no reason to go back. It would just be selfish. I have to make a real life for those boys. I have to take charge of our destinies—for me and my sons."

"What makes you so sure you can *choose* to make things different?"

"Because now, I have hope. I really do. And the craziest part of all is that you *taught* me to have hope."

I thought about how ironic it was that yet again, this man had swept into my life and had made me believe in marula fruit and time travel, and yet once again, I was saying goodbye to him—choosing a life with Rob instead of a life with this man who had always had the power to make time stand still for me.

Was this just another botched farewell?

Was I getting it right this time?

I couldn't help but think only one thing over and over: *Only time will tell.*

Ian sat back in his chair and shielded his eyes against the horizon. "I can't get over this golden sunset."

"Lemongrass," I said quietly.

part three

today

TRUTH BE TOLD, while my memory is crystal clear about the events of that cruise, my perception of time has been altered dramatically, and I have very little memory about the weeks and months and years leading up to embarking on that cruise with Benton, Brie, and Max.

And Ian.

Michael and David are six and four now, the same ages I remember telling Ian my boys were on the way to the Bahamas. And even though those days and nights with Ian are the clearest memories I own most days, the fuzziness of my memory about the events leading up to that cruise have caused me to continue to question how much of my memories with Ian were real and how much were purely imagined.

When I left the ship alone the day after I nearly drowned, I looked around and around for my car, but it was nowhere to be found. I had asked Ian not to disembark with me. I rooted through the bag that Ian had packed for me, and things seemed so different than I remembered from when I had boarded the week before.

No well-worn copy of *Life of Pi*. No lemongrass ballgown. I finally put my hands on a set of keys and recognized them instantly. They were my "old" keys from the apartment I had lived in when I was single. The apartment where I had my miscarriage. The apartment I moved out of to marry Rob.

On the cab ride back to that apartment, I began to question what I thought I remembered from the previous decade. Those ten years had become a foggy blur. As I passed by the standing

Twin Towers in the cab, I shuddered involuntarily without understanding why. Years later, I remembered that shudder with such poignancy.

I got home to my apartment to find a message from Rob checking on how my vacation with Benton had been.

Hey babe. How was your trip? How was Benton? Same as always? Listen, I hope you had fun and got a little R&R. I love you. I miss you. I'll take you out to dinner tomorrow to celebrate your return. Welcome back.

I went to sleep in my bed alone, and when I woke up the next morning, it was a brand new day. A brand new day in 2001.

In fact, ever since I left the ship that day, I wake up every day and begin anew. It is not as if I know what is going to happen each day. Yet, I have these moments of strong déjà-vu where I stop and sit down and acknowledge that—*This has happened before.*

It is in those moments, when the boys are trying on clothes that I feel they have worn before, or when one of them brings me a picture, a carefully painted piece of art that I am sure I have seen before, that I gasp for breath and allow myself the thoughts that at all other times are buried just below the surface—*Did I really do this before? And is it all about to happen again?*

The hardest part, and the most surprising part—or perhaps not surprising at all—is that I cannot fully let go of Ian. I carry him with me every day.

Still.

After all these years. Usually, it is a vague memory of warmth and love and connection. Other times, it is very specific. If I let myself, I can very clearly smell the Bahamian ocean mixed with beer and fresh seafood. There have been times when the boys have drawn their names on a fogged up car window that I have been instantly transported to Ian's cabin room on the ship, with IC + KM scrawled on the window nearby. Sometimes I hear his voice in my head.

Kate Monroe, I love you. I have always loved you. You came back to me.

Sometimes, I nearly answer it aloud.

And I can tell you.

It is not altogether pleasant being haunted by these thoughts of Ian.

In fact, if I am being honest about my most tangible feeling for Ian, it is loss. Sometimes it is piercing as my heart burns physically in my chest like someone has taken a hot poker and tapped the edges all the way around. But usually—thank goodness—it is more manageable. A dull aching loss that I remember and then forget again throughout the day, each week, every month, all year.

In my mind, I liken the feeling to what it would be to lose a limb. I miss Ian and I feel strangely incomplete somehow. But still I soldier on. There are days that I wake with a start, certain that he is still there, certain that I just now *felt* his touch, his breath on my shoulder. On those occasions, if Rob instead puts his arm around me, misconstruing my confusion for a bad dream that requires his comforting presence, I have to shrug him off and splash water on my face in the bathroom just to get rid of the phantom feeling that Ian has *just now* been with me. Holding me. Loving me.

And so.

Because the loss is so palpable, so real, I am certain that there is something to these memories. Even though I am unsure how *much* is real and how much is *not*.

But here's the thing you need to know.

The feeling of loss, palpable though it is, does not shatter me, because I remind myself constantly that if I had chosen Ian, I would have felt loss every day for my boys. For Rob, even.

I would have missed Rob, too. I would have missed him so much, likely with the same burning heart and phantom limb feeling. I am now certain of that. Life is filled with loss. *One choice very often does exclude another*, I tell myself on days when the burning heart pierces worse than usual.

I play a game with my children, "The Question Game" that has me choosing flowers over candy, and chairs over tables. I pick one or the other without being wishy washy or equivocal. Because sometimes you really *do* have to choose. Clearly. Definitively.

I've learned that now.

And so, I push the pain, the vague memories, and the doubt about whether all of it even happened, to the back of my heart and my mind, and I continue forward.

Each day.

And I am committed to making *this* life work. When each of my boys was born, sobs of relief poured out of me. So grateful was I that I had not permanently altered my universe, crazy as that sounds. That I had found my way back to my boys—these boys. The very reason for my existence.

At each of our sons' births, Rob tenderly put his arm around me, chalking my tears up to post-partem emotions and trying his best to calm me, to comfort me. In these tender moments, I feel such love for and connection with Rob. I am propelled forward dramatically at the births of each of my sons.

I know you. I say to each one as he emerges from me, a bloody and familiar creature. *I came back for you. Do not ever question your mother's love for you.* I whisper to each boy as I nurse and rock him to sleep all those many months. *I love you. More than my own self. More than my own heart.*

I AM PROPELLED FORWARD, too, by my friends, Pam and Lex. I am committed to them as well.

I spend quite a bit of time with Pam. She is my best friend, after all. It's funny, I used to think you could not have a best friend if you did not find her in childhood. But my relationship with Pam has made me rethink that philosophy. It has made me rethink a great many things.

I confide in Pam, and in turn, she confides in me. And that brings us together in a way I have never known. I do not have to put walls up or facades when it comes to Pam. She knows that I am not a perfect homemaker, or a perfect anything else. When Rob and I have arguments or struggles, I can trust her with them, and she listens, without judgment or pretense.

I even confide in her about Ian. I don't tell her specifically about the cruise, because I don't know how to put that experience in words. But I tell her about our love affair in Manhattan all those years ago. About his leaving for Botswana and my choice to let him go. I tell her that sometimes I think about him, and that even though I know I am where I am supposed to be, I cannot help but miss him.

She pats my hand sincerely when I tell her that. "That is because he taught you so much about yourself. It's ok to hold onto those memories as long as you don't wallow in them. Treat them with respect because they are part of you."

And that makes sense, and I am grateful for her advice and comfort. I focus on my marriage, trying to make it what I want it to be. What I feel it can be.

When I confide in Pam that I am feeling unfulfilled by teaching, even though I had always assumed it was my life's calling, she listens, asking only one question over and over again: "What is it—specifically—that makes you disappointed in your job?"

Until one day, I know the answer. I tell her unapologetically, "It's the kids. Well, it's that they are not kids. They are adults. I feel ill-suited to be teaching them. They need someone else. Someone who is not me."

And when Pam asks, "Well, who needs *you*, Kate?" I know the answer and it all seems so clear, and I am surprised I have not thought of it sooner. I would be embarrassed if I were having the conversation with anyone other than Pam. But there is no room for embarrassment with Pam. Our relationship is filled with such honesty and support and love.

Which is why I find myself asking *her* questions, including about her mother, and inviting her to talk to me about her own fears, her medical history. I try to do nothing but be an open and receptive friend, just as she is for me.

So when Pam confides in me one day that she wants to have the breast cancer gene test, I tell her I will take her. I will be there for her, and I convince her to let in her husband, Greg, as well, knowing that he will help her come to the right decision, and that being part of the decision—part of the choice—will strengthen them in a way they cannot even imagine right now.

❧

Lex is also my best friend. This, too, has destroyed myths I grew up thinking about friendship. That you can only have one best friend, and that your best friend will mirror your viewpoint in every way.

Lex and I are similar in many ways, of course. We are mothers and wives and smart, strong women. But Lex is convinced that motherhood is weakening her. Is weakening many of us, in fact. She has this theory that motherhood defies the laws of Darwinism, and when she decides to explore this theory in a new writing project, I am thrilled for her.

Thrilled knowing that she trusts in me and that she enjoys my opinions, even when they are *not* mirror images of her own. I am thrilled also at the possibility that by exploring this topic in great historical and empirical detail, Lex will really come to see how incredibly strong—and not weak—motherhood has in fact made her.

And me.

I ADORE MY FRIENDS. I treasure them so much. My relationships with Lex and Pam give me so much peace and happiness.

And because Ian is such a big part of my consciousness after all these years, I wish I could count Ian among my friends, but of course, I cannot.

Even though I think about Ian literally daily, I have no contact with him at all. Deliberately.

Once, a few years ago, right after David was born—the timing was impeccable—Ian sent me a "Friend" request on Facebook. I wrote several versions of a responding message before declining the request; all the while, a pressure took hold of my heart that made it nearly impossible to breathe.

The first draft of my message said simply, "Please come find me. I need you and I miss you."

The second draft said, "I cannot click 'accept.' You know why. But I will love you forever. I swear it."

And the last draft said, "I must continue on with what I have started. I must make this imperfect life of mine work. I know no other way than to give it 100 percent of me. Which means I cannot watch you from afar or be watched by you from afar. I cannot love you. Indeed, I *must* choose not to love you any longer. There is no other way for me to go on with my life. There is no other way for *either* of us to go on with our lives. Godspeed. Goodbye."

And while there were tears streaming down my face as I typed, the fact that the pressure in my chest lifted instantly once I hit "send" was all the answer I needed to the question

"Have I done the right thing?"

It felt like a proper farewell. After so many attempts, it felt like maybe I am close to getting it right with Ian.

❧

Other than strong moments of déjà vu, my life goes about normally. Rob and I have struggles and moments of disagreement about his job path, about child-rearing.

But I greet each one with optimism. I do not look at our marriage as one that was thrust upon us by the unfortunate miscarriage, distraught as I was the day it happened.

Yes, it happened again.

Of course, it happened again.

Six months after I left that cruise ship, I miscarried again. The pain was unbearable. Like reopening an old wound I had tried desperately to pretend was healed.

And yet, I couldn't help but feel that day that my life's journey was back within my control. That Rob and I were meant to be together as Rob said in the emergency room proposal, and as only I could truly understand in a unique way. I felt finally that I could choose this path, willingly, with eyes wide open this time.

So, I now look at our marriage as one I chose. One for which I gave up Ian, and so it is imperative that I make this choice— this life—be worth such a great loss. Because I remember how Ian made me feel, how he looked at me, what he taught me, and how much hope he gave me.

As I said, I remember every detail from those days at sea in vivid detail, even though I have brought home no reminders. The clothes, the bags were all from 2001. None of the mementos of the trip seem to have made it home with me.

There is no dress.

❧

Many days, I stand in my closet, looking again for the dress.

A golden beaded sequined dress with a red velvet lining. I move hangers along the closet bar, looking for it. I think back all those years ago to the garment bag I brought off the ship after my near-death experience. There was no dress. Certainly no lemongrass ballgown.

One day, the absence of the dress overtook me. Because if there is no dress, could I have imagined it? And if I have imagined the dress, isn't it possible I imagined the rest of it, too?

I began asking all my friends and family about the dress. No one remembered it. Not a one.

Not Pam. Not Lex.

"A lemongrass ball gown? Really, Kate, I don't think you've ever owned a ball gown, let alone something that went by the term 'lemongrass.' Taffeta bubblegum pink, maybe. But that was senior prom and we need not revisit *that* one." Those were my mom's very words.

My dad laughed when she said that.

My dad.

∾

One night, my mom called to say she couldn't make it to a party I was having because my dad wasn't feeling well. I said "ok," and hung up the phone, but for the next hour, I was distracted somehow. Eventually, I called my mom back and told her to take my dad to the ER. That I would meet her there. I cancelled my plans and went to the hospital to meet them. Within two hours, a doctor was telling us that my dad had some serious blockages and was on the verge of a heart attack.

"You're very lucky your daughter made you come here tonight," the doctor told my dad. My mom squeezed his hand and looked at me with such gratitude.

One quadruple bypass later and my dad is still with us when

my kids are six and four and I have an eerie feeling that this both refutes and completely validates what I think happened to me all those years ago.

AND WHAT ABOUT ME AND ROB? Are we content? Am I happy? Truly happy versus talking-myself-into-it happy?

Isn't that a logical question?

Most of the time, although there is no tangible, palpable evidence that Rob ever cheated on me, I treat him like a proven philanderer. Like a man who once cheated on me, but I have forgiven him, chosen to move forward.

I am cautious with Rob. I do not hire young, nubile babysitters and I do not encourage him to go out late with the boys or colleagues from work. There is something that I remember that keeps me from becoming too lax in my marriage. And yet, I love him. I love how he is with our children. And I love how crazy they are about him.

And I pray that I'm wrong.

I pray a lot lately.

And I hope.

I encouraged Rob to stay at the small third law firm, Parker and Hall, and not make the move to Larter & Gold. When he told me he was afraid he will not make partner, I told him, "So what? Then you will have more time for us and more time to take care of yourself, and who needs a law partnership anyway?"

He looked so relieved and grateful the day I said that. Like he had been waiting for someone to say it all along. Like he had been waiting for *me* to say it all along.

❧

After Pam and I had that enlightened discussion about my

vocation, I left my college teaching position.

I left it for a high school history teaching spot in an inner city school, not too far from the one where my Dad was retiring from his Principal position.

The day I walked into that high school classroom with my fresh lesson plan, I felt the first certainty that I had made the right professional choice, since I sat on my bed all those years ago with my dad—weighing the pros and cons of taking a banking position.

My dad can hardly hide his pride, and I wonder why it has seemingly taken me an entire lifetime to figure out that *this* is the right path for me.

This is where I belong.

After my first semester of teaching high school, Rob said, "High school teaching seems like a great fit for you, Kate. I wonder why you and I didn't think of that sooner. I'm so glad you are happy."

I have stopped planning exit strategies. From my career. From my marriage.

I wonder if I have made all the choices and decisions necessary to change the outcome this time. And sometimes, I wonder if a changed outcome is what I even want.

I live in uncertainty, without any real answers. And then one day—today—all the answers came flooding at me at once in a tidal wave of revelation.

❧

Today, I dropped the boys off at school and was about to order some new school clothes for them. Unlike the boys' preschool and elementary school, the high school where I teach is closed today and so I have a day off at home, to catch up on some house chores. Order clothes for the boys. Maybe make some rice pudding.

The boys have grown so much—none of their pants fit, and none of their long sleeve tees. It is nearly winter, and I log onto the computer in my bedroom office to shop online.

I haven't been on Facebook in so long—so I scroll through, checking out old friends' pictures and even loading a few new photos of the boys. Belated back to school shots. Freshly scrubbed. Beautiful.

Something catches my eye after I upload the boys' photos. Benton is tagged in what seem to be wedding photos. *Whose wedding?* I wonder. I click through, read the captions, and search for familiar faces.

Ian.

I see Ian's face. He is beautiful and unchanged in so many ways. He is in a tux, with his arm around Benton, and he is looking right at me.

I could swear it.

I remember something then that I hadn't thought about in a long time. A pendant that I won in a raffle on the ship. In addition to the missing dress, I have never remembered seeing that pendant since I got home from the cruise ship all those years ago.

The garment bag I used on the cruise ship is somewhere in the attic—abandoned long ago for more durable luggage—larger matching sets for traveling together as a family—to places like Paradise Resort. The garment bag that Ian had packed for me all those years ago while I was lying on a medical cot, trying to figure out whether I had just traveled back in time a decade, since a man I trusted implicitly had told me it was so.

I head up to the attic and in a corner, I see the garment bag. I open it up, unzipping each compartment, running my hands along the inside, until my hand stops on a piece of fabric that feels out of place in the garment bag and some plastic bundles next to it. I pull out a drawstring bag with a gemstone pendant along with the plastic wrapped bundles, and take all the items back down to my bedroom. I carefully open the fabric bag and pull out the necklace. I rub my finger over its smooth and unusual shape, and I am transported to that evening on the ship. The night Ian taught me how to gamble. The night he walked me back to my cabin just before midnight, just before we entered The Devil's Triangle, and we held each other in a hug at my door that took my breath away and made time seemingly stand still.

Something else falls out of the fabric bag—a small piece of paper—and I reach down to pick it up.

How to care for your Botswanan agate.

I catch my breath as I remember my first date with Ian over Indian curry so many years ago.

"A mystic in the delta who swears that through some combination of the fermented marula tree fruit and Botswanan agate, he can make things happen."

"What things?"

"Well, time travel, of course."

I carefully unwrap the plastic bundles that had also been hiding in my old garment bag, and tears stream down my face as I look at the two snow globes I carefully purchased and had bubble wrapped for my boys years earlier. Boys who had yet to arrive, but whose arrival I was certain of nonetheless. Their "Soup and Ears."

Standing there, with my pendant and two snow globes catching the sunlight in the bedroom I now share with my husband, who is not Ian, I know.

I know that I did not imagine one second of my time together with Ian. Not one second of those weeks in Manhattan and not one second of those days on the ship. Or in the Bahamas. Each and every moment with Ian was as real as each and every one of my moments spent with my boys before and after that trip.

I know now that Ian and I traveled back in time. Something mystical happened to us as we passed through The Devil's Triangle, something that continued on the rest of the trip and has never really been undone.

I turn back to the computer and I look at Benton's caption next to Ian's smiling face. "Congratulations to Ian and Stella— so happy for you!" I keep scrolling until I come to a photo of the couple. It is dated only a few months ago. And the bride is looking at her groom with unmistakable love and devotion. They got married just a few months ago, and Stella is looking at Ian.

She most certainly is not blind.

AFTER I PICK UP THE BOYS at school later in the day, we head past the clothing boutique. I have stopped in several times over the last few years out of curiosity.

A golden ballgown with a red velvet interior? No Ma'am. We don't have anything matching that description. Sounds beautiful, though.

I haven't stopped in a while. Most days, I just drive by and take casual notice of the window as I slow down for the light at the corner. Today, however, I have to slam on the brakes at the red light, as I am too distracted to slow down properly. I'm distracted by the crystal globes, the agate pendant, and by the man I just saw out of my peripheral vision.

A tall dark-haired man coming out of the boutique and disappearing from view before I could get a good look.

But, my God. It looked like *him*.

At the red light, I catch my breath, and Michael is whining a little in the back seat that his tooth is wiggly and hurting him.

His first loose tooth.

"Boys, would you like to stop for some hot cocoa?" I pull the car over in front of a coffee shop down the street from the boutique, and as we head inside, Michael keeps wiggling his loose tooth until it pops out, startling both of us. "Here, honey." I wrap the tooth in a napkin quickly and hand it to Michael.

I feel him before I see him.

The rush of October air from the hastily opened door in the coffee shop blows the crumpled napkin containing the baby tooth out of Michael's hand, and makes me shiver at the same time. With my back still to the door, I reach down to scoop up the napkin, eager to quiet Michael's renewed tears after the napkin flew from his clumsy hands, and in doing so, I drop my oversized handbag on the floor where it flays open, all of its contents exposed somewhat grotesquely.

"Michael. It's ok." I stroke his hair. Still crouched down, I pull Michael to my chest, his tears and bloody slobber streaking my sweater like some horror movie version of a water color design. Michael's tooth remains balled up in my hand.

The tears, the moment, the crouching hug, and the balled up napkin feel familiar somehow, and my shoulders shake again with a sense of déjà vu.

I turn to check on David who is starting to play with an elaborate display of coffee mugs for sale, and find myself facing *him.*

I stare at him, waiting for him to notice me. See that it is *me.* And then—

"Kate." He looks sad—*defeated,* I think—as he says my name. *Or is that my imagination projecting on him?*

"I wish—" he says as he surveys the scene in front of him. *Wish what, Ian? Because I wish, too. I wish so many things.*

I pull both of my sons to me and glance over Ian's shoulder at the door, wondering if I should leave or try to start the overdue moment again. I stare at him, willing him to finish his sentence, so that I will not have to speak. So that I will not have to think of something to say. It doesn't work.

"Wish what?" This time I say it out loud.

"That we could turn back the clock again. Start over."

A phone buzzes then atop my abandoned bag and I instinctively glance at it in time to see it lighting up with a familiar but infrequent number.

Benton.

It's like she knows I'm here with Ian. She has the most uncanny sense of timing.

I pick up the phone to hear, "Kate! How are you? I was just thinking of you because I am planning a little get-together. A cruise to the Bahamas. Can you get away? It would be so wonderful to catch up—" I click the phone off, cutting Benton off in mid-sentence, just as I drop the napkin on the floor again and Michael begins whimpering.

"Kate." Ian is still staring at me. "Can't we turn the clock back again?"

My mind flashes through scenes like a movie. Ian and I dancing in the lemongrass dress. His boozy commands at the blackjack table. The swirling compass. The underground tunnels at Fort Charlotte. His hands in my hair. His lips on mine. The warm ocean sand under our toes. Making lunch with the fish fillet station just outside. The Bahamian waitress named Dee.

Kate . . . happy to see you.

How many times have you been here, Ian?

Many times, Kate.

Ian, have you ever brought another woman here?

Of course not, Kate. Only you.

A tightness comes into my chest. The pressure is almost unbearable, as I ask Ian.

"How many times did we go back? How many times, Ian?" Silence.

How many times did Ian try to get me to make a different decision? How many times did we go through the Devil's Triangle, Ian hoping against hope that I would do things differently this time around?

It must have been so many times.

After all, things are changed now. Those déjà vu moments are becoming less frequent. This time I picked up Benton's coffee shop call. Stella is no longer blind. My dad is still here. And Rob and I—we are different this time. *I* am different this time.

"Ian. Tell me. Please. How long have we been trapped in this loop?"

Ian won't—or can't—answer me.

I crouch down again to Michael and my eyes begin burning with disappointed tears, as I remember our discussion that night on the cruise, wrapped in Ian's arms for the last time:

"Do you think you are always stuck in the past, Ian? Do you think WE are always stuck in the past?"

"Kate, we're right here. Right now. Doesn't that answer your question?"

Yes, it does.

I realize then that Michael has stopped crying and is tugging at my bloody, slobber-stained sweater.

"Mommy. I want my hot cocoa. You promised. We need to call Daddy. We need to tell him I lost my tooth. Will the tooth fairy come? Can we call Daddy now? Come on, Mommy. I want my hot cocoa. You promised."

I blink hard at both of my boys who instantly and continuously pull me out of the past, out of the loop that Ian and I have been stuck in.

And I make the one choice I didn't even realize was mine to make.

I choose *now.*

❧

I walk past Ian and out of the coffee shop with my boys, and we call Rob together to tell him about the lost tooth and David nearly knocking over an enormous coffee mug display.

Small things have become big again.

After the boys give me the phone back, Rob asks me to get a babysitter and meet him at a restaurant in town. Not a favorite restaurant. Not a romantic restaurant. Just a restaurant in town. He wants to talk, he says.

"About what?"

"Later. Just meet me for dinner, Kate." His voice sounds

strange to me.

I call around until I find a babysitter who can come on short notice and I put on a red dress.

If I still had that lemongrass dress, I swear I would wear it.

I head out to the restaurant to bravely face my husband.

And my future.

❧

"I joined the 8th Avenue Gym," Rob says, after our drinks arrive, and as I am waiting on pins and needles to hear why he has asked me here. What he wants to talk about.

He reaches across the table and takes my hands in his.

"I'm going to take better care of myself. And you. I'm going to be a better husband, a better father, Kate. I get it. I really do. I'm so glad you convinced me to get off the partnership merry-go-round. It's like I was chasing something we didn't even need. That I didn't even want. And I am so grateful to you.

"When you called me today in the middle of the day, I had just had this epiphany. God, we are lucky, aren't we? We have our ups and downs like everyone. But we're just really, really lucky, Kate. Extraordinarily lucky, don't you think? I think it's really time to stop living in the past and the future and just live *now*. In the present."

Rob clinks his glass on mine.

"The gym." I laugh. I am so happy. I can't actually remember being this happy in a long, long time. Genuinely happy, and not talk-myself-into-it happy. Tears of gratitude are streaming down my face right there in the middle of the restaurant, but I don't feel embarrassed. No, I feel rewarded in a way I haven't felt in so long.

Sitting there with Rob, the father of my children who are the great loves of my life, I feel something that is unlike anything I ever had with Ian, beautiful and magical as that was.

Ours is the connection that transcends time.

"You're all streaky," Rob says, touching my face tenderly. I excuse myself and head to the ladies' room. I am still dabbing powder on my glowing face when she walks in.

❧

It is her.

Celeste Morrison.

She is standing right next to me at the bathroom mirror and incredibly, she begins talking to me. Apparently, she cannot see my heart beating in my chest or hear the throbbing in my head because she—

Just. Keeps. Talking.

"I love your dress, that's a gorgeous color on you."

I have stopped dabbing at my nose and am staring at her, but she doesn't seem to notice or at least, does not seem put off by my staring.

"You look familiar," she says. "Do I know you?"

I am still staring.

She seems to confuse my silence as thoughtful consideration of where we might know each other. "I'm new in town," she says, "but I just joined the gym. That's it"—she mistakes my reaction to her mention of the gym as assent—"it must be from the gym. The 8th Avenue Gym. Are you a member, too? I've probably run into you there," she says.

I manage to shake my head and steady myself long enough to leave the ladies' room. When I come out of the bathroom, I see a back exit to the restaurant and I walk through it in a haze. I sit on the curb outside in my red dress, and I weep. Deep, guttural sobs that take me back to the day I read about the policeman's widow, the day I stared at her face in that newspaper story looking up at me from my office desk.

I vaguely recall another widow as well, a widow named Max,

who once told me that "love is not ruled entirely by the choices we make, no matter how much we pretend it is so."

Adele's "Someone Like You" is playing inside the restaurant, and I hear the song's refrain like a soft memory through the screen door I am sitting near.

This is not déjà vu.

It is unlike anything I have ever felt.

It consumes me.

And I am no longer jealous of any raw widow grief I have ever witnessed.

I stop crying and I close my eyes. I cannot be sure whether history is about to repeat itself or not, but this I know for sure.

I have hope.

epilogue

Destiny.

That's what I am thinking about tonight as I look at this gorgeous—more than yellow, not quite golden—sunset.

No, that's a lie.

I'm thinking about loss.

Choices. Destiny.

But mostly loss.

It's ironic of course that I cannot stop thinking about loss since we finally—*finally*—found our way back to each other.

And I'm not surprised at all that this is where we find ourselves.

Right here. All over again.

Because again and again, we find our way back.

I have always been convinced that starting over was all we truly needed.

But like I said.

Tonight I'm thinking about loss.

Choices. Destiny. And loss.

Oh, and one more thing.

That dress.

I can't stop thinking about that damn dress.

Not my wedding dress.

Which would make sense, of course, since this *is* my honeymoon.

But that crazy dress I found in the back of Ian's closet one day. The most unusual, exquisite dress. Such a vibrant sunset color, with a red velvet lining. It was tucked in the back of his closet under a shelf that seemed to house only one item—a dog-eared copy of *Life of Pi* with a piece of foreign money—Bahamian money—as a bookmark in a page that seems to talk mostly of "botched farewells" and sad goodbyes.

I ask Ian when he has been to the Bahamas, but he waves it off vaguely.

"Come on, Stella, you know I travel so much. Who can remember exactly when I was where?"

I let go of the Bahamas, but I can't let go of that dress.

"Ian, wherever did you get such a dress?"

"In my travels," he answers vaguely again. "It was made by artisans in India—gorgeous handiwork, no? I've thought about selling it to a boutique but I can't part with it yet."

He does not offer it to me, and I do not point out how strange that is. I try to ignore it in the back of his closet, as I am sure I would never enjoy wearing it. It's not my style. And it is a strange shade of gold, a color that does not suit me at all.

When I mention to Ian the gold color of the dress, he corrects me quickly. A bit too quickly if you ask me.

"Not gold. Lemongrass. It's called lemongrass. It's supposed to be the color of hope." He says.

So you see?

You see why I feel such loss?

This utterly hopeful man of mine.

I cannot be sure at all of what he is hoping for anymore.

Or whom.

acknowledgments

SO MANY "Thank You's," so little space. Here goes anyway.

First. Thank you to my publisher, Nancy Cleary, for your unwavering support and for championing this project so enthusiastically. Thank you, too, for analogizing this project to marriage and then saying "I do." I adore you.

Thanks also to Caroline Leavitt, for her invaluable feedback in editing this novel in its early and later versions, and for leaving me breathless with excitement when she called it a "unique" love story, and for loving the color lemongrass almost as much as I do.

Thank you to Beth Smith, my mentor and inspiration in so many things, not the least of which has been this project.

Thank you to ALL my writer friends, especially Jackie Hearing, Heather Christie, and Sarah Pekkanen, for cheering on this project and nurturing my confidence in that way only fellow writers can.

Thank you to my sister, Megan, the first person I ever let read the manuscript, after swearing to a vow of secrecy. Which she promptly violated by bragging to our mother and sister, Katie, that she was permitted a sneak peek.

Thank you to my dad and mom, Mike and Kathy Shelley, my original and biggest fans, who will probably sell more copies of this book than me and my publisher combined.

Thank you to my late grandmother, Lois Hunter, for paying me $10 when I was eight years old for the rights to a quote that she used to headline a poem published in the local newspaper, thereby giving me my first crack at navigating the world of commercial publishing.

Thank you to all of those extraordinary family members and friends (yes, this means YOU) who never, ever told me I was crazy when I told them I was writing a novel, and for asking constantly when they would get to read it, inspiring me to finish something worth reading.

Thank you to my Book Club gals (Kelly, Maureen, Sharon, Amy, Kathryn, and Eleni) for loving the title of *Lemongrass Hope* from the first second they heard it, and for pushing me to finish it so we'd have a new book to discuss over New Zealand sauvignon blanc.

My biggest and loudest thank you to my husband, Paul, upon whom the characters of Rob Sutton and Ian Campton are not even loosely based. Except for the good stuff. I am so very grateful to him for being the kind of brutally, unflinchingly honest person that he is so that when he told me my idea for *Lemongrass Hope* was "actually a really good one," I believed him.

And best for last—I owe a debt of gratitude to the central characters in my own real life love story—my children, Paul, Luke, and Grace, each of whom I knew. Even before I met them.

the author

PHOTO: JENNIFER BRETON PHOTOGRAPHY

A REFORMED CORPORATE LITIGATOR with a powerful background of survival and renewal, Amy Impellizzeri has been writing since childhood, but ended a long hiatus from personal writing after a plane crashed in her residential neighborhood in 2001, killing everyone on board and five of her neighbors, as she started on a journey of guilt and healing, detailed in her essay, *Unscathed*.

After 13 years in the cutthroat world of corporate law, including a decade at a top Manhattan law firm, Impellizzeri left to write and advocate for entrepreneurial women, eventually landing at the investor-backed start-up company, Hybrid Her, named by ForbesWoman as a Top Website for Women in 2010 and 2011 (and recently re-branded as ShopFunder, LLC) while working on her first novel, *Lemongrass Hope*, and her first nonfiction book, *Lawyer Interrupted*, scheduled to be published by the American Bar Association in 2015.

Her essays and articles have appeared in *The Huffington Post*, *The Glass Hammer*, *Divine Caroline*, and ABA's *Law Practice Today*, among more. She lives in Pennsylvania with her husband, three kids, and a menagerie of small animals.